Bricks without straw

Kendrick Foden

© 2009 Kendrick Foden. All rights reserved.
ISBN 978-1-4452-1990-5

To June with best wishes,
Ken Foden
13 June 2010

For Jan, Sarah and Michael

Contents

1 Maelstrom 7
2 Rice or couscous 16
3 Scourge of the staffroom 25
4 Count to ten 33
5 A soft spot 42
6 Stop digging 51
7 A great equaliser 59
8 Ambush 67
9 So what? 76
10 Buckets, bins and hard-hearted Henry 84
11 Leaky roofs and cold buildings 94
12 Zero, three, zero, eight 104
13 Splintered *biro* 113
14 Scum 121
15 Blood brothers 130
16 Not enough Sharons 141
17 Spectre 150
18 Edgar 158
19 Scoop 164
20 Nothing at all like a clown 171
21 The way they once had been 179
22 Petrol on the fire 183
23 Metaphor 187
24 The irritation of salt 194
25 Wide eyed innocence in the presence of worldly experience 201
26 The dull ache of suspicion 207
27 The increasing intensity of murderous uncertainty 214
28 Chips and scraps for tea 219

29 Grasping the wrong end of the stick 224
30 Don't they teach discipline in schools nowadays? 230
31 Deliciously unsaid secrets 235
32 Buzzing again 240
33 Still Alison 246
34 Spring madness 255
35 Bye-bye, Pepsi 261
36 Twenty per cent less fat 268
37 ILY 274
38 Whistling like Ashley Hardman 281
39 Mingled tears 290
40 No room a refuge 297
Post scriptum 300

1 Maelstrom

"Come here. Come here at once!" Alison Lister's heart was beating rapidly. This is what she had been dreading all morning. She had taught in several schools previously. She knew that however well respected you had been in your last school or however far up the promotion ladder you had climbed, you would still have to go through the ritual of *establishing yourself with the 'kids'*.

Three urchins disappeared around the corner of the building and into the staff car park. Alison broke into an undignified jog and arrived at the corner in time to see three elfin figures trying, unsuccessfully, to blend into the background.

She tried again. "Come back here!"

This time they did; sauntering over, their disdain barely disguised.

"Yes, miss?" These words were uttered, with mock seriousness, by a freckled, ginger-haired lad. His two companions, one at either shoulder, smirked their approval. "Do you call out to all teachers in that manner or am I a special case?"

"Just being friendly, miss." His companions smirked, with renewed vigour, at their spokesman's daring.

"Do you know who I am?" Alison regretted it as soon as she had said it. Her reference for this job had spoken of her as a calm, unflappable person, who was well respected by colleagues and pupils alike.

At present she was breaking all her own rules. Not only had she made a spectacle of herself by running through the yard but she was now playing the status game.

Her mouth was in automatic pilot. "I'm Mrs Lister - the new Deputy Head. How dare you talk to me like that?"

"Sorry, miss," lied 'freckles'. His two pals beamed impertinence. It was time for Alison to cut her losses. Make the point. Call a truce. Retreat with dignity. Any sort of a relationship was better than none at all. Next time she would not be starting from scratch.

"What's your name?" "Robert, miss."

"Robert what?" "Robert Walker, miss."

"What year?" "Y9, miss." Alison could have guessed.

"Whose class?" "Miss Faulkner's, miss."

"And you two?" "Darrell Williams." "Simon Higginbottom."

Alison was beginning to recover her composure. "Class?"

"Miss Faulkner's," all three intoned.

"Well, I'm sure Miss Faulkner will be interested to hear about your cheek."

"Wasting your time, miss. She's never here."

The bell had gone. Alison made her way through the car park, scooping up assorted snack wrappers as she went. That was the worst thing about starting a new school: not knowing names. Furthermore, there was always a slight divergence in the interpretation of rules from one school to the next. The youngsters sensed this and would exploit the element of doubt mercilessly with new members of staff, if they could get away with it.

Alison went inside through the pretentious, nineteen-fifties, grammar-school-type, rear entrance, mysteriously known as the 'front' of the school. She threaded her way through the remnants of youngsters reluctantly returning to their classes and rediscovered the sanctuary of her office.

It did not feel like home. Its prior occupancy still pervaded the room. Timetable and duty rotas shrouded the pin-board. Twin cocoa tins, improvised organisers, bristling with dried-up pens and stubby pencil ends, and a wire basket in-tray were the only items on the crinkled, green leather top of the solid wood desk. Faded ink stains and the circular indentations of numerous snatched coffee breaks simply emphasised her predecessor's enduring presence.

Alison eyed the virtually empty wire basket and wondered if she had made the right decision. An excellent academic record and a glittering career as a classroom teacher and head of department had done little to prepare her for the inadequacy and isolation that she felt at present.

A knock at the door intruded upon her soul-searching.

"Hi, I'm Duncan Lewis. I teach maths."

"Yes. Yes, I know." She had been researching the staff photograph with the help of the woman who worked the photocopier.

Duncan appeared somewhat baffled but continued: "I was wondering if I could have next Thursday afternoon off... to take my driving test."

Oh no, a decision to take. She looked at Duncan's face, trying to weigh him up. Was he checking her out to see if she was an easy touch? Anyway, what *was* the school's policy on leave of absence?

She lowered her gaze. "No... er... no," she faltered. "I don't think that's a good idea. Can't you re-arrange it for half-term holiday?"

A cloud passed across Duncan's face, then he smiled weakly. "Of course, if you think that's best. Sorry to disturb you."

"No. No. Not at all."

Duncan left the room and closed the door crisply behind him.

Alison continued to stare, for a few seconds, into the space that Duncan had left behind him, then, recalling her previous boss's literal open door policy. She walked deliberately to the door and set it wide open before regaining the threadbare elegance of her recently inherited, ageing, high-backed swivel chair.

The chair's previous occupant had been Ted Lambert. Though he had retired, his reputation had haunted Alison's thoughts during the days leading up to the start of term. Ted never had any discipline problems. Most of the youngsters in school had respected him. Those who did not, feared his biting wit. He could stop a sixteen year old tough-guy, dead in his tracks, at a hundred yards, with his booming voice. He had taught most of their parents. Tales of clippings, cloutings and canings were legend in the village.

Universally known as the 'Gaffer', Ted was one of the old school of deputy heads. His trade mark was the screw driver in the top pocket of his tweed jacket. Ted could repair anything in the time it took the caretaker to consult his job description.

Ted loved kids. He liked to tell them stories about what life was like when he was a lad. They would never have dared not to listen to him.

He was in his element when a fire drill needed arranging. In his later years, he spurned the advances of the desktop publishing person and insisted on stencilling the evacuation instructions himself, just as he always had done.

He liked to organise school camp and ran the under fifteen soccer team for every one of the thirty-two seasons he had spent at Southdale Comprehensive School.

He hated the term 'comprehensive'. As far as Ted was concerned, Southdale had started life as a secondary modern and that is what it would always be.

Development plans and budgets and local management of schools had left Ted behind. The new head with his talk of consultation and deadlines and action plans had made Ted feel out of his depth. It was with great reluctance that he had finally agreed to accept the offer of a golden handshake and taken early retirement at the age of sixty-three.

Alison fumbled through the few bits of paper in the in-tray. There was a memo from the 'boss' welcoming her to Southdale and wishing her good luck, an appointments sheet for a forthcoming Y9 parents' evening and a glossy leaflet from a company offering consultancy on all matters educational.

It was paradoxical that one of the tests during her two day interview for the post had been an 'in-tray exercise'. Half a dozen tricky theoretical scenarios to deal with in fifteen minutes. "It's nine o'clock on a Monday morning and the caretaker reports a gas leak in the kitchens. You are in charge of the school. What do you do?" "An angry parent bursts into your office, unannounced. Her son has been beaten up on the school bus and she demands that you do something about it. What do you do?"

No such meaty melodramas this Monday morning. Merely a past its best wire basket and a few insignificant papers.

A pale, watery, early January sun was labouring to reach its zenith. Its diluted rays cast a yellowy radiance on the table in front of Alison.

For the past fourteen years, Alison Lister had been a full time science teacher. She had spent part of every term-time Saturday and Sunday preparing lessons. Long evenings had been dedicated to marking work. Countless meetings had been devoted to addressing the politicians' current 'big idea' for state education. She had stretched Jake's patience to the limit by reading education management volumes, under the parasol, during their annual escape to southern France. She had spurred his wrath by spending numerous weekends at conferences and courses on how to be a successful senior manager.

Had it all been worth it? None of the books, none of the courses had prepared her for this immediate reality; this sense of guilt at sitting idle in an unfamiliar office waiting for the lunch bell to ring. Doubtless, all around the school, classrooms thrummed with activity. Teachers plied their trade. Youngsters sat transfixed in awe or numb with boredom. Some classrooms hummed with discussion, others screamed out discord but everyone out there was actively engaged at the chalkface. Everyone, it seemed, except Alison Lister.

A cacophony of sounds greeted Alison as she ventured out of her office into the corridor. The bell had had the effect of a starting pistol. The corridor was alive with pupils, running, pushing, dodging, weaving; all heading in one direction: the canteen.

"Miss, who's on first sitting?"

Alison looked down to find a diminutive figure tugging at her sleeve. Alison had not the faintest idea who was on first sitting. Before she could say as much the tiny figure had disappeared, carried along the corridor, as if by a tidal wave.

Here and there, bobbing up and down like buoys on the swell, dinner supervisors tried to stem the flood. Their neat, blue and white checked overalls disappeared and reappeared and disappeared again.

"Stop. Don't run!" they shrieked, unheeded.

Few teachers were rash enough to risk their dignity in this maelstrom. Those who did yapped a few stock instructions before bolting into the staffroom or out of the exits. They had little heart for putting their authority to the test with the mob.

Alison was at once fascinated and horrified. Southdale had quite a reputation locally for unruliness. When she had first applied for the deputy head's post, some of her colleagues had expressed doubts about her rationality. "Southdale! You must be joking. The kids over there eat iron bars and spit nails."

Alison gritted her teeth. She stepped into the raging torrent. She waved her arms. She yelled at hurtling bodies to "Take it steady!" She grabbed despairingly at passing sleeves until, at last, the surge subsided and calm returned to the corridor. The chaos had transported itself elsewhere. Alison could easily picture the noise and the flying food in the dining-room.

Alison made her mind up quickly. She strode along the corridor in the opposite direction from the dining-hall until she came to a door, firmly closed, with an elegant name plate: W P H Rogerson PhD, Headmaster.

She rapped at the door with rather more impatience than her first day status would normally have dictated. No response. She rattled on the door.

"Come," pronounced an unperturbed voice from within.

Rogerson was seated at his splendid desk, a delicately prepared cheese sandwich part way to his mouth. A paper tissue spread out on the impeccable desk top served as a napkin. A fine white china cup with a pink flowery pattern rested on its matching saucer. The sound of Classic FM added to the impression of calm and well-being.

Dr Bill, as he was known behind his back, gently placed his lunch on the tissue, clasped his hands on the desk in front of him and said: "Oh, it's you Alison. Do come in, my dear. Take a seat. How can I help you?"

Alison was not of a mind to take a seat. She objected to being patronised but she let that pass for now.

"It's horrendous out there, Dr Rogerson. The kids are just like animals." She croaked; her voice was a little hoarse with yelling and tremulous with anger.

"Calm down, Alison. There is no need to speak about our students in such a disparaging manner. You can't expect them to be as biddable and compliant as the middle class children you were used to in your last school. Southdale is a different kettle of fish altogether. You'll soon get accustomed to it."

2 Rice or couscous

James Lister arrived home just before six o'clock. As he slipped into the hall, he was surprised to smell onions and garlic frying. In the ten years that he had been married to Alison, he had got used to being in, as regular as clockwork, just before six o'clock, and starting the evening meal. He threw his heavy top coat on to the telephone table and called out, "Hello. I'm home." He jogged up the stairs, disappeared into the bedroom to re-emerge minutes later in denims, pulling a baggy sweater over his head.

Alison was standing at the hob absently stirring a meaty concoction. A glass of red stood on the unit at the side of her. He slid his arms around her from the rear and gently brushed his lips across the back of her neck. "Hi, sweetheart. Had a good day?"

"Hi, Jake."

"Rice or couscous?"

"Couscous. It's quicker."

Jake filled the electric kettle and clicked the switch. Alison continued to agitate the food without looking round. Behind her, on the breakfast bar, was an uncorked bottle of *Fleurie* - the only one left from the case they had brought back last summer. The bottle was scarcely two thirds full. It must have been a hard day, Jake thought to himself but he kept his peace. He knew better than to ask when she was like this.

They ate their meal to *Mozart*. They traded suggestions for Thursday's shopping list, concurred that the couscous from the exotic foods stall on the market was almost as good as the stuff they brought back from France and bemoaned the fact that neither of them had remembered to buy anything sticky for afters. They settled for fruit, finished the wine, and eked out the amaretto coffee - Jake's favourite.

Jake relived his day at the town hall. It was business as usual in the legal department: a dispute over a plot of land, a citizen suing the council because he slipped on the icy town hall steps, the prospect of more redundancies among the council workforce. Alison listened without enthusiasm. Jake could tell a story but tonight's audience was not a responsive one.

He drained his stone mug, savouring the last hint of almond, and chanced his arm. "How did it go then?"

"Not good." She was prepared to talk. That boded well.

"Jake, I'm in above my head. I can't cope with this management business. And the kids, they're just horrific - took no notice of me whatsoever."

"Come on, sweet, this isn't like you," Jake fibbed. He knew she had to be handled carefully when she went into self-doubt mode. He also knew her well enough to be sure that she would bounce back and come out fighting. The relative speed of her recovery often depended on Jake making the right choices about what to say, how much and when. He had made a good start. At least she was communicating. By next morning she would have resumed her alter ego: confidence personified.

Alison was not one to skimp on detail. A moment by moment account of her day would have switched off a less dedicated partner than James Lister. As it was, Jake fixed his eyes on her face and concentrated on concentrating. His resolve failed him from time to time and his mind wandered to his mates at the pub - after all Monday evening *was* quiz night - or to planning his next working day. His face, however, was the image of the seasoned counsellor and Alison warmed to the therapy.

What was wrong with kids nowadays? Didn't they have any respect? And what about the staff? Why didn't they do something? How could she possibly work with Rogerson? He didn't seem to have the first idea about how to run a school. And then there was that staff meeting, after school...

"Ladies and gentlemen... er ... ladies and gentlemen, could I have your attention, please? It's nearly ten minutes to four and I should like to make a start."

The conversations wafted away and eventually Dr Rogerson was able to begin.

"I know most of you will already have bumped into her but can I formally introduce Alison... er...Alison...," glancing at the scrap of paper in his hand, "...Lister, who has replaced Ted Lambert as Deputy Head. Welcome, Alison, I hope your stay with us is an enjoyable one. Would you like to say a few words, my dear?"

Several colleagues cringed at his obsequiousness.

Alison, on the front row, rose awkwardly to her feet and half turned towards the staff. She was taken aback by the profusion of pallor around her; one day back after the holidays and so many worn out, fraught, disillusioned faces.

"Well, yes, of course. I'm sorry, I wasn't expecting to be invited to speak. I... er... I'm delighted to join you and look forward to a happy working relationship with you all."

A few colleagues faintly smiled their support. Most continued to look downwards, shuffling whatever papers they had in their laps.

Alison, relieved, sank into the faded, armless, staffroom easy-chair. Dr Rogerson regained his feet and, peering over his reading glasses, disclosed the agenda.

"As you are all aware, the Office for Standards in Education will be inspecting us after half term. During the week beginning 26 February, to be precise. There are a number of after school meetings I would like you all to attend, so please have your diaries at the ready. Friday 9 February will be a Baker Day, so, please make a note of that. The purpose of these meeting slots is to enable us all to do some preparation for the week of the inspection. The school is, of course, doing as well as could be expected, given the nature of our clientele and the pitiful level of funding."

Alison felt she had been pole-axed. Granted her interview had been back in October, but the staff and governors would have known about the proposed inspection then. Why had no one mentioned it? Why had she been so stupid as not to ask? It was only eight months since her former school, just thirty minutes away from Southdale, had been put through an inspection and had been given a grudgingly clean bill of health. She remembered the extent of her exhaustion, as head of department, after the last time. She recalled the interminable build-up, the stresses and strains of the week itself, the tears and the soul searching, and the hours of follow-up time devoted to putting right the issues thrown up by the OFSTED team. The kids' behaviour had been almost faultless at the time of the inspection but they certainly made the staff pay for that in the aftermath.

Alison fought to concentrate on what Dr Rogerson was saying. A few half raised fingers around the room indicated a desire to speak. Rogerson ignored them until he had said his piece; he hated being interrupted, and then, removing his clear rimmed plastic spectacles and chewing for comfort on one of the arms, "Yes, Henry?"

Henry Appleton was head of science. He went back nearly as far as Ted Lambert but, unlike Ted, Henry was hated by almost everyone. Parents remembered his cruel sarcasm. The clips and the clouts handed out by Ted they could remember indulgently.

"Old Lambert would clip your ear as soon as look at you. I remember the time he slippered the whole class when the PE teacher made us late for his lesson. But it never did us any harm. That's what missing nowadays: a bit of discipline. A bit of discipline never did us any harm and we wouldn't have got away with that bare faced cheek, the way you youngsters do."

Henry was a different case altogether. Former pupils, at parents' evening with their offspring, shuddered at the sight of Henry sitting augustly at the same table, in the same place in the hall, as he had always done. They shied away from visiting him for fear that his mortifying stare would trigger off the distress and embarrassment they had felt all those years ago. Those who did manage to summon the courage to approach his table, left convinced that Appleton himself had perfect recall and had inwardly enjoyed reliving their past discomfiture as he spouted 'falling standards of behaviour' and 'incompetent parents'.

Henry despised Rogerson and had done so since the head took up his post some six years earlier. Rogerson had had cause, within his first few days, to call Henry into his office, in response to a parental complaint. Henry had never forgiven him and never would.

"I can't see what all the fuss is about, Bill." He delighted in using the head's first name, in front of as many others as possible. He knew Rogerson wished to keep a suitable distance between himself and his staff, especially during school hours. The head had occasionally relented at school camp, while enjoying a comradely cup of cocoa, after hours, but had quickly brought to book any colleagues who dared to maintain that degree of familiarity 'back at the ranch'. Indeed, a female colleague, who had shared a lift with 'Dr Bill' for practically all of his eighteen terms at the school, had been more than a little offended when her assumption that travelling together should entitle her to speak familiarly was brusquely rebuffed.

Since their early run-in, Rogerson had been afraid of Henry and Henry knew it.

"I shall not be putting on anything special for that set of failed ex teachers and accountants, so they can like it or lump it." Henry added.

Henry was not at all popular with his colleagues but several of them could relate to his feelings about OFSTED inspectors. They had a deep distrust of any outsiders but were particularly opposed to any who, while not doing the job themselves, were prepared to express an opinion on how it should be done. This group included pupils and their parents, governors, LEA officers and advisers, social workers and psychologists, OFSTED inspectors, but above all councillors and members of parliament.

Edith Barker, modern languages teacher, raised a diffident finger, in Dr Rogerson's direction.

"Go ahead, Edith."

"I don't know if anyone else shares my concern, headmaster, but, from what I've heard about inspection in other schools, it's a pretty horrible prospect. I've not had anyone in my classroom since I was a student teacher and the very thought of it gives me the shakes."

"Well, that's something we are all going to have to come to terms with, Edith, and I am certainly proposing that the head and deputies observe all of you teach in the next few weeks to give you a practice run."

Dr Rogerson called the meeting to a close at exactly four thirty. It was his photography club evening and he did not wish to be home late. He strode to his office and was just slipping his tupperware sandwich box into his leather executive briefcase, when someone tapped at the open door. He looked over his shoulder to see Alison. He swallowed his frustration at not being able to get straight off and forced a barely welcoming smile.

"Come in, my dear. I hope it won't take too long. You see, I've got an important appointment later this evening."

"I'll not keep you long. I was just wondering why no one told me about the inspection. It came as quite a shock, I can tell you."

Rogerson sighed inwardly but his face remained impassive. He did so hope that his new deputy was not going to make a habit of interrogating him about the way he ran the school. He remained resolutely on his feet and did not offer Alison the opportunity to seat herself. He thought for a while.

Alison had not been *his* choice. He had not had much time for Ted Lambert's managerial naivety but at least Ted's discipline had been strong. He had known how to handle the difficult kids. How could someone so relatively inexperienced, who had only taught in middle of the road comprehensives, possibly be right for a school like Southdale? The LEA governors had wanted to get a woman in and that deputy director of education, whose children Alison had taught, had, in Rogerson's opinion, unduly influenced the panel to a point where he, himself, had been unable to secure his own preferred candidate.

"It's quite simple really. A school in this sort of area gets few enough applications as it is. Why should we put off the few decent applicants we got with an extra complication?"

"You mean important information regarding the post was deliberately kept from us?"

"You could put it that way, I suppose."

Jake smiled and shrugged his shoulders. Alison had got it off her chest and she would soon start to think positively again.

"I think I should have stayed where I was or, at any rate, looked for a head of faculty job first before going in at the deep end."

"I'm sorry, love, but that *is* nonsense. Everyone knows you were ready for that promotion. It'll take a few days to get used to the change but you'll do it."

"I wish I had the faith in myself that you appear to have."

Jake suggested a stiff drink before bed. Alison declined and they agreed on an instant coffee. Unusually they were both showered and in bed by eleven. Alison leaned across Jake's chest to set the alarm for six fifteen. He stroked her loosened, crinkly, auburn locks and breathed in their blow dried freshness.

"Good night, Jake." she said pointedly and turned to face the wall. Jake took the hint. He switched off the wall mounted lamp and rolled on to his side, effectively doubling the distance between them as he did.

3 Scourge of the staffroom

Alison hated offices that looked like offices. By the end of her first week at Southdale, she had stripped her notice boards of their charts and replaced them with black sugar paper on to which she had lovingly transferred part of her treasured collection of postcards. She had cards from all over the world. Whenever she and Jake went on holiday, she would buy more cards to keep than to post. When her friends went on holiday, she would plead with them to bring a card back, personally, and without a message, so that it would remain in pristine condition.

On her desk, she established a yucca and a palm sort of thing. Other plants were deposited on the window ledge and on the cupboards away from the window. Jake was the one with the green fingers. He had told her which plants would flower and which ones would look nice but just stay green. He had given her written instructions on how to water them and how often - "Not straight from the tap, far too cold, leave water to reach room temperature before using it."

"Just like red wine." she had observed.

Jake had bought her a little plastic watering jug with a long spout and some liquid in a small brown bottle. He had gift wrapped both to cheer her up.

Alison folded Jake's instructions into four and placed them reverently under the Welsh slate paper weight, that she had filched from their study at home.

Alison had met Ted Lambert just fleetingly before he retired. She had come into school for a morning, before Christmas, to try to ease the change over. She had taken an instant shine to him. He seemed the epitome of the perfect granddad.

"I've cleared out both filing cabinets," Ted announced gleefully, "to give you a fresh start."

Alison had been grateful for the sentiment but uncertain about the wisdom of such a gesture. Her uncertainty had later changed to downright frustration. There was nothing in the office to give her an inkling about the school and what really made it tick. She had to find out everything by asking.

"When is the next round of departmental meetings?"

"Heads of department call them as necessary. No agenda - no meeting!"

"Can I see a copy of the school development plan?"

"The what?"

"Is there a schedule for Baker days?"

"Dr Rogerson hasn't made his mind up yet."

"Who is the appraisal co-ordinator?"

"It'll probably be Brian Ingleton, the senior teacher. He tends to deal with stuff like that."

Alison pinned up her *Friends of the Earth* calendar, printed on recycled paper, and circled, in red, 26 February. She traced with her index finger back through the weeks and sighed: "Six weeks today."

Brian Ingleton was the third member of the senior management team. He was gentle by nature and easy to approach. Alison guessed that he was nearer fifty than forty but she found it difficult to tell with men who had begun to lose their hair. She learned that Brian had a boy of ten and a girl of eight. Perhaps he was younger than he looked. Alison felt instinctively that she and Brian would get on. Brian had his finger on the pulse more than anyone else she had met at Southdale and he was prepared to spend time filling in the background details for her.

Though the roll was at present around the six hundred mark, and falling, as little as nine years ago, Southdale had had over a thousand students, including a small sixth form of about seventy. Financial cutbacks had rendered the sixth form non viable. The arrival of local management and competition between schools had increased the pressures, particularly since Southdale's nearest secondary neighbour, a former grammar school, had been blessed with an aggressive, go-getting businesswoman of a head. She had used every trick in the book to sell her establishment at the expense of Southdale. She was rumoured to have privately vowed not to rest until Southdale had closed.

Time was clearly on her side. Tempted by middle class values and inflated promises of academic success, ambitious parents had deserted the community school, in droves, to seek the greener pastures on the other side of the hill.

Six years ago the LEA had colluded with the governors to convince Southdale's previous head that his 'love the little darlings to death' approach would be more suited to the advisory service. Rogerson had been brought in to stop the rot. The rot had not stopped.

Rumours had been around for three or four years that, under government pressure to get rid of surplus places, Southdale was the council's number one target for closure. Brian felt that a damning OFSTED report would be as good as Southdale's death warrant.

Alison's starting mid-year at Southdale had been a problem for the timetabler. It was a bigger problem for Alison. As the timetabler, Verna Richardson, Head of Maths, said, "We don't have any spare science classes to be taught. You will have to pick up Ted's classes and do the best you can."

Ted had taught twelve periods out of twenty-five in the course of a week. He was one of those teachers who could turn his hand to most things. He was always very proud of being given the toughest, most disaffected Year 11 classes and having them eating out of his hand in a couple of weeks.

He was not particularly gifted as a teacher. His lessons were not exciting and, indeed, on many an occasion, they would have induced dormancy in even the most heedful of students. Ted had something, though, in addition to the customary authority bestowed on the position of deputy head. No one ever complained about his boring bits.

When, from time to time a youth, emboldened by success with lesser teachers, decided to try his luck with Ted, it just fell flat. The hapless miscreant was simply greeted with impatience by his peers. Ted would give him the famous look which had withered a thousand would-be troublemakers and carry on with the lesson in the sure and certain knowledge that the individual would not risk a second encounter.

Ted was a hard act to follow as Alison soon found out.

Personal and social education had been Alison's second-string subject during her teacher training. She had taught a few lessons on school experience but now she had to pick up Ted's Year 11 PSE group, last lesson on a Wednesday.

Teachers and pupils hate Wednesdays. The weekend before has long evaporated in the mists of time and the weekend to come still seems light years ahead.

True to form, Verna Richardson had given Ted a regular handful of a PSE group. It is one of the great mysteries of education how, despite the best efforts of all and sundry to come up with socially well balanced forms, there is always one class that defies all expectations and makes teachers' lives an utter misery.

Henry Appleton had been form tutor of 11HA since they started in year seven. As if predisposed by Henry's ghastly eminence they had immediately assumed the mantle of scourge of the staffroom. Several exclusions, over the years, and a number of changes of personnel had not improved the situation. The group had fought hard to preserve its corporate image and continued to revel in its success at bringing teachers to their knees.

It was Wednesday afternoon, three weeks into the term. During Alison's first lesson with 11HA, there had been some preliminary sparring. Lesson two had taxed Alison's strategies significantly further. As she entered the arena for the third time it was immediately obvious that something was 'in the air'. That sixth sense that teachers acquire made Alison uncomfortable from the moment she set foot in the classroom.

Alan Sumner had tried his luck with Ted Lambert, in the early days of year ten. He had, of course, failed to ruffle Ted's feathers and had contented himself with baiting easier targets. With the arrival of the new deputy head, Alan saw a golden opportunity to do what he was best at: winding teachers up.

Alan took great pleasure in his own physique. It certainly was not through any effort of his own, but he had developed hugely muscular upper arms and delighted in wearing sleeveless t-shirts that threatened to shred if he inhaled too energetically. His well built torso tapered to narrow hips which almost fused into endlessly slim legs. At a little over six feet tall, Alan cut an impressive figure.

Those pupils who did not despise him admired him for his looks, for his power or for the effect he created. All of them feared him. Most teachers were wary of Alan. Some of the more macho males occasionally tried to put him down but nearly all were careful not to overstep the mark. A hot-headed, rugby playing student teacher had once got himself into a confrontation with Alan. Only a timely intervention by Brian Ingleton had allowed both parties to disengage without losing face.

As she faltered into a lesson on 'preparing for the world of work' Alison felt thankful that the class had already completed the module on sex education.

Her sensation of discomfort and unease continued to grow. She dare not look in Alan's direction but she was intensely aware of his eyes burning into her body. It was as if he had X-ray vision. Even the unflattering clothes that she carefully chose for school could not disguise Alison's firm, still young figure. She had always recognized the power that an attractive female teacher could bring to bear on teenage boys and, unlike some of her colleagues, she had always repudiated its use.

Alison got through her opening talk. As the class started to weary of concentration and become a little fidgety, Alison invited general discussion. The degree of indifference was bewildering - the stuff of which many teachers despair.

"OK, then, give me a couple of examples, from your work experience, of how the world of work differs from school."

"It was even more boring and I had to get up earlier."

Guffaws from the class.

"Thank you, Erica, but please try to remember that you do not get any credit for an answer, in my class, unless you put your hand up."

"I didn't have to put my hand up on work experience."

"That's quite enough, Erica."

"Well, I've given you three answers. What's the point of asking our opinions if you aren't going to listen to them?"

Eventually, Alison risked a glance in Alan's direction. He was sitting back on his chair with his feet on the desk in front of him. He pursed his lips in her direction. She motioned at his feet. He looked quizzical, pretended not to understand.

Unsettled, Alison made the mistake of stating the obvious.

"Your feet are on the table."

He stared at her defiantly for what seemed an age. Alison would not wilt. She was made of stronger stuff than that. She motioned towards his feet once again and asserted, "Take your feet off the table."

Alan delayed. Alison could sense the reaction going through his mind: "What if I don't?" Alan detected the steely determination in her eye. He relented.

He balanced for a second on the back legs of his chair while he deftly pushed the desk forward with the toe of his shoe before allowing his feet to crash to the floor for maximum effect.

4 Count to ten

It was so awful that Alison could not even tell Jake what Alan Sumner had said to her. At first she was bewildered, then she felt ill and finally fear gave way to intense anger. She had smouldered all evening. Jake's hour in the kitchen had been a pointless one. She had barely disturbed the mound of rice on her plate and the lamb cutlet looked only slightly mauled. The half-full glass of Australian red completed the testament to Alison's dark mood.

After dinner, Jake tactfully volunteered to load the dishwasher while Alison fiddled perfunctorily with the contents of her well worn leather briefcase. She would be locked in the privacy of her own thoughts for the remainder of the evening and Jake knew this only too well.

When she was feeling normal, Alison really did appreciate Jake. Five years ago when she had first taken him to visit her parents, her mother had cornered her in the kitchen to get the low-down on her latest and most promising attachment.

"Well, *he's* a bit of all right. I should hold on to him, if I were you."

"Mum, don't interfere, I've only known him for three months. There's more to life than living with a man."

"I'd only known your dad for six weeks when he popped the question."

"And look at you two now!"

"Don't be cheeky. We've a lot to be thankful for, me and your Dad. Most of your friends' parents had split by the time they reached sixteen."

"Yes, I know, Mum, settling down was just right for you and Dad, but that doesn't mean it's the best thing for all of us. I've been bitten once before, you know."

"Jake is different. It stands out a mile. He's not one of those macho types, always using women to boost his own ego. He's quiet and gentle and not in the least like Clive."

"Don't mention *his* name, please. I've just about succeeded in getting him out of my mind. You're right, though, Jake is different. Hard as I try I can't have an argument with him. He just refuses to argue and that completely takes the wind out of my sails."

Days later, Alison had popped the question to Jake. Jake's response had been delayed only sufficiently long for him to recover from his surprise. They had married quietly, at the start of the summer holidays, and had taken Jake's beaten up old tent to France, a ritual they had repeated each subsequent year. Alison had not once regretted her decision but when she was feeling playfully annoyed she was sometimes frustrated by Jake's total refusal to take the bait. It took all the fun out of arguing, a pastime that Alison revelled in, if she were being honest with herself.

That evening Jake's reaction was just what Alison needed. It gave her the time and space to sort things out in her own mind. By eleven thirty, she knew exactly what she had to do. Drained by the mental effort of the evening and relieved at the glimpse of a way forward, Alison crumpled on the bed and fell asleep while Jake was still cleaning his teeth. He rolled her gently under the bedclothes and lay looking at her for some minutes before switching off the light.

At four thirty, Jake gave up the struggle to sleep and went downstairs to make coffee.

Friday morning, 19 January, Alison arrived at school at 7.45. She dumped her battered briefcase on her desk and made straight for Dr Bill's office. The door was closed. She knocked. No answer. His car had been in the car park. She knocked again. Dr Bill's private lavatory flushed. She allowed a decent interval to pass and knocked a third time.

"Come."

Alison strode in. The boss was wiping his hands on a paper towel. Two paper tissues were spread out on his desk. On them were a freshly prepared bowl of muesli and milk, a glass of orange juice and a mug of coffee. Rogerson barely managed to conceal his annoyance.

"Ah, good morning, Alison. You've caught me at it, I see. Like to get here early. Traffic gets bad about eight. Excuse the breakfast."

The 'Today' programme droned quietly in the background. Rogerson sighed, pressed the button on his radio and moved to the easy chairs surrounding his coffee table.

"Do take a seat, my dear."

Alison obeyed without a word.

"What can I do for you so bright and early?"

"It's about the incident."

"The incident?"

"Yes, yesterday afternoon ... Alan Sumner."

"Oh, *that* incident. Yes, I've had a word with the boy and spoken to his year tutor. You won't have any further trouble from him."

"It's not good enough."

"I beg your pardon?"

"It just is not good enough. That boy has humiliated me. I'll never be able to walk past him again without thinking about what he said to me."

"You know what it's like with boys of his age: bravado and all that. I'll get him to apologise and that will be the end of it."

"With respect, Dr Rogerson, you're missing the point. Students cannot be allowed to talk to members of staff in that disgusting way and get away with it."

"Were there any witnesses?"

"Are you doubting my word?"

"Not in the least but if it were to go any further there would obviously be questions asked by his family."

"Such as?" Alison could feel the anger welling up inside her.

"Well, for example, was there anything in your demeanour that might have encouraged his behaviour?"

"Of course not."

"He would dispute that."

"I can't believe the way this conversation is going. If he gets away with it, it will be all round the school in no time and no female teacher will feel protected against such abuse."

"You said yourself that there were no witnesses."

"Alan Sumner is not the sort of person to keep a victory to himself."

"No matter what we do, Sumner will spread his side of the story on the grapevine."

"All the more important to be seen to take effective action."

"I can't risk it blowing up into a major crisis not with the inspection coming up."

"I can't think the inspectors would hold it against you for making a stand against such indiscipline."

Rogerson had had enough. He did not respond well to criticism, constructive or otherwise.

"That is quite enough Mrs Lister. Please do not overstep the bounds of your role. As far as I am concerned, the matter has been dealt with. I would ask you to respect the finality of my decision and return to your duties."

Alison was seeing crimson. She fought to remember Jake's advice: "Count to ten. Don't lose your cool. Lose your cool and you've lost the argument." Her lips tightened. A prodigious effort subdued her instincts. She controlled her voice. Defiance misted her eyes.

"Thank you," she intoned and quit the head's office.

In the comfort of her own room she gave vent to her emotions and hated herself, for the rest of the day, for breaking down in tears.

The fire alarm went half way through the final period. Brian Ingleton was teaching and no one knew where Dr Rogerson was. It was left to Alison to try to inject some order into the chaos that ensued. She scanned the corridor. Classroom doors were opening and youngsters were spewing out. She ran to the office.

"Is it a drill, a false alarm or is it for real?"

"No idea, love."

Alison turned on her heel and hastened along the corridor in the direction of the mounting storm. Kids were pushing and jostling and calling out smart remarks. The exits were rapidly filling up and those youngsters nearest to the doors were at risk of being trampled or crushed. Rushing here and there, Alison had some success in reducing the commotion. Beyond the exits anarchy ruled. Youngsters rivalled each other in silliness.

Once the heaving mass of bodies had propelled itself, toothpaste like, into the yard, Alison slipped outside and joined two or three colleagues who were seeking to round up the flock and direct it towards the allotted tarmac, some fifty metres from the buildings. Bit by bit the great mosaic emerged as the form groupings reluctantly reassembled alongside the appropriate initials, greying-white on the crumbling asphalt.

Some staff yapped orders into the air. Some entreated, others implored. Some cajoled, others led by the arm or warily shepherded. Painfully, the school took shape.

Miriam Stewart, stalwart of the PE department, who would not have been out of place in a boot camp, had had enough. The 'commandant' was nowhere to be seen. The other two 'senior officers' were running around like headless chickens trying to restore calm. It was time for an 'NCO' to take charge. She extracted the 'Acme Thunderer' from her tracksuit bottoms and gave a piercing blast. Colleagues standing nearby shielded their pain racked ears. Silence cut through the cacophony like a carving knife. Stunned, the students remained in shock for a few seconds and then nervous giggles led to the resumption of the chatter, this time at a level more befitting the seriousness of the situation.

It was then that Dr Rogerson made his appearance. Gripped in his fist, magnum like, he carried the ageing loudhailer, the relic of times when sports days were still imaginable. He strode across the yard and joined Alison in the central position she had assumed, ready to pass on her instructions to the calmed masses. Rogerson said nothing to her. He raised the loudhailer to his mouth, pressed the trigger and proclaimed:

"Hear this, everyone. Once your register has been checked, you are dismissed. Return to your classrooms only to pick up your belongings and then go home."

Shrieks of delight greeted his final words. Form tutors fought vainly to call their registers against the rising excitement. Unable to contain themselves longer, individuals leaked away from the group. A trickle became a stream and then a surging torrent as more and more youngsters walked, then jogged and then, free from any restraint, sprinted towards the buildings to retrieve their possessions and then disgorge into the unsuspecting streets.

Teachers and support staff threw up their arms in despair. Alison had gone to Rogerson's elbow. Her advice fell on ears deafened by the crescendo.

"What are you doing?" she heard herself say. "This is madness! We must get them back inside, in an orderly fashion; discover what set the alarm off; find out if anyone was out of class and why..."

It was too late. No one could have reversed the flood, once Rogerson had opened the gates. Alison stood and watched until nearly everyone had left and then returned to her office without speaking further.

As Jake had remarked the same evening, "Hindsight is an abundant gift in any organisation." The next morning the staffroom was greatly endowed with hindsight. Brian Ingleton and Alison held their own post mortem before sharing their findings and their opinions with the head.

The tell-tale splinters of glass had confirmed that the alarm was a malicious act. Brian, who was safety officer, confessed sheepishly that the statutory fire practice had not been held in the autumn term. In fact he could not quite remember when the last intentional drill had been held. There were enough false alarms, usually, to help satisfy the basic requirements of the law. Alison had to concede that, in her short time at the school, she had not noticed the absence of fire instructions from most of the classrooms. Petty vandalism and natural wastage had accounted for them.

"Do the year sevens get told what to do about the fire alarm, when they first start?" she asked.

"In theory, yes. But you know what it's like at the start of term."

Alison did indeed know what it was like at the start of term but there were some things that simply could not be ignored. The inspectors would have a field day. How could she, personally, feel so answerable for the school's shortcomings?

5 A soft spot

Clive Holdsworth had been a competent geography teacher back in the early eighties. Young people did not mess around in his lessons. On the other hand they did not particularly enjoy them either. Examination results were always above the school's average, which gave Clive an exalted rating with the senior management and governors. On a personal level very few colleagues, governors, or parents and students for that matter, felt comfortable in any sort of sustained exchange with him. No matter what the question, he always had the answer.

As the eighties advanced, unemployment and the politicians' habitually voiced carping criticism of schools began to corrode the ambition of staff and students alike. Many boys, in particular, lost the will to strive. Clive, uneasy about his GCSE statistics, had carried out numerous home visits. Repeatedly, when he called during his free periods, he encountered dads and older brothers sprawled out in front of the television, in smoke-filled, greasy living rooms. Often, mum was out cleaning or washing hair at the local salon.

Ordinarily, he got a reasonable reception. The parents' mouths declared solicitude for the success of their children but far too often their eyes spoke of resignation, despair and hopelessness. The kids themselves were more forthright.

"You're telling me to do geography homework and revise so I'll get a D grade in my GCSE but what's the point? Everyone in my family is on the dole since the pit closed. Where am I going to get a job?"

Clive felt powerless. What could he do in the face of growing disaffection? His examination results were tailing off. It was time to get out. When a neighbouring Authority advertised for a Humanities Adviser, he jumped at the chance. His head's glowing reference and Clive's undisputed flair for speaking well of himself won the day.

Clive, delivered from the everyday burden of doing the job himself, had enjoyed telling others how do it. His courses were often oversubscribed and most of the evaluation sheets were positive. Clive was in his element. It was his first taste of influence at the chalk face without a can to carry.

This interval in his life was all too short lived. The government's renewed pressure on local council spending saw massive economies in LEA spending. Jobs were at risk. The simultaneous blooming of national inspection of schools afforded Clive his escape route. He retrained for OFSTED.

The telephone in Dr Rogerson's office had exasperated him by ringing all morning. As it sounded, yet again, he moved reluctantly from his bookcase where he had been scrutinizing his accumulation of management volumes and breathed "Yes?" into the mouthpiece.

"I have a call from OFSTED for you, Dr Rogerson."

Rogerson grunted concurringly.

"Good morning, Dr Rogerson, Holdsworth here, Registered Inspector."

Clive savoured these calls. He could discern the rise in the recipient's heartbeat. It accentuated his status.

"I'm just calling to make sure the arrangements are in place for the OFSTED parents' meeting. Wednesday, 7 February? In the school hall? At 7pm? OK. Thanks. I should like you to be there at the start to introduce me and my colleague, the lay inspector, but you will have to leave before the meeting starts, of course. Yes, yes, I look forward to meeting you, as well. Goodbye."

When the telephone rang again it was the last straw.

"What is it?" Rogerson growled into the receiver.

"I'm sorry to disturb you again, Dr Rogerson, but it's the chair of governors on the phone. She'd like to see you this afternoon."

"What about?"

"She's being a bit cagey but she did say something about Mrs Lister."

"Oh, very well. Two o'clock."

"She's seeing Mrs Lister at two."

"Two thirty," he retorted.

Alison had not wasted any time in taking things further. The weekend had only bolstered the impression that she was in the right. On

Monday morning she had telephoned her regional union representative and she had also expounded the situation to Gladys Ollerenshaw, Southdale's chair of governors.

Gladys was something of a local personality. She was politically active and spent much of her time supporting the various causes and campaigns espoused by Edward, her councillor husband.

Gladys was not herself a career woman, at least not in a paid employment sense, but her appetite for voluntary work was rapacious. Her husband's comfortable position as accountant with a local business permitted her to figure prominently on the local charity and community action scene.

She respected a woman who knew her own mind and was prepared to speak it. During the interviews for the deputy head post she had fostered a soft spot for Alison and had experienced a sense of personal satisfaction, having persuaded the male dominated panel that Alison was the best person for the job.

"Ugh! What's that floating in my coffee?" Tina Chatham pushed aside a half corrected pile of geography exercise books to get a closer look at the flake of off-white paint which had drifted with such accuracy from the staffroom ceiling."

"Bloody flat roofs."

"I beg your pardon?" Tina half turned towards the track-suited figure in a battered easy chair near the window.

Simon Cunliffe, feet on a low coffee table, *Daily Mirror* unfurled across his lap, was chomping on a *Granny Smith's*.

"Flat roofs. When they built this dump it was cheaper to give it a flat roof. Now it fills up with water until it leaks through. The council patches it up and the water finds another way in. They patch it up again and again until the ceiling falls in. Then we make the front page of the *Chronicle*. The council huffs and puffs about government cut-backs, patches up the roof and we start all over again. In local government circles it's known as strategic planning."

"Oh, Simon, you are a cynic."

Tina used the blunt end of her red *biro* to flick the paint flake on to the pockmarked table. She slurped her coffee and decided she had done enough marking for one free period.

"I hear our new deputy's making a right fuss about Alan Sumner. They say she's getting the union in. Old Rogerson's throwing a *dicky-fit*."

Simon misjudged his aim and the already browning core of his apple cannoned off the ugly, angular, dark green, metallic rubbish bin before skidding under the staff pigeon holes. The inside pages of the *Mirror* slid to the floor with the recoil.

"I don't know what she's getting excited about. Some of the old bags on this staff would be only too grateful to cause a stirring in some young buck's loins."

"I see equal opps. is lost on you, Simon."

Simon snorted.

Tina continued. "She *has* got a point though. Why should staff have to put up with that sort of crap from kids?"

This time Simon's snort was less convincing. "That prat Sumner just needs a good beating. Ten minutes in the showers with me would sort him out."

Tina knew it was pointless to comment. Simon would not even notice her silence. She took her cold coffee to the sink and poured it over the collection of used mugs already in residence there.

"I hope Mrs Lister gets her way. At least she's prepared to stick up for herself and the message might get through to some of the kids and their parents."

Simon deposited the remainder of his newspaper on the decaying carpet and turned his thoughts to lunch time rugby practice.

Brian Ingleton's declining *Cavalier* spluttered into life at the third pull, expelling a toxic billow into the immediate atmosphere. On the passenger seat was a rather under-ripe banana and a sliced bread, grated cheese and *Branston* sandwich, in one of those impractical triangular plastic containers that seemed to be at the cutting edge of school meals provision.

Turning right at the school gate, Brian drove deliberately towards *the shops*. His lunch hour had followed this regular pattern, since he had been promoted to senior teacher four years earlier. He parked in front of the boarded-up florist's and headed towards the *chippy*. Though the school bell had barely stopped reverberating through his head, a gang of youngsters was already beginning to coagulate on the pavement.

An old woman, hauling a shopping bag on wheels, exchanged insults with the group as their presence intimidated her into the road. Spotting Brian, she waddled towards him.

"It's disgusting, Mr Ingleton. You ought to do something about it up at the school. We never dared to talk to older people like that in our day. We'd have got a clip round the ear. That's what's missing nowadays a bit of discipline."

A few animal-like noises emanated from the group of youngsters. Brian looked up, his stare charged with unheeded disapproval.

"Leave it to me, love. I'll have a word. We do our best, you know, but if their parents don't teach them right from wrong it's an uphill struggle."

"I wouldn't have your job for all the tea in China."

Brian approached the sneering group. They were on their own territory and numbers made them brave. For Brian it was just another role play and years of experience had taught him how to come out of these skirmishes relatively unscathed.

"Now then you lot, what's going on? You've upset that old dear."

"*She* started it, talking to us as if we're rubbish."

"You should show some respect for your elders."

"They don't respect us. All we're doing is standing here. They think they own the place, telling us what to do all the time."

"OK, let's calm down a bit shall we? All of you know you're not supposed to be out of school unless you go home for dinner. Hang on, hang on, don't all talk at once. How many of you go home? OK. Right. You lot get off home or you'll be late back. What about the rest of you? Why have you left school without permission?"

"It's our free time. You can't make us stay in school. My mum says I can do what I like at dinner and if you try to stop me she's going to come up and see Rogerson."

"*Dr* Rogerson to you, Mandy. If your mum doesn't like the rules at our school she'll have to find somewhere else for you to go."

"My mum's boyfriend says Southdale is crap anyway and all the teachers are crap too."

"Give it a rest, Mandy. If you don't shut up, I'll have to put you in detention."

"My mum says you can't put me in detention. It's unlawful imprisonment."

"Mandy! On your way!"

In the dining-room, Alison left her lukewarm plate of chili and chips for the third time to enter into negotiation with a group of rowdy Y8s.

"Didn't your parents teach you how to behave at mealtimes? If I see anyone else throwing chips they'll be coming to see me at home time."

"It wasn't me, miss. It was him."

"No it wasn't. It was him."

"Was it?"

"Shut up and get on with your meal or I'll chuck you out right now."

Returning to her table, Alison found it populated by chattering Y7s. A supervisor had cleared her plate away.

At a safe distance from the dining-room, behind the closed door of his office, Bill Rogerson was studying his bulky copy of the *Head's Legal Guide*.

6 Stop digging

"For goodness sake get off your high horse, Bill. It's *me* you're talking to now."

Gladys Ollerenshaw replenished her cup from the delicate china teapot. She helped herself to another *arrowroot* biscuit and immersed it in the lukewarm liquid, just long enough for it to soften without disintegrating, before transferring it to her ample mouth. She paused to allow the brownish mass to dissolve before continuing.

"Give the lass a break. She's the best chance you've got of turning this school around."

"Don't do this to me, Gladys. I've taken my decision and I as good as told Sumner's mother that it wouldn't go any further. What credibility will I have in the community, if I go back on my word?"

Gladys opened her mouth to speak, thought better of it and dived for the pile of *arrowroots*, once again. Through a gentle spray of humid crumbs, she went on, "Most of the people in this village are the salt of the earth. All they want to know is that they are sending their kids to a school that will teach them right from wrong, how to add up and how to write proper. Convince them of that and you've got them eating out of your hand. The folks around here aren't thick, just because they don't have a fancy education. They know what's what. They know all about Becky Sumner and her sort. They don't want their kids being influenced by her foul-mouthed, ill-mannered offspring any more than Alison Lister and the rest of the staff do. Think about it, Bill. If you let the Sumners get away with that sort of unpardonable behaviour, you've lost it. Other kids will think staff are fair game and the school will have a succession of similar problems to deal with. Take action now and I guarantee you'll get support from staff, governors, the LEA and most of the parents and pupils as well."

"And if I decide not to take your advice, what then?"

"I hope it won't come to that. However, as you know, I've spoken to Mrs Lister and she's pretty determined. It's just the type of situation the unions would like to get their teeth into. If it goes any further than this office, you know what the press will do to us, with an inspection coming up and all. Come on, Bill, see sense. You're in a hole, so stop digging. It's much better to give way gracefully now than have to back down publicly after a mauling from the *Chronicle*."

Rogerson was hurting inside. "I'll give it some thought."

His attempt to alleviate the pain was to no avail. Gladys Ollerenshaw was fired-up and she would not take *no* for an answer. "The time for thought is over. I need your answer now."

Becky Sumner did not make a habit of going up to school. She *did* go to parents' evening once, when Alan had just started at secondary school, but by the time the fifth teacher had told her what a thorough nuisance he was becoming, she had already decided that she would not, in future, ask questions if Alan did not bring home the invitation to attend.

She was used to letters in manila envelopes. She knew they meant officialdom and usually trouble for her hard-pressed, one-parent family. It was with some trepidation that she tore open that morning's letter to reveal the school's impressive crest and the head's wire coat hanger of a signature. Her presence was required, the following day at nine-fifteen, in the head's study to discuss her son's future.

What had he done now? There was that silly incident recently when he had tried to chat up that bitch of a new deputy head and she had taken it the wrong way. He had probably been in a fight or perhaps he had been picking on that black boy again.

"I don't know what it's about, honest, mum. I haven't done nothing."

Secretly, Alan searched his memory. No, he decidedly did not know what it was about. In truth, he had not been to school for the last few days, preferring to wander the streets and shopping malls of the nearest town with his cronies. You didn't get your mum called to old Rogerson's office for just wagging it.

Becky and Alan hastened along the school drive, ploughing through the trail of discarded drinks' cans and food wrappers. If you were in the upper school and stopped for dinner, it was customary at Southdale to smuggle supplies past the supervisors and eat outdoors, summer, winter, spring or autumn. Only torrential rain forced these hardy picnic lovers into a dilapidated bus shelter or a stale telephone kiosk. Anything was better than that echoey dining-hall, with the younger kids throwing food around and those wretched supervisors yelling at them.

It was nine-thirty. Becky swore under her breath. Why was it that her best intentions always came to nothing? She had set the alarm in good time but one too many *Diamond Whites* the night before had dampened her resolve to get out of bed the first time it rang.

She cursed out loud. Alan, the butt of her resentment, replied in kind. She swung an arm at him and easily missed, losing her balance in the attempt.

"Don't think you're too big to get a clip round the ear, if you talk to me like that!"

"You started it."

"Shut it! Why didn't you get me up? That stuck-up Rogerson will be gunning for us right from the start. I'm going to ring up about those bloody buses. Most of the time they're late and then they come early when you're not expecting it."

"Give it a rest, mum! There's kids watching from the science block."

Bill Rogerson was drumming nervously on his desk.

"Shall I go and 'phone?" enquired Ricky Tomlinson, Head of Year Eleven.

Ricky was older than he looked. His casual mode of dress annoyed Rogerson. Those pants were only the next best thing to jeans. The shirt was denim and the baggy jumper incongruous in Rogerson's company. Tomlinson did get results though. He had this knack of getting through to the kids. He did not talk down to them and they respected that. They would take stuff from him that they would not take from most teachers.

When he had heard about Alan Sumner's abuse of Alison Lister he had sought him out and told him how disappointed he was. Outwardly, Alan's bravado was the same as ever but he could not disguise a temporary inward pang of regret.

Ricky repeated the question: "Shall I go and phone?"

Rogerson, locked in gloomy thought, did not respond.

Ricky looked at Gladys. Gladys nodded, sympathetically. Ricky left the room.

If Becky Sumner was flustered on arrival, she was not about to let it show. In her childhood home, an apology had implied weakness. Ricky Tomlinson hailed her from afar.

"Hi, Mrs Sumner. This way!"

"Who's that?"

"Tomlinson. Year Tutor."

Tomlinson ushered them into the head's office. Becky suppressed a shiver. She had been in that office some years before.

Rogerson was on his feet, as oily as ever.

"Do come in, Mrs Sumner, Alan. You know Mrs Ollerenshaw, Chair of Governors, I'm sure. Take a seat. You sit there, Alan, next to your mother."

Becky contemplated the used china, on the tray, on the coffee table. The roof of her mouth was like grit. Breakfast was not part of the normal routine in the Sumner household.

"Welcome." The greeting rang hollow. "I'm sorry I've had to ask you to come in, this morning, but you'll remember that little problem Alan had with our Mrs Lister. There's a thing or two we need to get sorted out. Mr...er...Tomlinson, would you bring Mrs Sumner up to date?"

Ricky recounted the story. He quoted precisely from Alison's statement. Alan stared straight ahead as if absorbing the titles on Rogerson's neat bookcase. His mother stayed impassive.

"That's about it, Dr Rogerson. Over to you."

Tomlinson's informality irked Rogerson.

"Mrs Ollerenshaw, would you like to add anything at this point?"

"No, thank you. Becky knows what I think about that sort of carry-on."

Rogerson swallowed hard and continued, "You'll appreciate how ...er... serious this incident is, Mrs...er...Sumner. We can't allow that type of behaviour in this school and I am afraid I will have to permanently exclude Alan from Southdale."

Becky was momentarily dumbfounded. The moment soon passed. Her retaliation was swift and awesome. Her response was punctuated with expletives but her message was clear. Rogerson was the worst head teacher that had ever walked the face of the earth. They could keep their school. In fact they knew where they could stick it.

Becky Sumner in a rage was not a sight that Rogerson would like to witness every day. She marked the climax of her outburst with the grandest gesture she could muster. Rogerson's prized china ware crashed about his ankles, staining his pale grey suit, pale brown from the knees down.

Becky gave Gladys a stare that would have frozen Ladybower and flounced from the study. Alan, emboldened by her example, came so close that the unfortunate Rogerson could feel his heated breath on his forehead. He hissed sundry insults into Rogerson's face and then strode haughtily in pursuit of his mother.

Rogerson had to go home to change his suit. It was good to be in the sanctuary of his seventeenth century cottage to regain his composure. When he and Cynthia had first visited, with the estate agent, there had been something church-like about the cool, heavy stone walls.

Thankfully Cynthia was not at home. She must have been out doing good or having coffee with the bishop. At any rate, it was to be on his own that Bill needed at that moment.

Shock gave way painfully to seething hurt and hurt gave way to burning anger. How dare people treat him, the headteacher, in this manner? In days long past, the head of school was someone to be treated with respect, to be spoken to with deference, to be obeyed.

By the time he had showered and pulled a fresh set of clothing from the walk-in wardrobe, the hatred had burned itself out, leaving only dull embers of resentment.

Had he had it within him to empathise, even Rogerson would have been moved by the sight at Scargill Court. Behind their bruised and battered front door, locked in each other's arms, Becky and Alan, mother and son, wearied by the hand life had dealt them, sobbed uncontrollably.

7 A great equaliser

The big snow of the winter came on the following Monday, 29 January. As usual it took everyone by surprise. The weather forecast early that day had spoken of "flurries and a powder coating". By mid-morning the local radio station was covering its tracks with "heavier localised falls by early evening".

As morning break approached, Brian Ingleton surveyed the carpet of white on the school sports field, from the window of his converted store-room office.

The school's ailing central heating system, failed to penetrate the iciness of Brian's cramped work space. An ageing, two bar electric fire took the chill out of the air. Brian stepped over its dangerously stretched, fraying flex to get a better view of the deteriorating conditions.

Snow was a great equaliser. In snowy weather Brian took a perverse delight in contemplating his neighbours' gardens. There was a delicious irony in his neglected patch taking on the same aspect as their manicured showpieces.

Brian chuckled wickedly out-loud.

Already the cans, bottles and packets on the playground had disappeared from view.

He could picture the chaos at Central Transport: the supervisor hastily trying to implement the snow contingency plan while the union convenor buttonholed him about conditions of service and stand-by payments. It would be some time yet before the gritters and ploughs hit the streets and by then they would be so clogged with incompetent drivers and abandoned vehicles that they would be wasting their time.

Brian sighed. "I suppose I had better do something." He knew that it would be dangerous to leave any arrangements to Dr Bill, and Alison, well Alison, she was a good lass but being a former Head of Department, a *curriculum* person, she would not have much idea what to do with a practical problem.

He sent for a couple of pupils who had forgotten their PE kit. There were several to choose from so he picked the two most reliable youngsters. He quickly scribbled a note in duplicate and sent a message around the classrooms.

"Are we going home, sir?" asked one of the messengers hopefully.

"Wait and see, lad. Wait and see."

It was to be *wet break*. Students were to stay in their classrooms. Exceptionally, toilet visits would be allowed but there was to be no loitering in the corridors. Tuck shop was suspended. No one, but no one was to venture outside. Staff may take it in turns to grab a coffee and go back with it immediately to their area.

Brian may as well have instructed the snow to return from whence it came. When the bell rang, everyone needed the toilet. The stronger staff held the fort for a while, as their less determined colleagues gave way to the pressure of thirty bursting bladders. The corridors filled rapidly with squealing adolescents, as excited as pups at their first sight of snow.

With little supervision on the corridors, it was a matter of seconds before a handful of bold year elevens burst out of bounds into the untouched softness of the deepening snow. The younger students needed little encouragement to follow their example.

Snow began to fly in every direction. Self-styled victims were buried in the stuff. Bullies, unfettered, revelled in the liberty to persecute all and sundry, as long as there was no risk of retaliation.

The teachers knew better than to interfere at this stage.

It was a good fifteen minutes after the official end of break by the time the exuberant youngsters had rejoined their classes. Brian, playing the sheep dog, intercepted a red-faced man, in a thick sheepskin coat, inside the main gate.

"Excuse me, can I help?"

"No."

And the man continued to slog through the snow in the direction of the school buildings.

Brian had not been emphatic enough. He slithered after him.

"Hang on a minute, sir. Can I ask what you want?"

"What's it got to do with you, pal?"

"Well, I am senior teacher here, sir and I don't think it's unreasonable for me to ask why you are about to enter the school?"

"I've come for our Natalie."

"Is there some sort of a problem, sir?"

"Problem? What do you mean a problem? I've come to take her home before this snow gets worse."

"This is very irregular, sir, we don't just let youngsters go out of school because of a bit of snow."

"Well, I'm taking our Natalie, whether you like it or not. So get her down here right away."

"I'm sorry, sir... I simply can't..."

"I'll get her myself then."

The man's face was even redder. Brian stood and watched in amazement as he wrenched open the door of the main entrance and launched into the corridor, spreading a trail of white in his wake.

Brian went back to his converted store-room. He plugged in and switched on the ancient radio, a relic of the time when live wireless programmes had been regularly used in schools. After some seconds of hisses, wheezes and crackles he heard the familiar jingle of the local station.

On days like this the local radio station took pleasure in its community role. It announced events that were off and those, presumably with hardier (some would say foolhardy) organisers, which would go ahead regardless.

After several minutes of information about cub packs, line dances and old folks' clubs, Brian was rewarded with an update on the weather situation. More snow expected. Vehicles having difficulties in some hilly urban areas. Certain bus companies taking buses off the roads or circumventing the worst affected areas.

Brian's assessment was confirmed. He shut off the radio. It expired with a gurgle, half a second after he flicked the switch.

He hoisted his telephone receiver and punched a two digit number.

"Hello, Bill." Brian Ingleton was one of the few privileged to use the Rogerson forename. "I think we ought to close after lunch and send the kids home."

"Do you really think it's necessary?"

"Absolutely. The forecast is terrible and the roads are getting blocked up. We have to think of staff as well as pupils. We'll be here all night, if we don't act soon."

The thought of spending the night away from his snug cottage focused Dr Bill's mind. "Very well but why wait until after lunch? Let's get them off site now."

Brian sighed inwardly. "I don't think so. They wouldn't be very pleased in the kitchens if we let the kids go now. The food's supposed to pass over the kids' plates before it goes in the pig swill."

Rogerson did not appreciate Brian's earthy sense of humour. Brian moderated his tone. "And then there's the kids on free meals. Some of them won't get anything decent until after the snow goes."

"Fine. Fine. You'll see to it for me then, Brian?"

"Of course."

Brian strolled over to Alison's slightly more spacious office. Together, they worked out their action plan and, without going back to Rogerson, put it into practice.

Selected youngsters took a memo to all staff. School would close at lunch time. Those who had ordered a lunch should eat it before leaving school. Those who went home for lunch need not return. Those who had nowhere to go should report to Mr Ingleton in the library and could stay there until normal closing time. Staff could leave school after the majority of youngsters had cleared the building.

Brian and Alison deserved a cup of coffee. They had got it just about right.

Within minutes of the bell the school was nearly deserted. Brian, weary of waiting in the empty library, sauntered down to the dining hall. He knew it was a mistake as soon as he set foot inside and observed the mere sprinkling of young people tucking into overdone chips and garish baked beans.

"Hey, Mr Ingleton." It was Cook. "Can I have a word?"

Brian sidled over.

"What on earth am I going to do with all this waste food? You told me they'd be in for lunch before going home and just look at it. Hardly anyone has bothered. I don't know what you teach them in schools today. Manners and consideration for others don't feature very much."

"The pigs, Mrs Hartley. Feed it to the pigs."

A waif knocked at the door of Alison's office.

"Excuse me, Mrs ...er   ...er. I can't find the library."

Alison chuckled. The waif blubbered.

"What do you mean you can't find the library? How long have you been at Southdale?"

"It wasn't where I thought it was and the corridor was all sort of spooky."

Alison came over compassionate. "Come on in here. You can wait with me."

By three o'clock the caretaker was anxious to lock up. He hovered on the admin. corridor.

"You get off, Al. I'll wait until Becky's mum picks her up." Brian and Alison were the only teaching staff left on the site.

"Are you sure?"

"Of course. I'm only just up the road. You've got much further to go."

"Thanks, Brian. You're a love."

Brian watched Alison creep out of the car park. The telephone rang. Brian let himself into reception.

"Hello. Southdale Comprehensive School. How may I help you?" Brian had learned the patter from the office staff.

"I want to speak to somebody."

"Somebody speaking," replied Brian, ill-advisedly.

"I *mean* someone in charge."

"Well, I'm the only one here, so I guess that puts me in charge."

"It's all your fault then!"

"I'm sorry. What is?"

"My Jamie. Poor little mite's soaking wet and half froze. I don't know what you're playing at letting him walk home in all that snow. Couldn't one of you teachers have given him a lift in one of your *posh* cars?"

Alison's *Clio* finally lost traction on an incline about a mile and a half from home. She abandoned it and walked the rest of the way. The house was cold and dark. Jake would be ages yet. The traffic would be atrocious.

Brian Ingleton did not bother trying to get his car on to the main road. No one would trouble to pinch it. He got out his walking boots, put on his daft black, woolly hat, pulling it down over his ears, pulled up his shabby collar and trudged out of the school gates.

8 Ambush

"I hate you, Daddy! I wish mummy were here. She doesn't shout at us like you do."

Katie flew from the kitchen and threw herself sobbing on the settee.

Mummy was Beth Ingleton. Beth taught primary school, in the outskirts of the City, some ten miles from Southdale. She had rung to let Brian know that the roads were bad and that she would be stopping over at a colleague's house.

Brian had done oven chips and fried sausages for Katie and her older brother Luke. The sausages had not been to Katie's liking. Blackened on the outside but rather chewy within. Katie had pushed them moodily around her plate and Dad had exploded.

"Get them eaten at once before I send you to bed."

Brian had regretted his outburst as soon as it was over. Stress was like a virus. It attacked him when he was at his weakest, run down by another exacting day at the 'chalkface'. He would never actually lose his temper with the students at Southdale, though, goodness knows, some of them warranted it much more than Katie did.

He tried to make peace.

"OK, Daddy. It's all right." She stuck her thumb in and curled up sulkily in front of the television until bath time.

Alison was up at five o'clock the next day, Tuesday 30 January. The snow had desisted but the streets of their village had not been cleared. She hiked back to her car, her briefcase in one hand and a shovel in the other. She dug out the wheels of her *Clio* and a kindly butcher on his way to work gave her a push and eventually got her spinning wheels pointing in roughly the right direction.

The main roads were slushy but passable. Alison reached Southdale Comprehensive by seven-fifteen. Brian Ingleton was sitting in reception, his feet on the desk and the telephone receiver permanently to his ear.

"Good morning. Southdale Comprehensive School. Yes, we are open. Thank you for calling. Good morning. Southdale Comprehensive School. Yes, we are open. Thank you for calling."

"Good morning, Brian. I'll take over for a while. Go and make us some coffee."

Forty-five calls later, the receptionist arrived and assumed her place in front of the switchboard.

Thirty-two calls after that, Bill Rogerson passed through on the way to his customary breakfast in the office.

"Good morning, everyone. Keep up the good work. I expect the attendance will be poor today."

The attendance *was* poor. Some classes had less than a fifty per cent turn out. Condoned sledging was a far more attractive proposition.

Most staff made it more or less on time. One maths teacher, who lived on the moors had let his wife take the four wheel drive and consequently 'phoned in to make his excuses. Alison and Brian shared the 'covers' for his lessons.

"The place seems a bit deserted today, Dr Rogerson. Students taking advantage of the snow?"

Rogerson might have known that the Registered Inspector would choose today to pay an impromptu visit. Clive Holdsworth waited, his stare burning into Rogerson's face."

"Yes, well, there is a lot of sickness about, you know. That strain of the 'flu that keeps recurring."

"Many staff off?"

"Umm, no... Five or six I guess."

"Seems quite a lot to me."

"About average for this time of year. Working in a school you are prone to every bug that's doing the rounds."

"Yes, believe it or not, I do remember what it's like working in a school. Anyway, I'm here to deliver the parental questionnaires. You need to send one home with every pupil and collect the responses for me. You can give them to me at the start of the Parents' Meeting."

"They'll never get home."

"I beg your pardon."

"Letters home. Most of them end up as paper aeroplanes or get left lying around."

"Well, I shall need you to emphasise how important it is that these questionnaires get home and are returned completed."

"I'll do my best."

Alison and Clive stood gaping at each other for an eternity. Neither of them knew how to break the silence. Alison had not yet bothered to look at the personal details about the inspection team that Rogerson had secured, by one corner to the chaotic staffroom notice board. Clive had seen nothing significant about the name A.L. Lister, Deputy Headteacher, on Southdale's staff list.

Clive took the initiative. "Good grief. Alison Forsyth. It's been ages."

"Lister actually."

"Lister. So, you married?"

"Obviously. What are you doing here, Clive?"

"Haven't you heard? I'm the RI."

Alison felt like the heart had been rent from her. She stuttered. "No, no.. I didn't realise."

"We'll be seeing quite a bit of each other over the next few weeks. Perhaps we could have a drink, to catch up on news?"

She was quaking inside. She hoped it did not show.

"Perhaps... I mean... I don't know. Things have changed so much since..."

Clive, the sharper to reclaim his composure, stared confidently into her face. He had not lost his power. She felt as if his eyes could reveal her deepest thoughts. He breathed charm from every pore of his body.

He knew exactly how to play it, "I understand. We'll wait and see, shall we?"

"Yes. Fine."

"I must get going."

"Bye."

Covering the mathematics lessons helped to take Alison's mind off Clive. Isolated in her office, it was a different story. She despised her own lack of resolve at not being able to dismiss his face. Not even the pangs of guilt that wracked her, when his face blended into Jake's, could dispel that peculiarly agitated feeling that she had first experienced in Clive's presence, some years earlier.

She pushed papers around her desk. She opened and closed her filing cabinet. She flicked through her in-tray. But nothing seemed to get done.

By lunch time the main roads were relatively clear. Snow-shy drivers continued to over-rev and slither on some of the steeper side roads. The lunch break passed by almost unremarkably: A gaggle of complaints from passers-by, peppered with snowballs; an elderly woman pelted as she got off a bus alongside the school fence; a year seven completely buried in the snow by some year nines; dinner supervisors hoarse with repeating instructions. "Don't throw near the windows!" "Do not bring that snow into school!" "Put it down, at once!" "Don't you dare throw that at me!" "Right that's done it. I'm reporting you to Mr Ingleton!"

Brian chuckled to himself. At least on a day like this the kids chose to wreak havoc on the school site, rather than terrorise the town centre. He had even had time to grab a sandwich from the dining hall and slosh it down with a mug of relatively warm tea, for a change. He had, of course, lunched on the hoof.

He and Alison had patrolled the corridors, their paths crossing from time to time. Occasionally they had risked a step or two outside the building. A few badly aimed, slush balls fell at their feet.

Brian strolled to the end of the English corridor and peered tentatively into the battle scene.

"Sir! Sir! Help me. I'm being bullied." It took Brian a fraction of a second to assess the situation. Darrell Williams, 9FR, was on his back. Half a dozen bigger year nines were pounding him with missiles. Brian did not hesitate. He set off towards the melee. Just too late the penny dropped. Ambush!

A massive ball of snow hit him on the right ear as he turned to leg it back towards sanctuary. Before the ringing had disappeared, another hit him full in the nose. It stung the boy within him into action. There in his sights was the ginger mop and freckled complexion of

Robert Walker, chortling at his own ingenuity. It was a temptation that Brian could not resist. Robert stood, transfixed, as Brian bore down on him.

"No, sir. You wouldn't dare! Stop!" His pleas went unheeded. Brian upended him with a perfect rugby tackle. Had he witnessed it, Simon Cunliffe would have been proud of his middle-aged colleague.

Brian rubbed handful after handful into the protesting face. He realised he had gone too far. The boy was crying. Brian released him and got to his feet, wiping the snow from his clothing. The boy lay still, sobbing dramatically.

"Come on young Walker. It's only a bit of fun. Get up and go and get dried off before tutorial."

The boy did not move. The sobbing grew louder. Brian reached down gently taking the boy's arm in an attempt to raise him from the snowy bed.

"You get your hands off me. I'm going to tell my Dad about this. He'll smack your head in."

Brian flared. "Well if that's the way you want it, son, that's the way you'll get it. If you can't take it, don't dish it out! Get yourself into school, get dried off and stop whining!"

From the security of his office, Rogerson had observed everything. Unable to hear the exchanges, he had observed the body language and the facial expressions of protagonists and audience.

Troubled, he returned to his desk and punched the off button on his portable radio.

The bus for the Scargill estate got through with no problem at the end of the day. Alison and Brian were pleased to see the kids on board and on their way.

"Fancy a cuppa, Brian. There are one or two things to do with the inspection that I would like to bounce off you."

"Bounce away. I'll do anything for a cuppa. Provided I can have a proper mug, not one of those paper thin china things that Rogerson has."

"*Had.*" corrected Alison, with a twinkle in her eye.

A quiet chat about work over a cup of tea. It was too good to be true and so it proved. The telephone rang. Alison answered.

"Yes. Yes. OK. Thanks, Constable Bransby, we're on our way."

Two lukewarm, half-full mugs added to the rings on the ancient, green leather desk top.

The school bus was parked up not a mile from the school. A panda car was parked across its bows. PC Bransby was standing near the folding door of the bus, next to a harassed looking, balding, slightly built bus driver, in an ill-fitting, burgundy uniform jacket. A dull chorus of chants and jeers could be heard emanating from the sealed bus. All the inmates were pressed against the nearside glass to get the best view of what was going on.

"I'm not shifting it."

"I'm sorry?" queried Alison, somewhat disingenuously.

"I said: I'm not shifting it. Not 'til you've sorted them buggers out, at any rate."

"What's the problem, driver?" asked Brian.

"Go upstairs and see for yourselves!"

Alison and Brian did as they were bid.

Suddenly, the youngsters were cramped back into their seats. Three to a double seat to comply with the law. Feigned innocence shone out from every face.

"There. Look what the little sods have been up to."

At the back of the bus, pointedly flanked by empty seats, stood, melting resplendently in an expanding puddle, a three-quarter scale snow man.

9 So what?

"Hello, Mrs Lister, I have a call for you from Sally O'Mahoney, education correspondent at the *Chronicle*. Are you available to speak to her?"

"What about Dr Rogerson? Shouldn't he be speaking to the press?"

"He's far too busy at the moment, looking at the new budget figures, and he thought it might be good experience for you."

"Very well. Put her through."

Alison had never met Sally O'Mahoney but she had read the *Chronicle* from time to time. In fact, she and Jake used to have it delivered until, one evening, Jake had torn the copy to shreds over an article to do with the council. Alison was very wary. *Teacher bashing* certainly did seem to sell newspapers and the *Chronicle* was always game to try anything that would boost its dwindling sales.

Alison had learned the lesson some years ago from a deputy head at her last school. No matter how serious the situation, it was always better to allow the press an interview and try to get your side of the story across. "No comment" was the worst possible response. The press could make whatever they wished out of that. Rogerson clearly had not got the *bottle* to face up to Ms O'Mahoney's call. It was up to Alison to remain calm and put the best possible gloss on what was bound to be an embarrassment for the school.

She allowed a thin smile to pass across her lips as she recalled one of her *mentor*'s anecdotes. A headteacher had answered 'No comment' to a journalist's query about the school's lowly position in the examination league tables. The very next day, the local paper bore the bold headline: *Head speechless over exam results.*

"Hello. Alison Lister, deputy head, speaking."

"Oh, hello, Alison. I was expecting to speak to the head."

Alison noted the disappointment in Ms O'Mahoney's voice. She had obviously missed an opportunity to give the boss a good mauling. Alison detested people who were over familiar when they spoke to someone for the first time.

"I am afraid he is extremely busy and has asked me to deputise for him. Now, what can I do for you?" Alison knew, very well, why she had telephoned.

"I understand there was some uncivilised behaviour on the bus, by some of your pupils, yesterday evening. We plan to run an item on it and I wondered how the school thought this type of conduct would go down with OFSTED inspectors. I am right in thinking that you will be inspected in a couple of weeks' time, aren't I?"

"You're quite correct, Ms O'Mahoney, the school will be inspected in the week beginning 26 February. I think all schools have this type of problem with high spirits, from time to time."

"Don't be so formal. Everyone calls me Sally. Just high spirits, you say? I believe that the police were called to the scene."

"That's perfectly true. The bus driver overreacted and refused to move the bus. The community constable was called out."

Alison knew she had blown it.

"Overreacted? So you believe that doing what your pupils did was just normal behaviour? People we have spoken to say that this type of uncontrolled behaviour is very frequent and they are afraid to travel on the buses at school home time. What do you have to say to that?"

If Alison's mouth had been any bigger, she would have got both feet in at the same time.

"Come on, didn't children get up to pranks when you were at school? I think it was quite ingenious really, to get all that snow on the bus without being noticed. They must have used plastic bags, so that it didn't melt too quickly. Hasn't the bus company got a sense of humour?"

"I've spoken to their security manager and he says that your pupils will be banned, if this sort of thing happens again. Are you telling me that you condone the children's behaviour?"

"No, I'm not saying that at all. It's just that I find it quite funny, really, that you should be making such a fuss about nothing."

Sally had got the angle she needed.

"Thanks a lot, Alison. Nice to talk to you. I should like to do an in depth feature on yourself, in the near future, the pressure of the inspection and all that. I'll give you a bell, right?"

Alison was furious with herself. She would not dare say anything to Rogerson. He had been even more than usually unapproachable since the Alan Sumner affair. She confided in Brian as they shared daily break duty at the point where the admin. corridor joined the main thoroughfare to the tuck shop.

"Slow down, please. Keep to the left. Don't overtake. Didn't you hear me, Jody? You'll be last in the queue, if you continue to ignore me. Pick up that crisp packet, please! I know *you* didn't drop it, Ricky, but I'm asking you to do me a favour, all right? You've seen me pick up enough litter and if I can do it so can you. That's better. Thank you."

The initial rush subsided.

"Do you think I should go and see Rogerson, Brian? He might be able to ring the editor at the *Chronicle* and get them not to use my comments."

Brian slurped his mug of tea. It scalded his lips and tongue.

"You'd be wasting your time. They've got about as much respect for him at the *Chronicle* as we have here."

"But I feel I should do something. I've let the school down."

"Listen, Al, the *Chronicle* has been gunning for us for some time now. If you were to ring back, they'd just think we had an even bigger story to hide. Just try to forget about it. The story may get buried, if someone robs a post office at lunch time."

"Are you trying to incite me to armed robbery?"

"Anything, if it'll take your mind off that stupid reporter. Oh, blow, there's the bell. Action stations. What do *you* want, Leanne? It's rude to interrupt when I'm speaking to Mrs Lister."

"Miss said it was important and that I should tell you straight away."

"Which *miss* would that be, Leanne?"

"The *miss* in the tuck shop, sir."

"And what is so important as to interrupt my *quiet* break, taking tea with Mrs Lister?"

"It's Simon Higginbottom. Miss saw him take 50p from the counter and he says he hasn't but he has."

"Here we go again. Hang on to my cup, will you, Mrs Lister?"

The remainder of the morning and most of the lunch hour were taken up with collecting written statements. The statements fell into two categories: *miss* and half a dozen girls who had been crowding around *knew* that Simon had taken the money. The other witnesses, all of them Simon's regular partners in crime, knew very little. Some of them searched their memories and stretched the teachers' patience by questioning whether Simon had even been there. "I think he was in the toilets, miss."

Brian knew he had done it. Alison knew he had done it. Simon knew he had done it but *he* was the only one who had actually seen it happen. The evidence would not hold up in front of the governors. One second the 50p was there. The next it had disappeared. A *turn-out-*

your-pockets search revealed several 50p pieces but none of them identifiable as the one missing from the tuck shop. Simon and his pals had plausible reasons for possessing them.

Brian and Alison knew they were beaten. They would have to content themselves with a *what if..?* routine and leave it at that.

"Well, Simon, we can't prove anything on this occasion but you know what would happen if you were caught thieving, don't you?"

"No. What?"

"You would get at least a three day exclusion from school and would probably have to go before the headteacher and governors."

"So what?" thought Simon but he said nothing and settled for a surly expression.

"If you'd been caught stealing previously, Dr Rogerson could chuck you out straight away."

"Anyway, you can't do nothing." ventured Simon defiantly. "And I'm going to tell my Nan and when she finds out she'll be up to school to sort you out."

"So what?" thought Brian. He had heard it all before.

Alison spent the afternoon teaching Y7. It was delightful. Most of them showed interest. Many of them asked questions. Nobody burned their fingers on the *bunsens*. Nobody set fire to someone else's pencil. Nearly all of them worked quietly on the written part of the lesson.

"I hope they are like this when the inspectors come," thought Alison. "What on earth do we do to them by the time they reach Y9, so that they change so much? How come all that enthusiasm and energy have to be subjected to the horrors of adolescence?"

All of the students had their *daily planners* with them. Alison joyfully dictated the homework and sent them on their merry way a minute before the bell. Another mistake.

Rogerson appeared at the laboratory door. He looked flustered. He was wielding a rolled up newspaper like a police baton.

"Kindly do not release the pupils before the bell, Mrs Lister. It is a bad example for the other staff and creates expectations in the minds of the children."

"I do apologise, Dr Rogerson. It won't happen again."

Rogerson unfurled the newspaper and with a grand gesture hurled it on to the bench in front of Alison.

"And what is the meaning of this?"

Alison's eyes focused first on the headline.

"SNOW JOKE AT LOCAL SCHOOL."

"Well, read it." howled Rogerson.

Alison scanned the text: "...scandalous behaviour...bus driver verbally abused...police sent for...teachers thought it a huge joke...what are our schools teaching children nowadays?...don't young people know right from wrong?"

"Well?"

"This is ridiculous, Dr Rogerson. I don't know where they got the impression..."

"From you, Mrs Lister. From you. I told them when you were appointed that we were taking a risk. Far too young and inexperienced. If that self-satisfied inspector, Holdsworth, gets hold of this, he'll really put us through the mill. If you can't handle situations, leave them to Ingleton. At least he knows what he is doing."

The injustice of it hurt Alison to the core. Long after Rogerson had stormed out of the laboratory, she remained, white knuckled, staring at the offending article.

"It's not fair!" she said out loud. "It's just not fair!" She was too angry to weep.

"Miss, miss, are you OK? You don't look very well."

Alison made a supreme effort.

"Yes...yes, Leanne... I'm fine. What have you come back for?"

"It's that homework, miss. I don't get it and if you don't help me, everyone will call me *thick* tomorrow."

"Come in and sit down, sweetheart. It'll be all right."

10 Buckets, bins and hard-hearted Henry

By Thursday morning the snow had all but vanished from Southdale. There were isolated mounds of icy crystals in the hedgerows. Here and there, along the roadside, were the remnants of the grimy, grey ridges left by the ploughs. A few inexplicable white patches, resistant to the pale winter sun, littered the fields.

At Southdale Comprehensive School the message went out at morning registration, "No snowballing under any circumstances. Those choosing to disobey this instruction will face serious consequences."

On the way to first lesson, a handful of students had found the vestiges of their previous day's sport and begun to bombard each other from close range. By five past nine a small queue of walking wounded had begun to gather outside the extravagantly named medical room. It was not the school nurse's day in school, so the office staff handed out cold compresses and cold comfort.

"Here hold this against your eye. It serves you right. You should do what the teachers tell you. I'm going to ring your mum and she can take you to the surgery to have it checked, just in case."

Henry Appleton was not, by nature, a happy person. Today, he was positively gloomy. The melting snow on the flat, heavily patched roof of his laboratory, had leaked through. Buckets and bins, strategically placed beneath damp patches on the ceiling, were busy catching drips. Ashley Vickers, that clumsy oaf in his form, had already sent one bucket flying during registration. Emma Inman had put her English homework down on the sodden bench top and the ink had run so much that barely a word was legible. Emma's tears threatened to fill another bucket.

Even hard-hearted Henry was moved by this pathetic sight.

"Come on Emma, love. Get a Kleenex from the box on my bench and pop along to see Mrs Brinkhurst. She'll not put you in detention, when you explain."

"She will, too. She always does."

"I'll have a word at break. She won't, I promise you. Now get a tissue and dry your eyes."

"She will, though. She did last week when our babby were sick on it."

"Come on, Emma. Get on your way. Oh, no. What are you blabbing about now?"

"It's these paper hankies, Mr Appleton. They're right soggy."

Appleton went into the prep room and dialled 34 on the internal telephone system.

"Hello. Technology. Breeze speaking."

"It's Henry, Kevin. Have you been on to Rogerson, yet?"

"What about?"

"My lab, what do you think? It's like trying to teach on the set of *Singing in the Rain*. It brings new meaning to the phrase 'tap' dancing. I expect Fred Astaire to come twirling through here at any minute, swinging his big umbrella around his head."

"Gene Kelly"

"You what?"

"*Singing in the Rain*, starred Gene Kelly."

"Er, yes...she could have been in it as well. But let's not get hung up on detail. What about my lab?"

"Well, I made an official complaint last time and it didn't do any good."

"What do we pay our union subs for? If you don't keep nagging them, they'll leave it 'til the ceiling falls in."

"You know the council's strapped for cash. The roof is the LEA's responsibility not Rogerson's."

"We all know that but if you put enough of a squeeze on Rogerson, he'll get Lister or Ingleton to ring the office and get something done about it."

"Leave it with me, Henry. No point in bothering with Rogerson. I'll go straight to Brian. He knows who to talk to."

9FR was baying at the door. Henry glared them into line.

"Winfield pick that toffee paper up."

"But, sir, it wasn't me. It was....."

"Winfield."

"All right then but it's not fair."

"Winfield!"

"But..."

"Winfield! Do it! One more word and I'll tear you limb from limb and feed you to the piranhas in Mrs Kenning's aquarium."

9FR could see Appleton was lusting for blood. Only a lunatic would take him on today.

"Get inside, you lot. Not a word and keep well away from those buckets."

Darrell Williams was not of a nature to be put off by a few sharp toothed fish or a teacher with homicidal tendencies. Before Appleton could follow the class into the room, he gave a red plastic bucket such a booting that it showered its contents over several metres of the worn parquet flooring.

Appleton could not be sure of himself. He remained remarkably calm, though his lips did twitch a bit and his face deepened its normal reddish hue.

"Try to be more careful, 9FR."

Darrell Williams was well removed from the scene of the crime.

"Winfield, go and get a mop from the caretaker's office and be quick about it."

"But, sir, it wasn't me. It was..."

"Winfield!"

"I'm going but it's not fair. Darrell Williams..."

Darrell Williams gave Winfield his famous 'you're dead at break' look and Winfield swallowed the end of his sentence.

"Right, 9FR, bring your stools forward and gather around my bench. I want to talk to you. I just know I'm going to regret this but today we are going to do some practical work and I need to do a demonstration first."

Clatter! The door fell open and Winfield tumbled in.

"Oh, please, give me strength! At least you've managed to find a mop but why have you brought the bucket. We're overrun with buckets in here."

Twenty minutes into the lesson everyone had settled down in front of Appleton. All eyes were, at least most of the time, fixed on him. He insisted. Anyone who did not look at his ugly mug got the sharp end of his tongue and had to sit and look at his mug at break, in any case.

Darrell Wiiliams could not resist temptation. On the floor near his stool was a *Tesco* bag. The bag yawned open. In the bag was a nylon pencil case, gaping, packed full of likely weapons. Darrell stooped; selected a pair of compasses. He straightened up, chose his target and jabbed.

The class thought someone's pet poodle had been run over on the dual carriageway. Winfield let out such a yelp, 8SC woke up in Mrs Kenning's lesson, two labs along the corridor.

Appleton went apoplectic. No one needed to tell him it was Williams. He *knew* it was Williams. When anything of this sort went off in class, it was *always* Williams.

Henry grabbed him by the sweatshirt and lifted him off the ground. He pulled Darrell's face so close to his that their noses all but touched. Last night's garlic made Darrell squirm with displeasure and brought tears to his eyes.

"How dare you, you little worm? How dare you assault Winfield in *my* lesson?"

"It's not fair, sir, Darrell Williams is always ..."

"Shut up, Winfield! Come and see me in the prep room at break, Williams, and be there immediately after the bell. Got that?"

Darrell did his best to nod. Henry dropped him to his feet. Henry walked back in front of the class. There were no giggles, no slyly exchanged glances, no "Come on Darrell, have a go at him!" When Appleton went berserk, it was serious.

Appleton carried on with the lesson as if nothing had happened

"Kirsty, it's getting a bit dull in here. Go and switch the lights on, will you?"

Kirsty slid off her stool and walked to the bank of switches near the door. Suddenly, a pistol crack and a blinding blue flash. Kirsty screamed a short scream and then erupted in tears.

"Oh, my giddy aunt, when will it end? Don't our lords and masters know that water and electricity don't mix? Stop snivelling, girl. You're still alive. Alison, fetch the caretaker. It looks like we will need to finish this experiment another day. Get your things together we'll move into the dining-room for the rest of the lesson."

There was no doubt about it, Darrell Williams was scared. He would not let on to his mates, of course, but he was trembling inside at the thought of another confrontation with Mad Henry, as Appleton was known, well behind his back.

He arrived at the prep room almost before the bell had stopped ringing. Appleton made him stew for a few minutes and then he showed him into the small, windowless room and closed the door, dropping the catch. Darrell gasped. It was not right. Teachers should not put the wind up you like this.

"Take your trainer off, lad."

"Why?"

"Don't ask questions. Just do it."

Darrell pushed off one trainer with the toe of the other, without untying the lace. He left the trainer on the floor in front of him and rested the unshod foot on top of the shod one.

"Give it to me!"

Darrell hesitated for a moment. He bent forward picked it up by the lace and handed it gingerly to the teacher. Appleton was not angry now but, somehow, he was so much more frightening.

"Bend over that table."

"Sir, you're not allowed to..."

"Do it!"

"No. You're a nutter. Let me out."

Appleton clutched the youngster by the back of the neck and forced him, struggling, and swearing over the table. He raised his arm three times and three times brought the sports shoe crashing down on the boy's buttocks. The pain was insignificant. The indignity was more than the lad could bear.

He jerked himself free. He released a torrent of abuse. He uttered outrageous threats about what his father, brothers and cousins would do to Appleton when they found out about this. He fumbled with the *Yale* on the door and stumbled, tearfully, along the corridor in the direction of Dr Rogerson's office.

"You're for it now. You'll get the sack for this. I'm going to tell Rogerson."

Appleton watched the pathetic figure struggle, in his anger, to the end of the corridor and then disappear from view.

"You do that, son. You just do that!"

Bill Rogerson cautiously unlocked his filing cabinet. He bent double to search behind the files in the bottom drawer. He withdrew a half-size bottle of scotch and took a couple of gulps. He replaced the bottle, making sure it was well hidden and felt in his waistcoat pocket for a nearly finished packet of extra strong mints. He slipped two of them into his mouth and crunched hard, pounding them into fragments.

There was a confident rap on the door. Rogerson positioned himself behind the elegant desk.

"Come."

The door flew open and Henry Appleton swaggered in.

"Blimey, Bill, you need to open a window. It stinks of whisky in here."

Rogerson ignored the remark. "Take a seat, Mr Appleton. There's something I need to say to you."

"It's a rare honour to be invited in here, these days, Bill. What can I do for you?"

"It's that...er...Williams boy in Y9. He's...been to see me and he claims that you assaulted him. Is this true?"

"Assaulted him?"

"Well, did you?"

"It depends what you mean by assault. I prefer to say that Williams got what he deserved."

"He says you hit him with his own sports shoe."

"Tanned his backside. Slippered him, as we used to say in the good old days."

"You mean you freely admit having struck a student?"

"Oh, yes, quite openly, here and now, just me and you, no witnesses. But you take it any further and it'll be my word against his. And everyone knows what a lying little so-and-so Williams is."

"We won't be able to keep this under wraps. It'll be all over the school and Williams will bring his family in or even report you to the police."

"Don't you worry about that, my old flower. Good for my reputation. Remember I taught Billy Williams. Darrell will never tell him in a month of Sundays. Billy would give him twice as much a thrashing as I did. And even if he didn't, Billy would never come up here. I've got too much on him and he knows it."

"You think you're clever, don't you, Mr Appleton?"

"A damn sight cleverer than you, Rogerson. Go ahead and accuse me if you wish. You'll be wasting your time and think of the bad publicity, just before the inspection. You could do without that, couldn't you? Might put your cushy lifestyle on the line, hey?"

Rogerson refused the bait. He motioned to the door. Appleton hesitated just long enough to maintain the upper hand and then strode haughtily from his presence.

11 Leaky roofs and cold buildings

Cynthia had been watching her husband for several minutes. He had pushed the *Chicken Chasseur* dutifully around the china and had forced a few pieces between his resistant lips but the rapidly cooling meal remained largely untouched.

He stared straight ahead. She placed her hand gently on his. He was gripping the fork like an inexperienced climber grips the rope.

Twenty-eight years of better or worse had not eroded her love for the man that she had known since Cambridge. They had rarely been apart since then. His *first* in English Literature had eased him into his first post, in a private school, in a well-heeled suburb of the West Midlands. She, equally successful in her own field, had found a position with the *Halifax*.

They celebrated the end of his first year in teaching with an August wedding, the type of wedding that they knew their parents would insist on. She had been twenty-three and he just turned twenty-two.

They had always seen her career as subordinate to his and Cynthia had no hang-ups about this. She followed him around the country to a succession of promotions and found what paid employment she could, as soon as they were settled.

He had made the leap into the state system, some twenty years ago, when he had become Head of English in a high achieving comprehensive in North Yorkshire. Five years of outstanding 'A' level results had been his fast-track to deputy headship in a neighbouring Authority.

His early years as a deputy had been exciting ones. His boss was one of those leaders that you only meet once in a lifetime. She carried him along in her whirlwind. Her success rubbed off on him. If she came up with an idea one day, it was implemented the next. Staff morale was sky high. Parents worshipped the school. The children did what they were told and the results proved it.

The next few years were marked by an enthusiasm to emulate his mentor's successes. He sent in application after optimistic application for the types of schools that he knew he would enjoy working in. A part time doctorate boosted his currency in the job market. He had a seventy-five per cent success rate on references being taken up and got interviews for over a third of the posts. Frustratingly, he never got beyond the last three.

The next phase of his deputy headship evolved into desperation to secure a post as head of school. Desperation unrequited gradually subsided into disillusionment and finally passivity.

When all had seemed lost he had applied for Southdale. It was a somewhat whimsical application, against Cynthia's better judgement and against the advice of his colleagues and friends. A governing body looking for a short cut to academic success failed to heed the warning words of the LEA representative on the interview panel and appointed Dr William Rogerson as headteacher.

The honeymoon had lasted about eighteen months. The staff and the parents had given him the benefit of the doubt. The students were not so easily satisfied. The governors worked hard at justifying their appointment but when Gladys Ollerenshaw joined the board and was rapidly elected Chair, she was sharp enough to spot Rogerson's flaws but pragmatic enough to realise that a headteacher could not be got rid of easily. It was far better to work with what they had than to harbour a forlorn hope of re-appointment.

Left to his own devices, Rogerson had struggled. Indecision had been his hallmark. What teamwork there had been in the school had dwindled away. The students, sensing the weakness at the top, had pushed and pushed and got away with it. Acts of gross indiscipline were met with dithering. Teachers took the odd day off without challenge. Parents felt free to question anything and everything. Scenting blood the local press had been on Rogerson's tail for some time.

Appleton's bare faced defiance and undisguised hatred had been just too much, as the pressure mounted towards the dreaded 26 February. Rogerson had drunk most of a bottle of wine on Friday evening and that had dulled the pain. Saturday had begun with his neighbour pulling out of the round of golf that might have put him back into better spirits. He had moped around the winter-paralysed garden and found not much to do to the frozen earth.

A walk in the afternoon, while Cynthia had been to town, had encouraged brooding. By evening meal a deep hopelessness had descended and Cynthia had no idea what to do about it.

She gripped his hand more firmly.

"Do you want to talk about it, darling?"

"Talk about what?"

"Whatever's getting you down. You seem very low, this weekend. Is it the inspection?"

"Yes, I suppose it is in a way."

"But it's more than that, isn't it? You usually lighten up at the weekend."

"Everything is crashing down around me, Cyn. I feel as if I am losing control."

Cynthia was no fool. She was well aware of how things had been at Southdale, for some time. A snippet in the newspaper, the increasing frequency of Bill's depressions.

She did not visit Southdale very often. Two or three times a year. The Carol Service, Prize Giving and, until the drama teacher lost heart, the Annual Production. On those rare occasions, she had felt embarrassed, frustrated, angry even, on Bill's behalf, at the way he appeared to be sidelined, by-passed by other members of staff.

His little closing speeches, his official thank-yous were received with polite indifference. His presence was an irrelevance.

"Losing control?" She tried to sound surprised. "What do you mean? Are the children behaving badly again?"

"No more than usual. But there was that Sumner business, you'll remember."

"That's resolved?"

"Yes, sort of. The lad's been permanently excluded."

"I think you made the right decision."

"That's just it. It wasn't *my* decision. Alison Lister threatened union action and Gladys wasn't strong enough to hold the line."

Not strong enough? Cynthia had met Gladys at functions where they shared an interest. She would never have described Gladys in that way. She paused to allow Bill to continue.

Bill stared into his glass of claret.

Cynthia, being a proponent of the 'get it off your chest' theory of counselling, tried to keep up the momentum.

"There's something else?"

"Well, you'll think it's stupid ..."

"Tell me anyway."

"It's just that, since Alison Lister arrived, I feel as if Brian has deserted me."

"You always got on well with Brian. He's a nice chap."

"The two of them seem to have really hit it off. They're always going into a huddle over something or other. I always seem to be finding out about things after they've happened."

"That's their job, isn't it? To deal with the day-to-day running of the school, while you get on with the creative thinking side of it? That's always been your strength, thinking."

"Rather than *doing*, you mean?"

"I didn't say that."

"You didn't need to."

"Is there anything else?"

"Just Henry ..."

"Oh, *that* man. What's he been up to this time?"

"We will magnify, we will magnify the Lord enthroned in Zion." Brian rattled the strings of his acoustic guitar with renewed vigour as the last song reached its crescendo. Beth crashed her 'knuckle duster' tambourine against her right thigh. On Sunday afternoons, she often wondered why that spot was so tender.

The music group leader slung his guitar behind him, rock star fashion, and removed the microphone from its stand. "We will magnify...," he yelled, urging the congregation into a final frenzy of praise.

Brian, Beth and the kids did not go into the church hall for the usual milky coffee (well diluted orange for the under fifteens) and plain biscuit. "Got to rush. No, no, haven't got time now. I'll see you before prayer meeting, Tuesday evening. We've really got to go. Friends coming for lunch."

Brian and Beth enjoyed having an open house. They were always the first to invite new arrivals at church, new neighbours and new colleagues. Alison and Jake had been on their hit list since Alison had been appointed but, somehow, their diaries had not coincided.

"Sunday lunch," Beth had exclaimed one evening while she and Brian were watching television. And so it had been settled.

Traditional Sunday lunch was not a tradition in the Ingleton household. Beans on toast was a regular option and this was popular with the children. Luke had been suspicious when Mummy had tossed a joint of meat into the supermarket trolley on Saturday morning. His suspicions were confirmed when she wrapped it in foil and rammed it in the oven, before church.

"Mummy, what are we having for lunch?" he asked warily.

"Roast pork with apple sauce, potatoes, peas, carrots and gravy, followed by blackcurrant cheesecake."

Luke chose to ignore the cheesecake.

"Oh, Mummy, what do we have to have that for? What's wrong with beans, as usual?"

"Nothing, sweetheart. It's just that one of Daddy's colleagues and her husband are coming for lunch and grown-ups don't like beans as much as you and Katie."

"Oh, Mummy." He rushed off, delighted at the prospect of breaking the bad news to his little sister. He would keep the blackcurrant cheesecake up his sleeve for the moment.

Jake and Alison were expected at one but they arrived at one-twenty. This was a blessing to Beth who had burned the gravy and had begun to get in a state.

Jake and Alison had rowed. The row had continued in the car. "If you were going for a run, why didn't you go earlier? You were ages in that shower."

"It would have helped if you'd had your shower while I was out instead of lazing in bed."

"I hate being late. We're always late when we go anywhere."

"Hi, Alison. Welcome to our humble abode."

"Hello, Brian. Sorry we're late. Got a bit lost."

"Oh, sorry. Wasn't the map any good?"

"On the contrary, it was spot on. It's just that I can't tell my left from my right and Jake has to keep shouting 'knife' and 'fork' and when that doesn't work 'my side' and 'your side'. This is Jake by the way. You must be Beth. Delighted to meet you. Lovely house."

"Do come through. Would you like an aperitif?"

"Sounds lovely."

"Brian, see to it, would you, while I finish off in the kitchen."

Everyone agreed that the remaining sliver of blackcurrant cheesecake should be divided equally between Luke and Katie. Katie had sucked her thumb, shyly, through most of the meal and Luke had refrained from making sick noises when the vegetables had been served.

The ice had been broken. The meal had been a relative success and the conversation had steered clear of education.

By the second cup of coffee, however, a slight lull had led to Jake letting slip that unsavoury word, *inspection*. From then on they had wallowed in a feast of fault-finding. The government, the local authority, children, parents, governors, the press, Rogerson himself, incompetent staff who could not be got rid of, all bore the brunt of their criticism.

Brian was in his element. "It's all right for them to blame what we do in schools but I'm sure they don't really know what it's like. They went to posh schools themselves and they expect all young people to be as motivated as they were. It's one thing coming from a well-off family and knowing that you'll walk into a well paid job, if you conform and do your homework. It's another story altogether if you come from a home where there's been no work for years and you don't have any prospects either. What kind of an incentive is that to come to school or give a damn about exam results?"

Beth gave Brian one of her little warning frowns. He knew what it meant but he was in full flow.

"If you'd seen some of the sights I've seen, Jake, when I do home visits, it would break your heart. I don't know how some of the kids cope with what they have to put up with at home. You'd think that a so-called civilised country like ours wouldn't allow people to get into the kind of mess that some get into. And we're expected to put it all right. The graffiti, the bad language, the poor standards, the violence...the despair. And where's the money to do it? One tatty textbook between three. Leaky roofs and cold buildings. Huge class sizes. Crap furniture. Bricks without straw, that's what they want!"

"Bricks without straw?" queried Jake.

"Old testament. Genesis, I think, or was it Exodus? What chapter was it, Beth? You've got a better memory for these things. Didn't you do it in RE at school, Jake? You know, Moses, the Children of Israel in Egypt. People being expected to do the job without the proper materials. That's the nub of it, in my opinion."

"Bricks without straw," breathed Alison.

"Would anyone like some more coffee?"

12 Zero, three, zero, eight

Jake's stomach was in knots. He knew he was being absurd but he could not get the demon out of his head. He gaped at the clock for the tenth time in as many minutes.

He trusted Alison implicitly. She had never given him any reason not to. He thought hard about the last words she had voiced before bolting from the house, still gnawing at the *Granny Smith's* she had preferred to the shop-bought, sticky dessert Jake had laid on the table.

"See you. I'll not be late. It's the OFSTED parents' meeting. We're not allowed in but Rogerson wants us to lurk purposefully in the foyer to 'welcome' the parents. Bit late to start trying to influence them, if you ask me!"

"What time?"

"About half-nine. We could go to the *Norfolk* for a swift half."

"See you."

Zero, zero, zero, one, read the little green figures, on the video.

Jake sighed. They were always open with each other, or so he thought. Up to now, Clive Holdsworth had only been a name, someone who had damaged Alison in a prior existence. Someone who was never referred to by either of them. Once, Jake had chanced upon some letters in Alison's drawer, addressed in a handwriting he did not recognise. He had been proud of repelling the temptation to have a peek. It made him feel good.

Now, he did not feel good.

He wished Alison had not introduced Clive casually into their conversation, the other evening.

"You'll never guess, in a million years, who's going to be our Registered Inspector." To Jake she seemed like a teenage girl, struggling to affect equanimity. "Clive."

Jake had experienced a sudden queasy sensation in the pit of his stomach.

"Clive?"

Her cheeks were flaming. "Don't pretend you don't know who I mean. You know... Clive."

It was Jake's turn to feign nonchalance. "Oh, *that* Clive. So?"

Alison snapped back at him. "So nothing. Just trying to make conversation. I thought you might be interested in what's going on at school."

"Of course, I'm interested."

Zero, zero, zero, three.

The beast was swelling within him. His insides tightened. He could not settle to anything. Several times he sought to scan the papers for the next morning's meeting but the words just stared back at him, glassy-eyed.

It was nothing new for Alison to be working late. That was how she had got on in education. This time, though, it did not feel right. Jake tried to picture what Clive looked like. He tried not to visualize Clive and Alison together but he could not help himself.

He fought off the fanciful images of them, this evening, locked in some improbable intimacy. The effort was more than he could endure. His folder of papers flew across the coffee table and skidded on the polished floor. His tiny glass of *Jack Daniel's* survived the tantrum. He gulped the contents down in one.

Zero, zero, one, zero.

Jake had not the heart to shower. He scattered his clothes on a bedroom chair and flung himself into bed, determined she would not discover that he no longer trusted her.

The OFSTED parents' meeting had lived down to expectations. Twenty or so questionnaires had been returned.

"I expect they were the only parents who could read," quipped Simon Cunliffe.

"That's good, coming from a PE teacher who can't even keep the score in a football match," retorted Tina Chatham.

Brian Ingleton could not resist having a skim through before putting them in the large Manila envelope, addressed to Clive Holdsworth, RgI.

None of the twenty had been particularly complimentary about the school. Some of the parents had been quick to pick up the tabloid tattle about parental rights and had much to say about what the school was doing or, more correctly, not doing for their offspring.

Rogerson had been reliably advised that it was good form to greet the arriving parents and to introduce the Registered Inspector and his lay colleague. Rogerson thought it would be extra good form to invite Brian Ingleton to come along, because he knew how to talk to parents. Not wanting to be left out, Alison invited herself.

As the parents passed through the entrance foyer the signs were not propitious. Most faces were glum. Those that were not glum were set stone hard or, so it seemed to the staff, distorted by scowling. The knives were out. The parents were on the warpath and they were looking for blood.

Brian had come up with a plan. Parents only were allowed to participate in the meeting. Betty Andrews, RE teacher, had a daughter in Year 7. She would be the staff 'mole'. Armed with reporter's pad, and two *biros* she made her way into the hall, exchanging knowing glances with Brian and Alison as she passed them at the entrance.

Once the introductions were over, Rogerson withdrew to his office. There was a concert on *Classic FM*. Alison and Brian went to Brian's office for coffee, in chipped mugs, and slightly soggy biscuits.

Betty Andrews took her task very seriously indeed. She wrote down everything *verbatim*. The result was ten sides of scrawling, speed-written notes. She hovered in the foyer as the parents, some of them even more glum or scowling than before, made their way out of the school.

"Dr Rogerson, I'd like to brief you *immediately* on what went on," she hissed secretively. Rogerson ushered her to his office. Brian and Alison slipped inside before he had chance to object.

If Clive Holdsworth had harboured any preconceived notions about what to expect, he would have been proved right. Parental opinion was vitriolic. Clive and his lay colleague had been meticulous in their preamble and had made it quite clear that parents should not refer to specific staff or specific incidents, that this was neither the time nor the place. They wasted their breath. Names were bandied around left, right and centre, in spite of the Inspectors' protestations.

"Mrs Dunstan, a child in Y7 and another in Y10. That Rogerson's a right plonker. We never get to know nothing. Take last September. My lass never knew what day school started. My lad didn't know either. When I rang up to find out I was told off like a naughty school girl for wasting office time. They think they're a cut above everybody else, in that office. And another thing, that form teacher of our Wayne's kept him in for thirteen minutes after school last week, without my permission. What're you going to do about that then?"

"Knowsley. My daughter's Rebecca in Y8. In my opinion, the teachers do a very worthwhile job, under difficult circumstances."

A groan rose from the fifteen or so gathered in the chilling hall. They all knew the 'stuck-up' Knowsley family. Robert Knowsley was a primary teacher, in the city suburbs. Born and bred in Southdale, he had never quite managed to break away from his roots. Rebecca was a show-off. Always came top in tests, a real boffin.

"Oh, shut up, Knowsley. You're one of them anyway. You would stick up for your own kind, wouldn't you? They don't know what a day's work is, these teachers. They want to try a day down the pit." The heckler had temporarily forgotten that the pit had closed years ago, just after the strike. "Nine till three and twenty weeks' holiday? And all they do is stand in front of a few kids, 'Turn to page 26 and copy it out'. I'd have some of that. It's better than writing begging letters for jobs just to get your dole money."

"Order, order," Clive interjected.

"You asked us here to give us opinions. We're giving them, aren't we?"

"He's right. Them teachers don't teach kids nothing. He's never got any homework, that lad of mine. I ask him every night, religiously, and he always says 'No, mum.' and off he goes out with his mates. I can't do nothing with him. If they had a bit more discipline in schools, we wouldn't have all this trouble at home. Bring back the cane, that's what I say. Never did me any harm."

"Would you please give your name and your child's year group?"

"No point, duck. My lad don't come here. I've just come to keep our Tracey company. It's our night out, you see. We're going straight on to the club."

It took Betty until nearly ten o'clock to complete her report back. By then, the three senior management members were thoroughly, though not unexpectedly downcast. Betty was revelling in her power. "And another thing, Dr Rogerson..."

"I think that's more than enough for now, Mrs Andrews. Please leave me your notes and I'll go through them in the morning."

"You'll never read my scribble, Dr Rogerson. I'll use our Stephanie's word processor and type it up for morning."

Rogerson was becoming mildly irritated. "That's quite all right, Mrs Andrews. Just leave your notes with me and if there's anything I can't follow, I'll get back to you tomorrow."

"Good night, Dr Rogerson, Brian, Mrs Lister." Betty Andrews left, still glowing with pride and excitement.

Brian murmured to Alison, shortly after they had left Rogerson's office. "Did you see that? Dr Bill has actually motivated a member of staff by giving her responsibility and he doesn't even realise it!"

Alison chortled.

Alison was last to leave. She thought Clive had left ages before but there he was, fiddling self-consciously with a sheaf of papers in the foyer.

"Hi."

"Hi."

"Seemed to go reasonably well."

"Come on, Clive, don't patronise me. It was an unmitigated disaster."

"Bit shirty, aren't we?"

"Sorry. I've had a very long day. I just want to get home to ..." Alison wavered and the sentence drifted away from her.

"I'm sure you've got time for a quick one."

Alison's sense of humour returned fleetingly. "I assume you mean a drink?"

"I should be so lucky!"

Why was her pulse racing? She wanted nothing to do with Clive. She was already late for her drink with Jake, her patient, so devoted Jake. She hesitated and instantly knew she was lost.

"Come on. It's only just after ten. Half an hour won't do any harm. For old time's sake."

Alison persuaded herself that it would be in the school's interests to have a harmless drink with the Registered Inspector. She would be able to counteract the parents' comments by communicating some of the positive things about the school.

Clive pressed home his advantage. Taking her arm and guiding her towards the car park, "Come on. I'll follow you. You know the local hostelries better than I do."

Alison stumbled over the milk bottle Jake had left on the step. Good old Jake. Once inside, she locked the door with excessive care. She slipped her feet out of her sensible, school shoes and tiptoed through the hall. The front room door was wide open. The little green figures on the video read zero, three, zero, eight. She winced.

She padded up the stairs. The bedroom door was pushed to but not latched. She went in. Jake was breathing heavily. "Jake," she whispered. He must be asleep. She slid her clothes to the carpet and slipped in beside him.

Jake's eyes were prickling. He felt numb and empty. His mind was bursting with imaginings. He carried on breathing deeply until he perceived that Alison had gone off to sleep. A warm tear wet his cheek and soaked into the pillow.

The next morning Alison woke with a start. Zero, seven, three, zero. She turned towards Jake. The bed was dimpled where he had been. She strained her ears for his whistling in the shower or his clattering of crockery in the kitchen. Nothing. Jake had gone to work before his time.

Alison went downstairs. His shoes and coat had gone from the hall. She lifted the telephone receiver and punched in six digits.

"Hi, this is Jake Lister. I'm out of the office at the moment but if you leave your name and number, after the third bleep, I'll ring you back later."

Alison Lister sobbed through the bleeps and then breathed, "Sorry."

13 Splintered *biro*

Thursday 8 February was not a good day at Southdale Comprehensive. Staff, sapped and wearied by pre-inspection preparation, slackened their grip. The youngsters, stirred up by the rapidly approaching holiday and rumours about the inspection were in the mood to take advantage.

Sheree Topham, who knew all about inspections from her Dad's newspaper, was holding court. "It's because we're a crap school. That's why them inspectors are coming; to sort the teachers out and tell them they've got to teach us proper. It's obvious. Take Besty for example: you don't learn nothing in his geography lessons. Everybody, like, messes about and nicks each other's stuff and chucks rubbers around the room. And when he tries to teach us something everybody, like, hums and when he gets louder we get louder, too. It's a right laugh. Ashley Whittaker says he was crying in geography last week. Besty, I mean, not Ash. But he, like, turned his face to the board so we couldn't see. A right whimp."

The morning registration bell struggled to make itself heard on the campus. Sheree's entourage, unperturbed, kept its attention acutely focused on Sheree.

She knew how to tell a story. Her English teacher had said as much in Sheree's last report. "Sheree is a very talented young woman.

She has the potential to get a reasonable grade in English Language, even at this late stage, if she knuckles down to some serious work."

Knuckling down was not in Sheree's nature. Spouting words of wisdom was.

"I think I could run this school better than old Rogerson. He hasn't got the foggiest idea. Remember what he did to Al Sumner, just because he tried to get off with Lister. She's an old tart anyway. They say that's why she left her last school to come here. You know - illicit relationship with Y10 pupil. My Dad says they're all at it. It says so in his paper. Ingleton's about the only decent teacher here." Sheree's mum went to the same church. "And *he*'s a religious nut. My mum says ..."

"Did I hear my name being taken in vain?" Brian Ingleton was in a mischievous mood. "Come on, ladies, late bell has gone. Don't you think it's about time we went to registration?"

Brian wondered what was wrong with Alison. Perhaps last night's meeting had got her down. She had passed him in the foyer with only a watery smile and had gone straight to her office. She did not appear at staff briefing. Brian tapped on her door on the way to first lesson. No answer. He tapped again and entered.

Alison was sitting at her desk with her back to the door. She appeared to be writing. She half turned to face him. Her eyes were pink, strained and moist. Her nostrils were red and flared.

"Not now, Brian. I need some space."

Brian nodded understandingly and gently closed the door behind him. He strode to reception. "No calls or interruptions for Mrs Lister, this morning, ladies. She's not well."

"Very well, Mr Ingleton," uttered one lady. "Lazy cow that Lister woman," added the other, barely allowing Brian the time to close the door behind him. "I've got a headache but there's a fat chance of me being left in peace. No calls or interruptions. She should try working in this place for a day. She'd soon want her cushy job back."

In the time that it took *lady two* to get that off her chest, *lady one* had answered two telephone calls.

"Southdale. Yes. Sandwiches, you say. This isn't a food delivery service, Mrs Higgins. It's a school. Well, he'll have to remember to bring his packed lunch in future. Nothing I can do. Goodbye."

"Yes? Southdale. Hello... hello... Oh, good morning, Mrs Ollerenshaw. Sorry to keep you waiting. I was on the other line. Awkward parent, you know. Expecting me to run errands for her. Dr Rogerson? I'll check if he's available. Hold the line please."

Line two rang, flashing red. *Lady two* sighed and snatched up the receiver.

"Southdale. No he's not available. He's just taken a call on the other line. Calm down a minute. There's no need to use that sort of language. If you don't calm down, I'll hang up. You might well be upset but I'm not listening to that sort of talk. Well, no you can't talk to her either. She's not to be disturbed. I don't make the rules, love, I just answer the telephone. You could speak to the year tutor, if she's not teaching. No, there's no point in you coming down here now. You'll have to make an appointment. Dr Rogerson's a very busy man. What's it about? Mr Best? He said what? Well, I agree it's not a nice thing for a teacher to call a pupil but you haven't heard his side of the story. No, I don't think it's a good idea for you to see Mr Best until you've had chance to calm down a bit. I tell you what, I'll see if Mr Ingleton's in his office. Hold, please."

"Bitch," exhaled *lady two* as she punched the *secrecy* key.

Brian was in the corridor outside his office, lecturing a Y9 that someone had sent to him for using foul and abusive language in class.

"Look, just shut up, will you? Surely, you've known me long enough to realise that if you've done something wrong and you own up and apologise, you'll be treated much better than if you lie."

"I'm not lying. It weren't me. Honest, sir. I wouldn't tell lies to you, sir."

"So, Mr Brown's lying then?"

"Well, he don't like me. He's always picking on me. He always has done."

"Look, son, when you're in a hole, stop digging. Are we going to get this sorted out now or are we going to have to contact home?"

"I never said what he said I said."

"What did you say?"

"Crap head."

"What?"

"Cra..."

"All right," I heard. Listen, Deke, you just sit there outside my office and I'll deal with you in a minute. I've got something else to see to."

Brian had been on his way to Modern Languages. The telephone in his office bleeped. He hesitated for a second and then, disregarding it, jogged off down the corridor and up the stairs to the extravagantly named *languages suite*.

It would have been clear to any observer that Brian Ingleton really was in a hurry. He bounded over the scattered, gaudy, metallic snack packets. He ignored the splintered *biro* and the empty *Wrigley's* wrappers on the stairs. He even pretended not to notice a huge, pink gob of still moist bubble-gum on the landing.

The languages' landing was a disheartening sight. Tattered sheets of bleached, brown sugar paper drooped from the wall at curious angles, revealing the cracks in the plaster, some gouged into channels, that the paper had been intended to conceal. Matchstick figures in faded felt-tip, on un-ruled file paper, with elementary French and German captions, had been pasted heavy handedly on to the sugar paper.

Brian burst into room ten. The room was heaving with strained silence. Several reddened faces were so swollen that Brian feared they might explode in nervous laughter at the slightest opportunity. Gaynor Sneap, French and German, in her second year of teaching, stood, as stern as she was able, in front of the class.

"What's up, Miss Sneap?"

"It's this lot. They've been *high* ever since they came in this morning; calling out, answering back and that sort of thing. And they keep asking to go to the toilet so, by the time it came to Gavin Watts, I'd had enough and decided to put a stop to it. I told him he couldn't go."

Brian got the gist of where this was leading. "I bet he's wet his pants," he thought.

"And?" Brian prompted expectantly.

"I'm so angry. He's done it out of the window."

The pupils could hold themselves back no longer. When the hysteria had died down, Brian turned on his heel without giving the boy the satisfaction of catching his eye.

"Gavin Watts, my office. Now!"

Break had come and gone. Deke had been dealt with. Gavin had been put on hold while Brian thought what to do about him. A Y10 parent had been placated. His daughter had complained about being called a slag by Mr Best. Brian managed to keep his opinions to himself and pointed out that the girl had been rather provocative in her treatment of her geography teacher but, nevertheless, a teacher should know better than to respond in kind and that he would have a word with Mr Best and make sure that it did not happen again.

"It had better not or I'll be round to sort Best out for myself. Understood?"

Brian knew this family of old. He understood *perfectly* and determined to make sure that Mr Best understood as well. He caught him at break in the toilets.

"Look, Richard, you just can't talk to kids like that. If Rogerson finds out he'll take disciplinary action and it'll go on your record."

"But she started it."

"Oh, for goodness sake, grow up!"

By lunch-time, Alison had not emerged from her office. Brian checked the corridors, checked the dining-room and had a quick walk around the yard, eating a tuna mayonnaise sandwich. All was relatively quiet. Some Y11s had pinched some younger kids' battered, deflated football.

"Come on, lads, find yourself something better to do than bullying the Y7s."

There were still smouldering fag ends behind the rotting storage sheds near PE but the smokers' club early warning system had worked again. Brian was pleased to have been saved another task.

A trio of unemployed local lads was on the look out for some Y10 girls they had met in a club the night before. Brian spoke jovially to them about security and the need to keep the site clear of intruders. They listened patiently and complied with his instruction to head towards the gate, at least until he had disappeared around the corner of the building.

Alison was Brian's priority. He was worried. In their short acquaintance he had not seen her look so low. He tapped on her door and went straight in. She was still sitting at her desk. She turned to face him. The eyes were dry but gloomy, the nostrils sore with blowing. It was clear that something was amiss.

"Are you all right?"

"Fine. Well, not exactly fine. I'm not too well so I thought I would catch up on some paper work today." The guilty glance at her nearly empty out-tray gave the game away. "I'm sorry if I've left you a bit in the lurch."

"Oh, don't worry about that. Nothing I couldn't handle."

It was apparent that she did not want to talk.

"Have you had anything to eat?" he asked, knowing full well that she had not.

"I'm fine, thanks. Really. I couldn't eat a bite. I'm sure I'll be OK tomorrow."

"Listen, Al, if there's anything I can do..."

"It's just a headache... a sort of migraine, I suppose... like I used to get as a teenager. A good night's sleep and I'll be fine."

She was an improbable liar. "Just ring," he said and left it at that.

Brian returned to his office. Lying on his desk was a yellow slip of paper. On the slip was a telephone number and the words: "Irate neighbour. Please ring."

14 Scum

At last Alison summoned sufficient courage to face Jake. She left school at 6.00pm and drove steadily home. The house was in darkness. The windows looked cheerless and full of foreboding. The house was empty. The rooms were bare and lifeless. Alison slumped on the unfriendly bed and wept.

Kind, gentle, patient, understanding Jake was the last person on earth she would wish to hurt and she had hurt him more than she could bear.

Jake, sitting bolt upright in his high-backed, swivel typing-chair, stared vaguely at the wall. Not much had been achieved in this particular enclave of the town hall on that day. Jake felt empty. His body was tensed against the searing torment in his heart.

At ten o'clock, Jake had to ring the caretaker to let him out.

"You've been working late, Mr Lister. You'll be after a pay rise next."

Jake grunted. The caretaker shrugged and watched Jake's back as he retreated towards the car park. Jake sat in the darkened car park for an hour before he turned the ignition and drove home. He pulled into the drive and sat again.

Hearing the engine Alison made an effort. She wiped her eyes with a tissue and came downstairs, flicking on the television. Jake faked a greeting through the open living-room door.

"Hi. Sorry I'm late. Worked late and then went for a pint with the lads."

Before she could pour out her bursting heart, he had gone upstairs and hurried into the shower. He showered with indecent haste and slithered into the icy bed, face to the wall.

Alison mounted the stairs, quivering. He had closed the bedroom door. She stepped inside. She watched him for an age, praying, willing him to turn to her so she could take him in her arms and cry tears of sorrow into his hair. He did not budge.

She abandoned her clothes and eased into bed beside him, as close as she dare. Surely he was not asleep. He remained rigid, determined not to weaken. She turned on to her other side and they lay there, a yard of no man's land between them.

An eternity elapsed. She rolled on to her back and raised her neck to look at the clock-radio.

"Goodnight, sweetheart," she sighed into the void.

The day before the holidays was traditionally a problem for teachers. For the youngsters, it was a chance to take advantage. Rogerson had tried since he got there to stamp out the flour and egg fights but many of the parents had fond memories of the ritual and enthusiastically condoned it.

"What's up with you, Mr Rogerson? Weren't you ever a kid yourself?"

There were always rumours of war between Southdale and its nearest rival, *The Andrew Pickersgill School*. Friday, 9 February was no exception. A mole had caught Rogerson alone in the corridor.

"Mr Rogerson, have you heard?"

"*Doctor* Rogerson, if you don't mind, young man."

"Yes, doctor. Have you heard though?"

"Heard what precisely?"

"That lot from Pick-us-nose School are coming to get us!"

"Hum, well I don't think you need to worry about that, young man. We've heard those tales before."

"It's true, sir. I know it is."

"How?"

"Well, it's our Neil. He's been going with one of them snooty girls from over there and the lads there don't like it and they're coming over here mob-handed to give our Neil a right seeing-to."

"You've been watching too much television."

"But, sir..."

Rogerson telephoned Pickersgill just to be on the safe side, though he hated talking to that self-satisfied, business woman, the headteacher."

"Come off it, Bill. My lot have all got their heads down, revising for their exams. Nose to the grindstone and all that. Very quiet here. I'll give you a ring if I pick up anything on the grapevine."

Break came and went without incident. Rogerson had confided in Brian.

"I'll keep my eyes open, boss."

Lunchtime was nearly over, with just a couple of random eggings, when it happened.

"Sir, come quickly. They're here."

Brian, showing no sign of emotion, strolled calmly to the playing fields.

"Good grief, hardly a need to call for the cavalry."

Coming over the brow of the hill was a cluster of a dozen or so Pickersgill scholars, readily identified by their bright green blazers and glaringly striped ties. The Southdale heavies were forming up to defend the school's honour.

"Go back to the yard and leave this to me!"

They took no notice and continued to match him stride for stride towards the interlopers. Both factions halted with about ten paces between them. Brian looked the Pickersgill kids up and down. They were better fed and cleaner cut than the Southdale contingent but this made them look, some how, more menacing than he expected.

They were armed to the teeth. Some carried lengths of chain and others sported filched rounders bats.

"What's it all about, lads? Why don't you just turn around and go back to where you came from before I phone up Pickersgill?"

No response. No foul-mouthings. Nothing.

The Pickersgill crowd inched forward. The Southdale lot held their ground. For the first time Brian felt slightly anxious.

"Now come on, lads. Let's not do anything silly."

His voice had gone up a semi-tone. The invaders sensed his fear and moved in for the kill.

"Hold it right there. Not another step."

The smallest of the uniformed kids stepped forward, carrying a bat. Before Brian could react the weapon crashed down on to his shoulder. A fraction of a second later, another blow, this time to the side of his head. He fell to his knees, his vision blurred and his senses reeling. A third youth came at him with a chain but he was stopped in his stride by a tall youth on the Southdale side.

"Alan Sumner! What's he doing here?"

Brian fell forward on to his face and consciousness left him.

The battle was on. The engagement was short and bloody. Pickersgill honour was soon satisfied, though the offending Neil was well out of the way, sitting, bored, outside Rogerson's office. The small war party disappeared over the horizon before Southdale reinforcements could arrive.

Alan Sumner pulled Brian's limp form into a sitting position.

"Come on, you lot, give me a hand to get sir back to school."

Alan supported his head and upper body while a couple of the other walking wounded grabbed his legs and they staggered with him back to the school buildings.

Rogerson's limbs turned to jelly as he saw Brian, half-walking, half-dragged, enter the admin. corridor.

"999. An ambulance, quickly," he squeaked through the open door of the office.

Rogerson espied Alan Sumner. "What are you doing on the premises, Sumner? You're banned. I told your mother that if you as much set foot in the yard, I'd call the police."

"Shut it, Rogerson. Can't you see Mr Ingleton needs help?"

Rogerson, banishing considerations of blood spots on the carpet, pushed open the door of his office and motioned for Brian to be helped through. Brian flopped into the easy chair and uttered a few choice declarations, the like of which Rogerson had never expected to emanate from Brian's mouth.

"Uh, what hit me? Is everyone else OK? Good job you were there, Alan. They might have made mincemeat of me."

Alan Sumner grunted an acknowledgement.

Rogerson, a quiver in his voice, advised Brian that help was on its way. Would he like a drink of water? He stopped short of offering something stronger from his filing cabinet. What on earth had happened? Could his wife be contacted?

Fifteen minutes later the ambulance pulled soundlessly through the gates. A bearded, jovial colossus ambled along the corridor and into Rogerson's office.

"Stand back, everybody. Let the professionals through. My, my, you're going to have a headache in the morning, aren't you, sir? Better get you to the *General* to get that seen to. Another week's holiday coming up soon, I believe. Can't have you teachers missing your holiday, can we?"

Brian moaned.

In a fluster of flashing lights and powerful sounds, the police vehicle screeched to a halt alongside the ambulance and two baby faced officers dashed into the school.

"What's happened to you then, sir?" queried the female.

"Had an accident, sir, or is there another party involved?" quizzed her male companion.

Brian groaned.

Rogerson stammered a few words of explanation. "This boy can help you find out what went on," he stuttered, turning to the empty space that had been Alan Sumner only seconds before. The wretched boy had sneaked off.

"We'll catch up with him later."

"We'll try and head off the assailants before they get back to base." They departed as recklessly as they had arrived - all noise and light.

The jovial giant took Brian by the arm and steered him towards the waiting ambulance. The driver, still behind the wheel, looked on with a carefully cultivated matter of factness that spoke volumes. It was all in a day's work. Nothing could faze him. He had seen it all before.

Two hours later, cleaned up and stitched, Brian called home from the hospital.

"No, honestly, darling, I'm perfectly all right. A couple of staff are going to get me home. One will bring me in my car and the other will follow on to take him back to school. There's no need for you to come out. No, really, I'll be home in about half-an-hour. Just a splitting headache and bloody angry with myself for getting into that situation. You'd think I'd know better after all these years."

Several miles away, at Scargill Court, the police car wailed to a halt. One officer, wary of stone throwers, braved the abuse while the other made a beeline for the Sumners'.

"What do you want?"

"Open up, Becky. We want a word with your lad!"

"He hasn't done nothing. He's been with me all afternoon."

"Don't talk crap. Open up before I boot it in."

The door opened reluctantly. The officer squeezed past Becky. Alan Sumner stepped forward.

"What do you lot want?"

"Alan Sumner, I'm arresting you in connection with an attack on a teacher at Southdale Comprehensive School, you do not have to say anything..."

"But it weren't me. I ..."

"Shut it, scum. Get in the car. You can do your whining at the nick."

15 Blood brothers

Ashley Hardman liked the school holidays in particular. He received deliveries and *signed* for them. He gave the cleaners their instructions. He strode up and down the corridors, finding dusty crevices that no one else had noticed. In short, he was master of all he surveyed. From time to time, he rang Rogerson at home to keep him abreast of graffiti or broken windows.

What he savoured most exquisitely was being free from all those arrogant teachers for a while. No need to be at their beck and call for jammed locks and dud light bulbs. No complaints about the heating. No requests to mop up vomit on the stairs. Oh, the ecstasy of real job satisfaction!

Hardman had been caretaker at Southdale Comprehensive for twenty-three years. He had seen staff come and go. In all that time he had never seen anything like this.

"I've been caretaker here for...oooh... twenty-three years, and I've never seen anything like this before," he explained to a long-suffering cleaner. She was leaning on her broom, sucking on an illicit cigarette, outside the staffroom.

"Can't get them from under my feet," she joined in. "Muttering to themselves in the classrooms, sticking things on walls. How are we supposed to get finished? Rogerson'll be kicking up a fuss if there's footprints on his corridor again, first day back."

Ashley spotted an opportunity to share his inside information. "It's this OFSTED thing or whatever they call it. Got 'em all running around like headless chickens. The word is they're all going to be in dead trouble 'cause the kids are mostly thick."

"Steady on, Ash, my lad comes here you know."

"Like mother, like son, I always say."

"Cheeky sod."

"Anyway, they're all working their socks off to try and con the inspectors. They'll never get away with. I mean, some of the classrooms are like bedlam. Teachers tell 'em what to do and they do exactly what they like. Sometimes when I go in to fix a light bulb or something, it's all I can do to keep my hands off the little so-and-sos. If I were in charge, I'd soon bring them to heel. 'Spare the rod and spoil the child,' our lass always says."

"Kids are kids and they always will be, as far as I'm concerned. Oh no, Ash, that little nipper of yours has brought his mucky dog into the corridor again. It's piddling on my floor!"

Ashley asserted his parental authority. "Darren, you little pillock, get that dog outside. Darren, did you hear me? What did you say? Who taught you that word? Just wait till your Mum gets her hands on you. You won't be able to sit down for a week!"

Southdale School really was a hive of activity. From the moment the date of the inspection had been announced, Southdale staff had been conspicuous by their absence from travel agents within a twenty-mile radius. Years old traditions of ski-trips to elegant resorts in the Alps and packages to warmer climes had been unanimously abandoned.

Fear is a great motivator and there was none more motivated than Bill Rogerson.

With Alison in tow, he personally inspected every corner of the school. Cardboard boxes had to be removed from the tops of cupboards. Table tops had to be sanded down to remove the etchings of multiple cohorts of Southdale scholars. The dining-room tables were turned upside down and thousands of chunks of hardened chewing-gum hacked away by hand. Reams of faded sugar paper were ripped from noticeboards and - what an extravagance! - replaced wholesale from Rogerson's secret supply of resources.

No sooner had the resources technician finished tacking up the pristine sheets than teachers emerged from classrooms armed with staple guns, *Gloy* and *PrittSticks*. Whole walls were pasted with outrageously recent pupils' work.

Rogerson, on his frequent rounds of the corridors, sang the praises of the gaudy illustrations but bewailed the myriad spelling mistakes. "Literacy and the ability of students to access the curriculum will be a key issue for the RI, Mrs Lister," he lectured, in a rare sortie into the educational vernacular.

*Grey*boards were thoroughly washed down and became *black* again. Whiteboards were sponged leaving the sweet odour of solvent thick in the air. The same solvent was used to remove felt-tip graffiti from walls and windows. The windows were washed inside and out.

Simon Cunliffe made a point of wearing his ski-ing goggles when he went into the gym. "Oh, the glare! I must speak to my union rep. Could put in an industrial injury claim and retire on three-quarter salary to Klosters!"

"Oh, shut it, Simon!"

Toilet doors were re-hung and re-painted. *Soft* toilet paper was placed in the cubicles. Ashley stopped short of replacing worn washers on the taps. No need to overdo it!

Litter bins were emptied. The grounds were cleared. Plastic bottles, glass bottles, foil containers, yogurt tubs, crisp packets, chocolate wrappers, cigarette packets, old cheese sandwiches, bits of tomato, bubble gum, spent matches - all suffered the same fate: bagged in black bin liners and taken to the tip in the caretaker's ancient van.

There was an uneasy peace in the Lister houeshold. On finding out about the inspection, Alison had unilaterally decided that jetting off was not number one on her priorities for half term. She had informed Jake that she intended to go into school every day to help get everything up to scratch. Jake had shrugged off his resentment and unbooked a week's holiday.

During half term, Alison had worked only marginally less hours than in a normal week. Jake had found it difficult to resist a peculiar desire to leave for work earlier and come home later. This had not gone unnoticed. Jake was afraid to share his worries with Alison for fear of hearing the worst and Alison was unsure what she could say that would put Jake's mind at rest. The result was a distance that neither of them had experienced in their marriage before.

Alison had telephoned Brian Ingleton every day since the incident. He did not make an appearance in school during the first three days of the holiday. He had recovered swiftly from the trauma but his head was sore. Alison called to see him on her way home one late afternoon. He looked as jovial as ever. You would not have known he had been through such an experience were it not for the shaven patch on the side of his head and the black, crispening scar in the centre of it.

"This is a good one, Al. It'll make you laugh. It's about the verger at our church. One of his jobs is to keep the tower clock going. Well, on Saturday, he remembered he had forgotten to wind it when he noticed the absence of the chimes. So off he went down to church to start it up again. When he got down there, he realised that he had left his watch at home and therefore didn't know what time to set the clock at. Suddenly, he had a brainwave. There's a telephone in the office bit, so he rang the speaking clock and spent a few seconds getting into the rhythm. 'At the third stroke, the time sponsored by Accurist will be five ten precisely. Beep. Beep. Beep. At the third stroke, the time sponsored by Accurist will be five ten and ten seconds. Beep. Beep. Beep.' At this stage he set off for the belfry. Out of the office, saying to himself 'At the third stroke the time sponsored by Accurist will be five ten and thirty seconds. Beep. Beep. Beep.' Out of the office and into the porch: 'At the third stroke the time sponsored by Accurist will be five ten and forty seconds. Beep. Beep. Beep.' Up the stairs on to the balcony and then up the wooden ladder and so he went on repeating the time until he got to the clock mechanism and adjusted the hands. The funny thing is that the time on the church clock looks pretty spot on to me."

Alison chuckled politely. After the niceties she asked him about the aftermath of the attack.

Apparently, Becky Sumner had managed to get his telephone number, on the Friday evening, and through her sobs had told him what had happened to her Alan. Beth had run him down to the police station. A few minutes of explanation to the desk sergeant and the intervention of his senior officer were enough to get Alan turned out of the interview room, where he was being questioned. Alan and Brian came face to face. They nodded curtly but said nothing. Some bonds transcend all else. They were blood brothers.

On the second Saturday of the half-term break, Jake and Alison had managed a walk to the pub in the next village and put up with a hot-sandwich-and-door-wedge-chips lunch, washed down with halves of bitter. Their interaction had been cool and banal. They were going through the motions. Their late evenings had been dismal. Alison had gone up for a shower and lingered while Jake had flicked the cable channels and retired only when he knew she would have slipped into bed and turned her back on his side of the bed. A gnawing desire to hold each other and return to normality had been resisted by both so well, that it had been replaced, imperceptibly with a determination not to give way the first. On the Sunday, Jake pottered around. Alison forced herself to read in a futile attempt to keep her mind off the return to school and the stalemate between herself and Jake.

Twenty minutes after returning to school on the Monday, it was as if she had never been away. The kids, bemused by the glowing splendour of the corridors, classrooms, toilets and yards, set about restoring normality with a vengeance.

Muddy footprints began to appear on the shining walls. Secret felt tips scrawled here and there. Photos were gouged, drawing pins pinched and sugar paper slashed. Staff patched things up as rapidly as the kids undid them.

At break-time the vending machines were rapidly emptied of their contents. The wrappers were torn from a hundred chocolate bars and deposited emphatically in the eerily undefiled yards. Discarded crisp packets floated by on the chilling north easterly breeze.

The Head of IT blamed the Internet. "Some little swines have learned that if you throw a two pence coin hard enough at one of those reinforced glass windows, it can cause a little crack that gradually spreads and causes the pane to explode like an old fashioned windscreen. It can happen quite some time after the coin has been aimed so it's almost impossible to track down the culprit. I'm sure they've learned how to do it from the Internet! You can find all sorts of disruptive stuff if you know where to look."

"It's obvious you do!" chipped in a staffroom wag.

Rogerson had ordered a council of war with his senior 'team'. Alison and Brian huddled in his office to await his words of wisdom.

"How's the head, Brian? Better now, I hope. It's obvious that Holdsworth is going to hit us on our statistics in the GCSE exams. and our SATs results. Brian could you fill us in on the details?"

"Well, if I'd have known that you were going to ask me, I would have looked them up. As it is I reckon ten per cent of last year's Y11 got five A starred to C grades."

"Nine per cent," chimed in Alison. "It was ten per cent the year before and the year before that it was twelve per cent."

"And the SATs?"

"I..er…can't quite remember the exact figures ..." said Brian, somewhat disconcerted by Alison's input.

"Very similar in Maths, English and Science really. Last year we were about twenty per cent below the local average and quite a bit more below the national average. Boys are doing significantly worse than girls, in line with the national picture. Even at this late stage we could probably con OFSTED a bit by drawing up some targets for improvement and circulating them around the staff, in case an inspector asks them."

"Mrs Lister," uttered Rogerson, shocked by her directness.

"Good idea, Alison. I'll see to it after lunch."

"We could sort of back date the paper so that it doesn't look last minute."

"No, that I won't do!"

"Oh, Brian, that honesty of yours will get us into trouble one day."

Brian smiled rather coyly. He hated OFSTED and would love to put something over on the inspectors but there were things that he just wouldn't do.

Rogerson suddenly realised that he had lost the reins.

"Well, that seems very satisfactory, you two. Can I leave you to get on with it?"

"Just a moment, Dr Rogerson. At least one of us is going to get a grilling over these stats. Hadn't we better get our story straight?"

"What do you mean, Mrs Lister?"

"Well, when the RI takes us to task over the low pass rates and the attendance and the unauthorised absence and the low 16-19 participation rates, are we going to take it lying down or are we going to go down fighting?"

"Explain."

"Well if they're going to try and label us as a failing school, we need to be able to make out a case for why we haven't turned it round yet and convince them that we are on the point of making a breakthrough."

"Careful, Mrs Lister, I don't like to hear the word *failing* used around here. It's not good for morale."

Alison swallowed her opinions on the morale of Southdale's staff and continued.

"It's absolutely no use giving them that crap about how the youngsters come from deprived homes and they can't be expected to do as well as kids from the leafy suburbs."

"But it is true to a certain extent, Al."

"True it may be, Brian, but that's not what those cynical so-and-sos want to hear. They want to hear about success against the odds. Phoenix rising from the ashes. Bricks without straw. That's your expression isn't it? We've got to play them at their own game. That's what they're looking for. They don't want ordinary teachers and leaders doing ordinary jobs with ordinary kids. They want *Superheads* dishing out *Superideas* to *Superteachers* who somehow work miracles with damn all resources and precious little thanks from the bloody government!"

"Go for it, Al. I wish smoothie Holdsworth were here right now."

Alison coloured. She went on more calmly. "Well, anyway, you know what I think now. I just feel we have to take them on the front foot. That's a cricketing image isn't it, Brian? You know about cricket. We've got to go on the attack. Convince them that we can turn it round. Play *their* game - for the sake of the school. If we don't they'll close us down, as sure as anything."

Rogerson's colour seeped from his cheek. He cast a nervous glance towards the door, as if Alison's utterance might have escaped into an unsuspecting corridor.

"I think we've taken the point, Mrs Lister. I hear what you're saying but I really do not think that they can close us down. There aren't enough places locally to cater for all the pupils."

"I mean close us down and reopen on the same site with a new name. They've done it to other schools already, you know. Sacked the senior management, brought in troubleshooters, appointed new governors."

"I see. You must do what you see fit, Mrs Lister, but I must ask that neither of you breathe a word of this outside of this office."

Alison turned on her heel.

"The staff aren't as naive as you think!" she hissed between her teeth, not caring whether Rogerson heard her or not.

Pretending he had not, he turned to Brian.

"Bricks without straw? That's biblical isn't it? Exodus, if my memory serves me well. What on earth did she mean?"

16 Not enough Sharons

At County Hall they were getting twitchy. Sarah Koszalinski was ringed by her acolytes.

"Who's the school's adviser? Why haven't you tackled this one earlier? For goodness sake, when OFSTED get in there they'll take *us* to pieces, let alone the head and governors. I can't believe how an LEA could be so lacking in its sense of responsibility. What about those children and their future?"

"It's me, Chief," ventured Bernard Horsfield, forty-something, balding, gingery-grey whispers on his temples.

"When was the last time you visited Southdale?"

"Not exactly recently," he squirmed.

"When?"

"Must be ... oooh ... two years ago."

"Two years! Give me strength."

"But I have been in touch with several Heads of Department in that time and I've chatted with Rogerson at Heads' meetings. He assured me everything was going all right. We do have to display an element of professional trust, Chief. Without it our school based colleagues become demotivated. We can't be breathing down their necks all the time. It's unhealthy."

"Bollocks!" Sarah Koszalinski always called a spade a shovel.

Bernard Horsfield had never been spoken to in this manner. His previous boss had been a *gentleman*. Deeply hurt, he went on, "I spoke to that new deputy…er… Angela Lister … on the telephone just a few weeks ago…"

"Did you ring her? To welcome her to the County, perhaps?"

"*She* rang me actually."

"About?"

"A couple of issues really. She was having some sort of a problem over a permanent exclusion with the head and she also …er… mentioned a few fears about the OFSTED inspection."

"And what was your response?"

"I told her, quite rightly in my opinion, that they were internal matters to be dealt with by the head and governors."

Sarah Koszalinski chewed her bottom lip ferociously. "Mr Horsfield, get me Rogerson on the telephone now." Turning to one of her 'trusties', "Denise, we are going to have to do a bit of subtle work behind the scenes. Get me the RI's telephone number."

Chief Education Officer Koszalinski had at least two things in common with Alison Lister. She was new to her job and determined to do it effectively. Her predecessor, Reg Houson had left, owing to very premature retirement, on a fat pension. He was now chairing committees and doing lecture tours. A highly intelligent individual, loaded with enthusiasm for education and young people, he had lacked the hard edge and single minded determination to get things done.

Ms Koszalinski constantly and vexatiously referred to him as "The Incompetent". She did not share his human weakness. Because of him there were colleagues in post, at LEA and school level, who were simply not up to the job. She was on a mission.

"Denise, Horsfield will have to go. Get me his file."

Sarah Koszalinski was a high flier. First class degree and PhD, though she spurned the title that went with it. Woe betide anyone who referred to her as 'Doctor'. She had started her career teaching but promptly tired of the company of children and passed hastily through the grades of Local Education Authority administration, leaving her mark on everyone and everything. When she applied for the post of Chief Education Officer, her tough facade and frank approach had stirred the councillors, weary of the wishy-washiness of Houson's regime. They had their hatchet woman.

Southdale had seen the busiest week of the term. On Alison's advice Rogerson had grudgingly called all staff together on the Thursday evening. Brian briefed them on how to respond when there was an inspector in class. He charged all form tutors to talk their classes through the need for good behaviour.

Head of English, Gareth Jenner hit the nail right on the head.

"Forget all this staffroom talk about letting them see a normal week at Southdale and not giving a damn. If they see a normal week in this place, we'll all be out on our ears. We've got to teach out of our shoes. Heads of Department should check lesson plans. No tests! No dictating notes or copying from the board! At least *try* and do something meaningful with the youngsters."

Dr Rogerson made his contribution. "I've put a copy of the school policies on the Current Noticeboard."

Colleagues looked at each other, mystified, and then at the transformed noticeboard with its word processed labels and neatly stapled white tape dividers. Alison had obviously been busy. She could turn out five policies a day. Ten a day in the week before inspection! "I want you to read them carefully and... well... learn them in case an inspector asks you about them."

"Can we have a copy each, Dr Rogerson?"

"I don't think I can justify that level of expenditure on photocopying. Our budget, as you know, is not sufficient and it's only through my effective financial management that ..."

Brian whispered in his ear. Rogerson coughed nervously and continued. "But in the circumstances, perhaps we could lift the tight spending restrictions. See to it, Mr Ingleton, will you? That's all, ladies and gentleman. Good night."

Alison had a sudden rush of blood to the head. "Excuse me, Dr Rogerson, could I add a word or two, please?"

"Well, it's a bit irregular, Mrs Lister. I have dismissed the staff and they've all got homes to go to, you know..."

Alison seized the initiative. "Hang on, folks. Sit down a minute, will you? Order. Order. I'd like to say something. Oh, for heaven's sake shut up and listen! Sorry. I'm sorry. I didn't mean to sound impatient. It's just that this means so much to all of us. We've got our jobs, our careers to think of. But just try to think what it means for the children and their parents. They've little enough security in their lives already. This school may not be much but it's all they've got. Most of them won't travel out of the area for their education. They're far too parochial. We've got to make a success of it for their sake. I've only been here a short while but I've seen enough to know that you care deeply about those young people. You've had the stuffing knocked out of you by the government and you're wearied through constant change. But deep, deep down you came into this profession, like I did, because you care. You care about their academic success but many of the kids around here, with all the pressures they face, will be lucky just to survive. We're not only educators. We're social workers. We're their friends! We're the only place they've got to turn to when they don't know where else to turn and I'm talking about the parents as well as the kids. Oh, I know it's just a jumble, what I'm saying, but I'm speaking from the heart. Let's go out there and do it - for their sake."

Alison raced from the staffroom, down the corridor, past startled cleaners and into her office. Rogerson, appalled by her impertinence, his insides churning with seething anger, shoved open the door and restrained himself sufficiently to utter the pathetic, "Mrs Lister, you may refer to them as students or pupils or even children but, kindly, not as kids."

Alison's eyes filled up with frustration.

Five minutes later Brian Ingleton rolled through the yawning door. "Well done, Al. That was just what we all needed."

"Like a hole in the head!"

Cynthia Rogerson was becoming more and more concerned about her husband's state of mind. He had sulked through Thursday evening and by late on Friday he appeared so disturbed that she just had to speak to him directly.

"What's eating at you again?"

Bill passed wearily through the customary denials but was only too relieved to have someone to listen.

"That Lister woman is taking over. She constantly flies in the face of my authority. At the staff meeting yesterday she spoke as if *she* were the head. The trouble is that some of the staff fall for all that emotional claptrap. There was even a ripple of applause as she stormed out at the end. It's obvious that I'm going to carry the can for everything that's wrong at Southdale. Goodness knows, I've tried but you can't imagine what it's like, Cyn, overcoming years upon years of apathy. You can't expect those youngsters to be able to succeed like youngsters from the leafy suburbs, who have everything going for them: parents who take an interest in education, books from an early age, trips abroad, expensive private lessons and so on. You know, two years ago we had a girl who got an A* grade in French and I was just comparing her with that niece of yours, Rebecca, who also got an A*. The difference was that Rebecca had spent six weeks every summer holiday in France with her parents, absorbing the French language and culture. The girl at Southdale, Sharon was her name, had never so much as set foot in France. Her parents couldn't or wouldn't even afford the price of one of those day trips we used to do. It's just so unfair, Cyn. Which of those two had to work hardest to get that top grade, Rebecca or Sharon? The problem is there are not enough Sharons at Southdale. Most of the young people want instant success... and if they don't get it they just give up. I haven't got much time for Cunliffe, that young PE teacher but he has this frustrating habit of hitting the nail right on the head with his cynical comments. I overheard him in the staffroom, one time, talking about the attitude of our students to sport: 'Our kids' motto should be not *who dares wins* but who *cares* who wins?' And he's right, oh so right. Ever since they were born they've had it rammed down their throats, by the media, that education is a waste of time; teachers are no good; there are no jobs when they leave school. How can we expect motivation from them? What is the point of them achieving exam results just to end up on benefit? They can do that without qualifications, just like their fathers and brothers. No wonder so many boys are underachieving. They have their dignity torn away from them. They're the modern victims of stereotyping, Cyn, young male adults in that kind of working class environment. For so long they've been expected to be the breadwinners and now the pits have closed and the steel works have gone all that's left for them is the Job Centre with its pitiful offering of part time jobs; women's work, as they see it. To make matters worse I had a phone call from the new Director of Education. Koszalinski, she's called. She berated me about the school's lack of success. Only concerned about her own position, as far as I could judge, and how an adverse inspection report would reflect on *her* LEA. How patronising. Went on and on about the futures of all the young people in my care and how they deserved a better deal than they were getting. She's never set foot in the place up to now. High expectations! That's what we should have. I've really had enough, Cyn, I can't take much more. High expectations! I had high expectations once about what the government and the council should be providing for these children. They put them in oversized classes, with insufficient resources and expect us to get the best out of them. Alison Lister put her finger on it. We're not just educators. We are expected to compensate for all that's missing in those young people's lives. I came into this job with such high hopes of what I could do for them. But they're right, Cyn. They're all right: Lister, Koszalinski, Ollerenshaw even Brian Ingleton. I've tried, but I've not got it in me. I've ... I've ..." He hesitated. "I've failed, Cyn. I've failed."

Cynthia looked lovingly at her man, through misty eyes. It was one of those times in a relationship when words were not enough to plumb the depths of emotion. She cradled him in her arms and they stayed like that until the warmth of her soul nearly dulled the hurt within him.

It was 9.30pm on Friday, 23 February. Brian and Beth Ingleton and their children had just got back from their weekly visit to Tesco. Beth was sorting out the shopping while Brian was sorting out the children.

"Come on, you two, time for bed."

"Aw, Daddy, can't we stop up? It's not school tomorrow."

Alison Lister was ignoring the dishes on the table and pretending not to be concerned over Jake's failure to appear.

Sarah Koszalinski was in her office at County Hall.

Clive Holdsworth feverishly rattled out the final sentences of the report of his previous inspection and closed the lid of his laptop. By Monday morning he would be back into a new cycle and this time it would be Southdale Comprehensive School.

17 Spectre

Ashley Hardman and Brian Ingleton stared at the front of the building in disbelief: letters a yard high, spray-painted in white.

"The little sods," exhaled Ashley.

Brian chortled. "At least they've reached level five at spelling. Not a spelling mistake to be seen. I'm proud of them. They must have read the inspectors' CVs to know so much about their parentage."

"Eh?" queried Ashley. "Better ring and get it cleaned off."

"Better had, Ash. It's not a very warm welcome for OFSTED, is it?"

Ashley scurried off to the dingy box he ambitiously referred to as his office.

Brian continued on his unhurried way into the school. It was seven-thirty a.m. on Monday, 26 February. A huddle of unfamiliar cars had gathered already in a corner of the playground. Rogerson was fussing around in the entrance foyer. There was no sign of Alison.

"Has Hardman got on to the LEA about the graffiti?" asked Rogerson, nervously?"

"He's on with it now, boss. It'll be off by midday."

"I wish I could get my hands on the little so-and-sos who've done this to me!"

"Don't take it so personally, Bill. I'm sure most of the inspectors know what the score is. They'll take it in their stride, provided we don't let it rattle us."

Alison rushed in, breathless. "Have you seen..? You have, haven't you? Is something being done to..?"

"Relax, Al. It's all in hand. Fancy a coffee?"

"You're laid back this morning. You put the kettle on and I'll have a quick litter check."

Rogerson, superfluous, returned to his fussing.

Staff briefing was an edgy affair. Rogerson appeared downcast and not a little befuddled. Sensing an absence of direction, Brian piped up. "Come on, folks. Let's give 'em what for."

No one was in the mood for being encouraged. There was fear in the air, mirrored in the anxious faces of some of the more vulnerable staff. They filed from the staffroom, heads hanging, as if a firing squad awaited them outside.

At registration, the kids were eerily restrained for a Monday morning, when they had been let loose to do as they pleased all weekend. There was not even much pushing and shoving on the way to first lesson.

Gaynor Sneap had year seven French. A charcoal-grey suited spectre glided into the corner of Gaynor's classroom.

The lesson set off well enough. *Bit of basic revision to warm them up after the weekend.*

"James, James. Listen, James, I'm trying to ask you a question.

"Yeh, miss. Let's go for it big time, shall we miss?"

James, comment t'appelles-tu, James?"

"Eh?"

"I'm trying to ask you what your name is, James."

"My name, miss? You know it. You've just said it."

"James!"

"See, you've said it again!"

"Just stop messing around and answer my question, s'il te plaît!"

"What was it again, miss?"

"Comment t'appelles-tu, James?"

"James, miss."

"En français, s'il te plaît."

"Oui, miss. James, miss."

"Stephanie, quel âge as-tu?"

"J'ai douze ans, miss."

Gaynor's frustration was growing.

"Non, non, *mademoiselle*!"

"Right...er.....J'ai douze ans mademoiselle, miss."

"Kirk, où est-ce que tu habites?"

"I don't have one, miss."

"Pardon?"

"I don't have a rabb*eet*!"

"Where do you *live*?"

"With my Gran, miss. My mum's buzzed off with her boyfriend."

"Natalie, où habites-tu?"

"J'habite à Southdale, monsieur."

The opening session had not gone too badly. A squint at the spectre showed that it was still present. The face was expressionless. It jotted down a few notes from time to time. One or two girls nearest the corner gave it sideways glances but it did not respond.

Now it was time to revise last lesson's work. "Alors, mes enfants, nous allons maintenant discuter l'emploi du temps de notre école."

"Eh?"

"The school's timetable, Joseph."

"Quelle est ta matière préférée?"

Darren Rowbotham had put up his hand. Dare she pick him? Darren was the slowest child in the class, at French, and everything else as well. Could be a feather in her cap with the spectre? Differentiation, special needs and all that. She dared.

"What's that smell, miss?"

"I'm sorry?"

153

"Oh, is it you, miss?"

Gaynor strategically ignored Darren....and the smell as well.

"Tracey, quelle est ta matière préférée?"

"He's right, miss, there's a right bad smell. It's Craig Crapper. He's pooed his pants."

"I have not."

"Yes, you have. You did it in the juniors."

"It's not me!"

Joseph joined in. "It's on his boots, miss. It's *dog* poo! He came across the fields this morning and they're full of poo."

"Show us your boots. Show us your boots," intoned Katie.

Craig stood up resolutely and with a flourish exposed the soles of both boots, one at a time, to the enchanted gathering.

"I was right," triumphed Joseph. Great big dollop of it stuck in the grooves."

"It's not. It's *mud*!"

"Why does it stink then?"

"Goodie poo shoes!" added Joseph helpfully.

It was too much for Craig. He launched himself at Joseph, arms flailing like a demented windmill. He missed his target far more often than he connected but Joseph was incensed.

"Right, you've asked for it now, Crapper!"

He seized Craig in a neck lock and wrestled him to the ground. The two diminutive figures rolled around to a collective accompaniment of jeers and exhortations.

"Smack his head in, Crapper!"

"Give him a good kicking, Joe!"

Gaynor was rooted to the spot, her face a portrait of powerless trepidation. The spectre roused itself. Lurching across the floor it grabbed both combatants by the relative scruffs of the neck, dragged them, still swinging and kicking across the room and deposited them in the corridor one at either side of the doorway.

"Don't you two dare touch each other again," it rasped.

"What's it got to do with you, you old git?"

"Yeah, pick on someone your own size."

The spectre spluttered for a moment and then, almost recovering its composure, "Miss Sneap, snap out of it, will you? Send someone for assistance before these two set about each other again!"

Matters lavatorial were very much to the fore elsewhere in the school. Richard Best had been up since four o'clock in the morning, creating the mother of all lesson plans; a lesson plan to fool the inspectors into thinking he knew what he was doing. Since arriving at school he had evacuated his bowel twice and had been amazed at the rate at which his bladder refilled itself.

At one minute to nine he had realised that getting through the lesson without paying a further call was optimistic to say the least.

Nature called and Mr Best had no alternative but to answer. He sprinted to the toilets.

Relieved, he flew to the wash basin, hygiene winning out over punctuality. The hot tap had had no top to turn for some years. He wrenched at the tap with the indistinct C and immediately regretted it. The pressure was high. A jet of water exploded from the pipe, swirled around the shallow basin and soaked the front of Best's trousers from the belt to the crotch.

Horrified, he grabbed a handful of faded green paper towels and dabbed desperately at the affected area. It was all in vain. The only option was to button his jacket, with the two buttons that had not fallen off, and hope.

He sidled into the classroom, three minutes late, his knees pointing suspiciously inwards and his hands lolling awkwardly in front.

"I'm sorry for being late...er...kids and Mrs...er...inspector. Urgent call... had to...er...respond immediately.

His dissembling was futile. Sheree Topham was rapidly on his case.

"Look at his trousers! Sir's wet himself. He's peed his pants."

Best, humiliated, abandoned all hope and rushed from the room.

Break could not arrive soon enough for Southdale's staff. The bell signalled a dash for refuge in the staffroom and a sharp shot of caffeine. Gaynor Sneap slammed the door behind her and emitted a huge sigh of relief.

"Had a good lesson, Sneapy?" called Simon Cunliffe hopefully.

"It was *crap*!"

18 Edgar

The so-called 'lay' inspector had been an accountant by trade. He had retired at fifty-five and had wanted something to occupy his time. When OFSTED was set up, it was just what he wanted. He applied for training and within a short space of time knew everything there was to know about educating young people and running a school.

He thoroughly enjoyed meeting teachers and discussing the issues. He had children in a state comprehensive and knew exactly what he expected out of schooling. He was not getting it at Southdale. The children made him uncomfortable, slightly threatened. They stared at him in the corridor. He could feel their eyes burning into his back. He was afraid to look around for fear of catching a pulled face or an offensive gesture in his direction. The children were as resentful of his presence as the staff were. The only difference was that the staff averted their eyes when he approached them.

Clive Holdsworth had experienced some difficulty in finding tasks that the lay inspector could cope with. Clive, himself, was unsure of the value of having someone on the team who had no direct experience of working in a school. Consequently he allocated jobs that merely flirted with the major issues.

The lay inspector inspected the buildings for graffiti and investigated their state of repair. He was sent out into the grounds to check for litter and general tidiness. He was asked to consider the appropriateness of the facilities for their intended purpose.

He went into the toilets, both male and female. In the latter case after calling out, "Excuse me! Is there anyone in there? If there is, speak now because I'm coming in."

A year seven waif scampered about her business, hurriedly adjusting her jeans and a year ten tobacco addict attempted vainly to depart without exhaling.

This was his sixth secondary school inspection, so he was quite confident in his capacity to generalise. Girls' toilets were always more likely to be subject to graffiti. There was always a thicker blue haze of stale cigarette smoke in the girls' toilets than in the boys'. The boys' toilets just smelled worse.

Southdale had that much in common with other schools.

He browsed over the slogans and the sexual libels on the walls of the girls' cubicles. He tutted at the obscenities and was secretly, though naively, glad that his own daughter did not have to read them. He noted the bin lids scattered around and the cold taps left running into cracked, 1950s basins. He observed the lipsticked messages on the antiquated mirrors.

In the boys' toilets, he turned up his nose at the smell of urine and retched at the chewing-gum and fag ends in the urinals. He noticed the doors off their hinges, the soiled toilet seats, leaning against the pedestals and the flimsy, pink toilet rolls stuffed into the bowls.

Raising his eyes to the ceiling, he observed messages fingered in the grime and wondered how the authors had reached up there. Here and there bits of paper towel papier mâché clung to the cracked and flaking plaster. The names of several football teams were etched into the metal of the emptied paper towel holders.

It was obvious that the staff had made an effort in the yard and on the field. There were only a few packets and wrappers, deposited on that morning, and a few more, well trodden in. Apart from the message of welcome to the inspectors, emblazoned across the front of the building, there was evidence of other graffiti, recently scratched, scraped and scrubbed into near oblivion.

A sudden movement and rustling among the nearby, overgrown shrubs distracted him from the serious business of inspecting.

"Who's there? Come out of the bushes at once or I'll report you to the Headmaster."

Further rustling.

"I've warned you. If you don't come out, I'm coming in. I'll count to three. One... two... I mean it, you know. This is your last chance... THREE! Right, I'm coming in!"

In he went, parting the shrubs with his forearms. One, two, three strides through crispy dead leaves. Then he came to a standstill, momentarily dumbstruck at what he saw: a perfectly bald, apparently naked, suntanned male, crouching. They stared into each other's eyes for an uncomfortably long time before the intruder sprang upright, turned and dashed away.

He was a well built man of about forty. His broad shoulders emphasised his well-kept waist. His well-oiled, muscles rippled impressively with the effort of escape. He was not, in fact, totally naked but was sporting a black, silky thong, the like of which the lay inspector had never before seen in the flesh.

Overcome by a sense of duty to the young people on the site, the lay inspector set off in pursuit of the shiny, athletic-looking buttocks.

"Stop in the name of OFSTED!" he is alleged to have called, in the version later relished in the staffroom.

The fugitive headed for the gate. He was wearing rubber flip-flops, with fluorescent, plastic straps between the toes but this did not impair his flight.

Leaning against the rusty gate post was a gleaming, silver bicycle: the drop handlebar, racing kind. In one movement he snatched it up, mounted and propelled the wheels into motion. Not even pausing to look round at the irate official, he pedalled furiously away.

The distance between the bike and the puffing inspector doubled by the second. The inspector halted, panting, at the exit. By this stage, his self-control had completely gone.

"Come back here, you pervert. I'll have the police on to you for this!"

Helpless, he turned on his heel and jogged back towards the main school building. He spluttered into the deserted foyer.

"Where is everybody? Ring 999. There's a sex fiend at large."

His ranting tempted the secretarial staff from their coffee break.

"What on earth is going on? Can't we have our break in peace? Oh, it's you Mr...er... What's wrong?"

"Get the police. I've just confronted a near naked man in the school grounds. Could have assaulted goodness knows how many children!"

"Did he have a thong?"

"A what?"

"Sort of underwear that just covers the bare essentials."

"Yes, that is correct."

"What colour was it?"

"Black but I don't see what this has got to do with..."

"Oh, black today. Edgar must be in a serious frame of mind. Sometimes it's red and others it's bright yellow."

"You know this man?"

"Yes, it's Edgar. He's well known around here. You don't want to worry about Edgar, love. He's harmless. Everybody round here knows Edgar. He always dresses or rather *undresses* like that. Even in winter. I don't know how he manages it. You'd think the cold would ... Well, never mind. He wouldn't hurt a flea."

"But this is ridiculous. I insist you call the police immediately."

"You can call them, if you like, love, but I'm not. Waste of time. They'll just laugh at you. Nothing they can do. His parts are covered up, you see. He even goes to Asda like that. Gives everyone a good laugh, does Edgar. Goodness knows, we need a laugh round here."

The lay inspector departed to consult his manual. There must be a section in it about this sort of thing.

19 Scoop

Sally O'Mahoney could sense a big story brewing. The *Chronicle*'s circulation was not what it could be. Keeping a job, as a staff journalist nowadays, meant sniffing out the big stories. Sometimes big stories had to be helped along and Sally had built her reputation on this.

She despised schools like Southdale: their whingeing about poor resources, their lack of discipline, their failure to provide decent results. She had little respect for Rogerson. Alison Lister had really got up her nose over the snowman incident - stuck-up cow!

It was obvious that Southdale was going to get a drubbing after the inspection and Sally wanted to be the first to put the boot in when it happened. She had been lurking around the school gates at home time, quizzing the kids about what was going on. She had knocked on some of the doors, in the local community, and posed a number of provocative questions. She had telephoned a source at County Hall, Denise, a former school mate, and had heard about Sarah Koszalinski's anger and Bernard Horsfield's perilous position. Not wanting to compromise her informant, she would keep that spicy titbit up her sleeve for the time being. She had tried speaking to several teachers but they had told her to get lost.

She had a brainwave. She inhaled a last chestful of smoke, stubbed the cigarette in the overflowing ashtray and abandoned her word processor to screen saver mode.

Sarah Koszalinski had been mortified. The RI from Southdale had dared to ring her and warn her to get her act together. "There'll be people running for cover when this lot hits the fan," he had volunteered.

Bernard Horsfield had cleared his desk. "Sorry to see you go, Mr Horsfield," said a young typist from the pool. "You always treat us so much nicer than some of the others."

Gladys Ollerenshaw had called a secret meeting, at her own home, of Southdale's LEA governors. "It's not looking good. The council is going to cop a lot of flack over this."

Kevin Breeze, main union rep. at Southdale had convened his members. Colleagues had concerns about the attitudes of some of the inspectors. "They're so cold," complained Verna Richardson. "The maths inspector can't even manage a 'good morning' or a 'thank you'."

Clive Holdsworth reported back to Rogerson at the end of each day. He liked to impress school staff by his dedication to duty and always did his best to outstay the head in school, every evening. In Rogerson's case, it was not difficult. He was not a workaholic. He liked to seek refuge in his cottage and be with good, reliable 'Cyn', who loved him, in spite of everything.

"See you at 6.00 this evening, Dr Rogerson," Holdsworth had asserted. "Got to write up my notes, first. The picture's taking shape now and, I have to say, it's not looking at all good. Better start preparing your version for the press."

Sally O'Mahoney parked her bright red Nissan Micra in a sidestreet close to Southdale Comprehensive. One of the school's boundaries rang along Station Road. Two or three of the school's sprawling classrooms came within a few metres of the old iron fence.

Sally strode along Station Road staring earnestly at the classroom windows. The view, albeit through the grubby glass, into one of them, looked promising. Thirty or so youngsters, twelve or thirteen year olds, she thought, were crammed into a room that looked slightly too small for the purpose. There were three ranks of double tables lined up, confronting a blackboard at one end of the room. Several of the tables had three youngsters sitting at them. Some of these threesomes were nudging each other, for extra space. It was probably a history lesson judging by the posters, pinned haphazardly on some of the notice boards.

A smallish woman, early forties Sally would have said, was standing, perfectly still, arms at her sides, with her back excessively close to the blackboard. Her lips were operating, goldfish like, and she periodically glanced down at a scrap of paper on the table in front of her.

Sally altered her position somewhat to get a view of the opposite end of the classroom. Sitting at the back of the room, intolerably close to some of the children was a tidily dressed, middle-aged woman. Plainly the inspector. She had a large, leather-backed note pad angled in front of her and she repeatedly applied her pen to the paper, in short, sharp bursts.

The youngsters were undoubtedly fed up and some of them were searching around for a distraction from national curriculum history, purveyed in a humdrum manner. One weasel-featured boy sitting close to the window engrossed Sally. Heedless of the fact that he was being spied on, from the road, he purloined his neighbour's pencil case, nudged the unlatched window until it yawned sufficiently, then dropped the pencil case outside on to the sparse grass. As it landed it spilled out its contents. Elsewhere, rulers were being prodded, goad like, into unsuspecting backs. A boy was staring at something black and plastic looking, that nestled in his lap. Sally took it to be a pocket-sized computer game. Some children were passing sweets or chewing-gum. Even the inspector looked bored. The teacher droned on, barely moving her body. On one occasion, she reached down and flipped over the scrappy piece of paper on the table in front of her. It occurred to Sally that she must have just passed the half-way mark in the lesson.

Mind numbing it may be, but it most certainly was not the stuff of which ground-breaking newspaper articles are made. Sally sighed. Perhaps she was wasting her time. She would make her way around to the main gate at home-time and ask a few leading questions about the staff and their lessons.

While she was still regretting her brainwave, her headline wrote itself. From the classroom next door to the one she had been watching came a tremendous crash and a splintering of glass. Three metal legs from a broken plastic chair jutted through the broken window. As Sally watched, a pair of hands grabbed the chair and used it to clear the shattered glass from the window frame. The chair dropped the short distance on to the ground and it was followed in a matter of a few seconds by a freckled, ginger-haired lad. He stumbled over the remains of the chair, pulled himself to his feet and yelped wildly into the space he had just vacated.

The figure of a young man appeared in the empty frame. "Robert, come back here at once! This will do no good at all. You'll get yourself into even deeper trouble."

Robert Walker took no notice. He was angry and when he was angry it took a long time for him to come down. His face twisted with childish rage, he hurled the most unpleasant words he could think of in the direction of the despairing teacher and made for a bent rail in the fence. He thrust himself through the gap and set off towards Sally. She blocked his way. "Just a moment, son. You can't just..."

The boy avoided her outstretched arm, ran into the road and disappeared through a gap in someone's hedge.

What a headline!

At the school gate, Sally had the greatest difficulty finding anyone who knew anything about the incident. The cleaners, on their way into the building, eyed her with suspicion. A youngish, senior looking woman, with crinkly auburn hair tried to get her to leave.

"I'm a journalist. I'm on the public highway. I've every right to be here. There's something going on in there that is clearly of interest to the public and I intend to find out what it is."

"In that case you'll need to speak to the head but he's very busy, at the moment."

"I bet he is! Trying to think up an excuse for this one, I suppose? What kind of a school is it where the students need to break out of the windows to get away from the teachers."

"That's a ridiculous statement to make. I can confirm that there has been an incident involving a member of staff and a Y9 pupil but the matter is currently under investigation, therefore I am not in a position to offer any further comment."

"What a load of claptrap! May I ask who I am talking to?"

"I'm Alison Lister, deputy headteacher."

"Oh really. You sounded so much older on the telephone. Pleased to meet you. I'm Sally O'Mahoney."

"The pleasure's mutual."

This type of incident was the last thing Rogerson needed. He did not normally deal with issues of pupil indiscipline and he had not the least intention of getting involved this time.

Alison tried to brief him. "It was in Glenn Jackson's history class. Robert Walker was..."

"Yes, yes Mrs Lister. Do I need to know this now? Give me the full details when you've sorted it out. If you need any support ask Brian. I'm afraid I'll have to get myself prepared for the meeting with Holdsworth."

"As you wish, Dr Rogerson. It is important you know, however, that the press are on to it. That O'Mahoney woman was sniffing around the gate trying to ask kids what went on. Fortunately all the kids who were in the classroom at the time are still writing their statements. I think we need to risk keeping them a little longer until the journalist goes."

"Do what you see fit. If their parents complain, you can sort that out tomorrow."

20 Nothing at all like a clown

The week dragged onwards to Thursday, 1 March. It was after school hours and Rogerson was sitting at his desk, the telephone receiver at an exaggerated angle from his ear. The mouthpiece was as far as possible from his mouth. Rogerson did not really believe that you could catch anything from the telephone and, in effect, he was the only person to use this extension but neither did he believe in taking risks.

"Yes, Mr Dobson, I quite understand your difficulty, Mr Dobson. I know it's not easy bringing up teenagers on your own but you have to remember that there is only so much that a school can do. As a parent, you have a... Well, no, Mr Dobson, of course I care about the situation you find yourself in but... If you'd let me get a word in, I'd ..."

Brian and Alison had dropped *Rogerson* in it for a change. The receptionist had buzzed each of them, in turn, and announced Mr Dobson's call. Both, wisely, had been too busy to take the call and Mr Dobson had insisted on speaking to the head.

"Hold it a moment, Mr Dobson. If you'd let me get a word in edgeways, I'd give you a response. Yes, we do have a policy on make-up. Our students, girls or boys for that matter, are not allowed to wear excessive make-up but I wouldn't let a daughter of mine wear any at all, at that age. No, I can't agree with you there, Mr Dobson. She looks nothing at all like a clown... Yes, I understand what you're saying. I regret that no-one challenged her today. It is her form tutor's responsibility, in the first instance but we are having a very busy week, with the inspection... The inspection, Mr Dobson, the OFSTED inspection. Oh really. Well let's not go into that now. Parents do have... I say, parents do have some responsibility in the matter as well, Mr Dobson. Well, if you can't get her to go easy on the make-up, how can you expect..? No, I'm not getting irritated, Mr Dobson. Goodness me, is that the time? I shall have to come off the telephone. I have an appointment at six p.m. And a good evening to you, as well, Mr Dobson. Goodbye."

It was five minutes to six. Rogerson was awaiting Clive Holdsworth's nightly visit. The three previous visitations had been stressful affairs. Rogerson had heard much about the school that he had hoped against hope no one would notice. Holdsworth's accounts had been full of inspectorial jargon. This or that percentage of staff had not matched up to this or that criterion. The proportion of teaching and learning considered to be 'sound' fell far short of the average of all the schools that had been inspected in a given time. The standard of behaviour of the youngsters was lamented over and over again.

Rogerson reflected on the week so far. He was decidedly uncomfortable. The headache that had begun on Monday evening was still lurking in the background. His whole body felt rigid and this was making his neck ache. He rotated his head, like they used to do in PE lessons and rubbed his wearied brow with the tips of his fingers. He found it difficult to concentrate. His mind strayed, time and time again, to the 'what if..?' scenario. Inside he felt slightly nauseous.

Thankfully, there had been no further incidents of the same magnitude as the Robert Walker affair. He had allowed Brian Ingleton and Mrs Lister to take the heat out of that and he was grateful for the burden they had taken off him. He had never thought to tell them so.

The headline in the *Chronicle* had been a damaging one but the story had been short on hard facts. Sally O'Mahoney had been reluctantly obliged to write that no one, at the school, was available to comment.

Though Rogerson would never be aware of it, Alison Lister had insisted on certain procedures taking place with regard to the incident. Firstly, she had obliged the teacher, Glenn Jackson and all the pupils present to write a full statement of what they had seen. In spite of their protests about missing buses and threats about mums, dads, big brothers and bruising grandads coming up to school to sort her out, she insisted on it happening there and then before they had the opportunity to collude.

Leaving Brian to keep a watchful eye on the proceedings, she had leapt into her car and sped around to Robert Walker's house. She managed to get there before he did. She had learned the advantage of doing this from a wise, old year tutor in the school where she started her career. Presumably Robert had stopped for a sob on the way or perhaps he was working out what to tell his mum.

By the time he pushed open the battered front door and stepped into the grimy kitchen, Alison and Mrs Walker were sitting together at the cluttered kitchen table, sipping insipid tea from dodgy mugs.

"Hello, Robert."

The last thing Robert Walker expected was bossy-boots Lister to be sitting in his own back kitchen, socialising with his mother. He tried to disguise his shock by wiping up the excretions from his nose on the back of his arm.

The situation was serious. He did not know what Lister had told his mum and he was not quite sure how much to lie and how much to tell the truth.

"Can I go round to Pog's house?" he asked optimistically.

"No you cannot, my lad. Sit down at the table at once.

"But, mum, I need to ask Pog about maths homework and he's going out with his dad at five."

Mrs Walker knew her son must be feeling very guilty if anxiety over his homework was the first excuse that came into his head.

"Sit!"

He knew it was useless to resist and he perched on the front edge of a worn-out dining chair, studiously avoiding Mrs Lister's eyes.

"You know why I'm here, don't you, Robert?"

"No."

"Think again."

"It were his fault not mine."

"Whose fault? Mr Jackson's?"

"No, Pog's."

"Pog's?"

"Yes, miss. Warren Pogmore."

"He's your friend, isn't he?"

"Yes, but he called me mum a tart."

"The little bleeder. I'll murder him."

"Let us deal with it, Mrs Walker. What do you mean he called your mum a tart?"

"He said she, like, went with other men, for money."

"That's not a very pleasant thing to say, is it? So what did you do?"

"I told him his mum was even worse and his dad wasn't his dad either."

"Well, that's true!"

"Please let me handle this, Mrs Walker. So what happened next?"

"He stabbed me."

"Stabbed you? With a knife?"

"No, his door key. And it hurt a lot."

"So what did you do?"

"I kneed him where it hurts."

"Where it hurts?"

"You know, his marriage tackle."

"Oh, I see and what happened then?"

"He sort of screamed and Mr Jackson looked up. Peggy, the grass, shouted, 'Sir, Walker's hit me in the balls.' And Jackson said, 'Get out, Walker. Go and see Mr Ingleton. I'm not having that.' And I said,

'It's not fair, sir, you're not doing anything about Pog.' Then he said, 'Get out at once!' and I said...I said...a bad word and he tried to grab me."

"Mr Jackson got hold of you?"

"I was too quick for him and I ran over to the other side of the room and then, well, things sort of got out of hand. This chair kind of went through the window and all I could think of was going home and getting our Cal to sort Jackson out...and Pog, as well."

Alison wanted to smile but she controlled herself.

"As you can see, Mrs Walker, it's quite a serious situation and unfortunately a newspaper reporter has got hold of the story. I think it would be better if Robert wasn't in school for a day or two."

Robert's ears pricked up at this.

"I'll deal with the paper work tomorrow and you'll have to come up to school to talk about it, some time next week."

"All right, love. Thanks for coming round. Now you, Robert, get up those stairs until I tell you to come down and do not dare switch on your television or your stereo or your computer. Is that understood? I'll be round to see that Pogmore woman and her little bastard later."

Back at school, Rogerson had reacted predictably.

"Let me remind you, Mrs Lister, that there is only one person around here who can hand out an exclusion."

He did not pursue it any further satisfied that another problem had been taken out of his hair. Alison bit her tongue and returned to her office without further remark.

As the second hand, on Rogerson's wall clock ticked to the hour, his office door opened, uninvited, and Clive Holdsworth walked in.

"Had a good day, Bill?" he asked, knowing that he had not.

"Yes, thank you, er... Mr Holdsworth."

"Good news, Bill. I've observed a first rate lesson, this afternoon: a *one*, if ever I saw one. That history teacher of yours, the one whose also head of Y11, Mr...er..."

"Richard Tomlinson?"

"Ricky, that's him. He has very good relationships with the young people. You must be very proud to have him on the staff."

"Yes, of course. How did his lesson go?"

"Better than anything else I've seen so far. Bit unorthodox, mind, but the youngsters clearly enjoyed every minute and, when I asked a few of them later, it was obvious that they had learned a lot of stuff. He sort of burst into the room like a whirlwind. I think that's the best way of putting it. No messing around with the 'Stop doing thats' and the 'What do you think you're playing ats?' that I've heard so often this week. The kids' eyes lit up when he came into the room. There was a sense of expectation. It was almost religious, if you see what I mean. He issued a few short instructions and kids were rushing hither and thither getting resources out of cupboards and handing out exercise books. It was lively but there was no excessive fuss. He settled them down in a trice and rattled off the objectives for his lesson: 'By the end of this lesson you will have learned about this and you will have learned about that and you will be able to do so and so.' He got the youngsters to recap what they had done in the lesson before and then they had to report back on last night's homework in pairs. Each pair stood up in turn and expounded on what they had done. Most of them had visual aids of one sort or another. Some had produced pretty, coloured pictures and others had what looked like computer generated info. It was most impressive. He then set the main work of the lesson which lasted about forty minutes and involved a whole range of different activities. He seemed to find time to talk to pupils of all abilities and give them help and advice appropriate to their needs. Not once did he seem the least bit flustered, though he was constantly aware of what was going on in every part of the classroom. If a kid went off task he just brought them back immediately with a kind word of encouragement or a funny crack. To cap it all, once he had got them to pack away at the end of the lesson, he disappeared into the stockroom and came out with a guitar. They all sang a mediaeval folk song related to the theme of the lesson. The kids left his room glowing with motivation. They love history because they love Mr Tomlinson. You could do with a few more teachers like him."

Bill Rogerson should have been encouraged but, as he drove home to Cyn, a curious blackness descended on his soul.

21 The way they had once been

The Lister household was riven with self-reproach. Jake despised himself for permitting the suspicions to fester. Alison, though mindful that Jake was hurting, could not bring herself to lance the boil. On plenteous occasions she came close to blurting out why she was so late that night but would it distress him more?

They were simply and painfully civil to each other. Alison asked if Jake had had a good day at the office. Jake, who had not, lied and asked about the inspection.

They were no longer close to each other. Their relationship was becoming portentously distant and neither of them knew why. In their private, fearful moments, both of them understood perfectly that, sooner or later, whatever it was would manifest itself in a way that would change their lives for ever.

Frantic breakfasts, brushing lips with each other between gulps of stinging pineapple juice and mouthfuls of singed toast had been replaced by excuses about being at work early or needing to pick something up from the newsagents. They nibbled their evening meal, no longer anything out of the ordinary, but accompanied sometimes by two thirds of a bottle of wine each, probing politely into each other's day. Their answers were given and received without enthusiasm. Juicy morsels of gossip were left on one side; news of mutual friends left undisclosed. Passionate early nights had given way to staggered bed times; drifting off in each other's arms supplanted by apparently cold-shouldered indifference. If only they could tell each other how they burned inside to be close again.

Thursday evening. Jake was showering. The indifferent hum of the electric shower tuned in and out of Alison's consciousness. Tomorrow was feedback day. Clive Holdsworth and his team would be still huddling in the adequate conference room of their basic motel accommodation. Trading corroborations of impending ruin. Synthesizing exquisite reproofs, high sounding recommendations. Issuing action points. Inserting evidentiary statistics. Declaring targets for improvement. Or was Southdale beyond all hope?

An excruciating drama was about to unfurl.

Mad Henry Appleton, tartar of the science department, cloistered in his capacious garret, was gluing in the last plastic particle of a model early flying machine. If only his fearful students were able to witness some of that childlike glee.

Brian Ingleton was hopelessly endeavouring to keep his mind on the business of a church sub-committee. Beth was convoking all the powers of an off-duty primary teacher to convince her offspring of the need to immerse themselves before retiring, giving Beth and Brian an hour alone together before bed time. If only Brian had had a greater sense of ambition he could have been in charge at Southdale and things would have been oh so different.

Gladys Ollerenshaw was pondering what could be done about Rogerson. It would be the easiest thing in the world to resign and leave the dirty work to someone else but Gladys was not a quitter. Gnawing away at her innards was the suspicion that she would actually enjoy doing the dirty work. Surely that could not be true? If only Edward were not at *Rotary* again, he would calm her fears and gently massage her throbbing temples the way he used to. The way he used to.

Ashley Hardman's ear, keen for the sound of breaking glass, had been exercised several times that evening already. He had chased away the little so-and-sos, unsurprised by their insulting suggestions about his private activities. He was even less surprised by the scornful way they dismissed his threats about getting the 'bobby' to visit their dads. They were untouchable and, in any case, most of them only saw their dads once a month or never at all. If only these kids had something, anything, but just *something* good in their lives.

Bernard Horsfield, fortyish, balding, wisps of gingery grey, stroked the uncomprehendingly content feline sprawled across his lap. Failed teacher, failed adviser, failing human being. Try as he might he could not hate Sarah Koszalinski. She was not the destructive force that he sensed invading his world. She was merely the channel for it.

Sally O'Mahoney was having an early night. She had been for a white wine and lemonade straight from work with a close colleague, Stephanie. Stephanie had wanted her to go round for the evening but Sally needed her sleep. Just around the corner was the break she was waiting for.

Clive Holdsworth cannot pay attention fully to the hatchet job he is orchestrating. Alison's face fills every nook and cranny of his mind.

The disturbing ripple of those silky tops she wears. That delicious exposure of calf as she walks away. And above all, *the way they had once been.* Had he missed his chance? She still felt for him. It was obvious. Why had she..?

He must concentrate on what his colleagues are saying. Tomorrow will be a taxing day even for one so used to handing out bad news.

Past one clock. Sarah Koszalinski looks scarily provocative in her clinging, scanty attire. She is intoxicated by the throbbing beat of the music as much as by the several straight vodkas she has consumed. No man dares approach her. She is out of herself. In a world that no one can share. The breathtaking, insistent bass, the hypnotic lights, the fevered, pounding movements of the mass of humanity around her carry her away to where her deeply hidden doubts and her penetrating sense of unworthiness escape her soul on the hazy wings of temporary oblivion. Tomorrow can worry about itself.

Cynthia Rogerson sits on the edge of a once comfortable easy chair. Before her the shell of a man. The mortal remains of W P H Rogerson, PHD. His ashen face. His eyes not focusing, blankly, on anything in particular. Oh where are you Bill? What uncompassionate world has destroyed your inner self? Where have you slipped away to, my love? My man. My life.

22 Petrol on the fire

Friday 2 March began like any ordinary day at Southdale Comprehensive School. Brian arrived very early. Alison nearly beat him to it for once but it was Brian who crossed the foyer first.

Brian had not slept. His mind was in turmoil. Turmoil. His face was pale and drawn but whose was not at this stage in an inspection? Brian's exterior was as calm as always. No one would know. The tuneless whistle was still there as he penetrated the dimness of the entrance. But Beth knew. She could tell what was churning around deep inside him. She could feel it.

Sitting grim faced in a dark corner of the as yet unlit reception area was a parent. Brian's heart was like lead. Alison, hot on his heels through the battered entrance doors was secretly relieved. Without even a *good morning* she shot off down the corridor and bolted into her office.

Brian steeled himself, made up his mind to be cheery and approached the parent, hand outstretched in greeting. "Good morning," he intoned. "Can I help? Got an appointment with Dr Rogerson?" he asked optimistically.

The friendly hand was ignored. Brian, resolute, stuffed it back in his trouser pocket. "Got a problem?"

"I'll say I have. It's our Clint. He's been set upon by a gang of thugs and I want them expelled. They've been robbing his bus fare off him. He had to walk home last night and who knows what pervert might have got him because of you lot."

The parent was warming to his delivery and sensed that a few choice insults might just help Brian to empathise with his son's misfortune.

"You're all the same you sodding teachers. Couldn't give a toss as long as you can get off home by 3.30."

Brian kept his cool. "Am I to deduce that you have informed a member of staff and they have refused to help your son? ... er... What's his name?"

"Clint... Clint Thistlethwaite, year 7. Deduce? Deduce? It's you that's dead useless, pal! I can see I'm wasting my time here. Come on, Clint, we're going home."

Brian could make out a diminutive figure sitting, forlorn, even deeper in the gloom of that corner of the foyer. Brian took a few steps and flicked a light switch. The fluorescent tubes spluttered and clicked for a few seconds and then burst into half-light.

"Hello, Clint," he chirped, trying hard to resist the parent's provocation. "Why don't you run off and wait for your mates while your dad and I have a little chat in my office?"

"He's staying with me and we're going down the *education* to get you lot sorted."

Brian's seething frustration translated itself into sarcasm. "Let me get this straight, sir." His lips curled on the word 'sir'. "Your little Clint got bashed by some big boys last night on his way home and they took his bus fare off him. Correct? Did you phone the police? No. Did you contact school? No, I suppose you thought we had all gone home by 3.30. You come in here this morning, dishing out your insults and expecting us to take responsibility for the way this rotten society of ours is going and before we have the chance even to investigate what happened you're going to the *education?*"

Brian was pouring petrol on the fire. He knew it but he could not stop himself. Years and years of biting his tongue under severe goading from angry parents had taken its toll. He did not care any more. He poured and he poured.

The parent was on his feet. "Hey, mate. You want to watch who you're talking to." His head came barely to the level of Brian's ample shoulder. "I'll take you outside and break your legs if you talk to me like that."

Brian took a deep breath and restrained himself. He took a step or two towards the corridor and the refuge of his office.

"Hey, where do you think you are going? You're not walking off on me like that." The parent imposed himself between Brian and the double doors of the mouth of the corridor. One of the doors was still wedged open, forgotten about after the comings and goings of the cleaners.

"I think it would be better, Mr...whatever your name is...if you waited to see someone else. We're both too angry and we need a cooling off period. I apologise for my loss of temper. We're under a lot of pressure, you know, especially with the inspection and all that."

The parent exploded in tears and expletives. "You're under pressure, you middle class git? You're under pressure? You don't know what stress is, pal. You want to think what it's like living on handouts since the pit closed. That would take away some of your smugness. What kind of a school is this that lets bullies get away with beating up little kids? When I were at school bullies were sorted out behind the gym, good and proper. And you, you think you're so good just because you had a bit more education than us. Why don't you get back to where you belong, instead of trying to force your ways on working class kids."

Brian wanted to burst. He wanted to proclaim, "My dad was a steelworker. He was killed at work when something hot and heavy fell on him. I do know what it's like. I do but I've run out of steam. My compassion tank is on empty. " Instead he put his arm on the parent's shoulder...

"Don't you lay a hand on me!"

Brian grabbed both the parent's shoulders in his large hands and pulled the sobbing man towards him. "Listen," he hissed into his face. "Listen. I do understand. I'm sorry. Come back and see me next week when it's all over. But not now. Not today. See someone else, please, to sort out your problems."

Brian released his grip and brushed past the man into the corridor.

"Bastard!" rang in his ears as he disappeared.

23 Metaphor

Simon Higginbottom broke wind with a retort like a hurricane rent tarpaulin.

"Aw!" groaned Kimberley Greenwood. "Darren's let off one of his bombs!"

The class giggled. Ricky Tomlinson would not be fazed. He waited for the titters to subside and asked a question. Ricky was covering Y9 English for a colleague who had fallen by the wayside.

"Tell me, Y9, which linguistic device was just used by Kimberley."

The class bright spark shot up her hand. "Sir! Sir! I know."

"OK, Marie, you tell us."

"Metaphor, sir," she pronounced proudly."

"Quite right. Take a merit. And as for you, Simon Higginbottom, if you ever do that again I'll take your head and shove it where that trump came from!"

The class roared its approval. Simon looked sheepish. Everyone got on with the English lesson.

187

There was an unexpected, eerie and unnerving air of truce around the corridors and classrooms of Southdale Comprehensive School. It was like the calm before the storm, the lull in the action, the night before battle.

The staff of the school knew the inspection was not going well. Indeed it was going disastrously wrong and had been doing so from the moment the first pre-inspection documentation was filled in. The teachers were on edge. The youngsters, who knew nothing about what schooling was like in any other environment, tuned into the vibes.

There was something in the air and whatever that something was it produced a feeling of togetherness. They were all in it together: one school, one community, one way of life. One stance against a common foe. Two fingers to the establishment.

The *suits* were barely in evidence around the building. One or two slipped into classrooms to give a second opinion or in pursuit of a theory. Others passed almost imperceptibly along the corridors, keen to carry out some mysterious errand. Others pecked at laptops, adding last minute refinements to their drafts.

A couple more hours and the inspectors would be moving on somewhere else. Some would be looking forward to seeing their own children, abandoned so frequently to the pursuit of ever higher standards. Others, sadder cases these, would be recycling the few clothes that they pushed into their worn suitcases and moving on to another inspection to start on Monday, a good train's ride away.

Soon only Clive Holdsworth would remain. His business was unfinished as yet. The draft conclusions of the inspection team had to be passed on to the management of the school.

Additionally, he would have to return in a few days time to take the governors through the skeleton of the inspection report.

Southdale offered him the opportunity to really make his mark; to play his part in transforming the lives of these forlorn youngsters; to bring new hope to this depressed community; to spur this failed comprehensive school to rise like a phoenix from the ashes. He would recommend special measures or perhaps even a fresh start, under new leadership.

Yes, that was it, Rogerson was past his *sell-by* date. In fact, Clive wondered how Rogerson had ever risen to headship: no creativity, no ambition for the school, no understanding of the multifaceted concepts of running a contemporary school. He should have stuck to the safety of academia where he could have fulfilled his middle class aspirations without harming anyone.

In Clive's book, Rogerson was simply not up to the job and should be disposed of as quickly as possible. What this school needs is someone with vision; someone with determination to succeed; someone who will not make excuses for failure, who will not see stumbling blocks but stepping stones to success. Someone like…Alison Lister.

Try as he might he could not spend five minutes alone without thinking of Alison. How foolish he had been to give her up so easily. In some ways the fact that she now belonged to another man made her an even more attractive proposition. He burned to be in her presence, to breathe in her fragrance, to hear her soft yet uncompromising voice setting the world to rights, to touch that silky hair, to run his fingers across her downy, blushing cheeks.

Brian Ingleton had never felt so low. He had been taken aback by the speed with which this all consuming depression had overtaken him. It must have been building up inside him for years. He had ached through the Thatcher years believing that it would one day be all right again, that common sense would prevail. He had shared the jubilation of many when the iron lady had strategically withdrawn into retirement. He tolerated that gentle man Major. He shed a tear at the loss of John Smith. He knew it would be all right one day soon.

But it had not been. At first he had comforted himself. Society is like a giant ship. You cannot turn it around straight away. You have to slow it down gently and then turn it in a massive arc before heading in the opposite direction. But hang on a minute, this vessel is not slowing down, it is speeding up and it's still going in the wrong direction. Watch out for those poor people under the bows! You ran them down. Stop! Stop! I cannot take it any longer. Stop the ship, I say! It's going faster still. Life jacket or not I must get off! Man overboard!

Brian was on the point of going overboard. Outwardly, he went about his business. He answered the telephone and spoke with barely a trace of tension in his voice. He visited troublesome classrooms as he always did and glared miscreants into compliance. He shared break time coffee with Alison, as usual, but deep inside he was on the point of going overboard.

When the warning signs had shown themselves before, Brian had resolved to do something. He must do something but what? He concluded that he would write to the secretary of state for education; no he would write to the prime minister. No, this was not enough. He ached to let the whole world know how he was suffering, how his principles had been trampled into the ground and how he, himself, had been forced to take part in the trampling. He wanted to scream about the injustice of the way things were going. It is not fair! His rebellion must be more public than a private, easily ignored letter to a politician. Brian's troubled mind fell upon the ideal solution. He would write an open letter to the prime minister via the columns of *the Times Educational Supplement*. His words would be a trumpet call to all like-minded individuals. Alone we can do nothing. Together we can change the world or at least slow down this ghastly ship of misfortune.

Brian mentally composed his missive.

Dear Prime Minister

I am sad that I need to write in these terms since I have supported your party at every election since I was old enough to vote. Sadly I have now reached the stage where abstention is a more attractive course of action than voting. I can no longer vote for your party on principle. I swore an oath to myself, many years, ago that I could never vote for the other lot. So what is left to me? I should probably derive most satisfaction from spoiling the paper. Perhaps a gigantic cross over all the names on the paper to show that they are all as self seeking as each other or, if I'm really tempted, a bold swear word, in letters an inch high. That would really make me feel better.

By this time, you have probably stopped reading, Prime Minister, and dismissed me as being the only person on this tiny sceptred isle who hasn't yet succumbed to your undoubted charm. However, I must advise you to look more closely, my dear Prime Minister. I am not the only one. I may not be in one of the groups that you wish to court in terms of securing your re-election but I do have a vote and it used to be yours. Are you interested in finding out why it is no longer?

All my working life has been devoted to young people. I've worked in schools with leaky roofs, with one textbook between three pupils. Even chalk has been difficult to come by on occasions. The furniture in some classrooms would not have looked out of place in Steptoe's yard! All that time I and thousands of others kept going because we believed in what we were doing and we knew that sooner or later you would come along, in whatever form, and you would make everything OK.

Well you did come along, and, to give you your due, your heart seemed to be in the right place. You wanted equal opportunities for all, or so you said. You promised extra funds for schools and you were as good as your word. You gave us extra funds, not necessarily sufficient as yet, but there was lots of catching up to do.

But then, Prime Minister, you blew it. I have to say you blew it!

I've never made it right to the top as a manager and I'm certainly no leader but what I know about leadership is definitely based on common sense. If you want the workforce to achieve for you, you have got to take them with you on the journey to higher standards.

Instead, presumably to court the middle class vote, you have decided that teacher bashing is flavour of the day, every day. You've named and shamed and you've blamed us for everything that is wrong in our society from sporting failures to teenage pregnancies and lager loutish carry-ons.

Now in spite of your performance related pay and increased funding, teacher recruitment is approaching crisis proportions and many, many good people, too many for it to be taken lightly, want to get out of the profession they once felt drawn to. They *came into the job not for high wages and performance related bonuses but because they loved working with children.*

All you had to say to get us on board, my dear Prime Minister, was WE have got it wrong in this country over the years. Let's all take our share of the responsibility for past failures and let's move forward together. You are doing a good job in the circumstances but together we can do even better.

That's all it would have taken, Prime Minister...........

Brian Ingleton mentally scrunched up his emotional outpourings and deposited them in his mind's recycle bin.

24 The irritation of salt

Alison and Brian had volunteered to be with Rogerson during Clive Holdsworth's feedback session on Friday afternoon. Stoically or perhaps out of a sense of shame, Rogerson had declined. He would face the music alone; take what was coming to him; smile in the face of adversity.

A few telling moments after 2.15pm, Holdsworth tapped on Rogerson's door and, in advance of the anticipated invitation to enter, did so.

"Good afternoon, Bill."

Rogerson winced at his familiarity.

"I'll not be too long, this afternoon. That is unless you keep interrupting me with questions. There'll be plenty of time for that at the governors' meeting next week. I'm afraid I can't hide it from you, the picture is not a good one. But you weren't expecting anything else were you? There are schools where not all members of the team are in agreement about the conclusion but, sad to say, this is not one of them. All of the team are of one accord. Under present management Southdale is going rapidly through a downward spiral of failure. Drastic action needs to be taken to get it back on its feet and, I have to say, I don't believe you are the man for the job. I shall be recommending that the school be closed and re-opened under new management and with a new name. That is to say I shall be suggesting to my masters a *Fresh Start* programme. I know you will find this difficult to accept but the future of hundreds of children is clearly at stake here."

Rogerson's insides were hollow. His mouth like emery paper. He brushed his lips with his leathery tongue, finding sufficient saliva to facilitate the vaguest of watery smiles. Expecting the worst, he had vowed to Cynthia over an unconsumed breakfast that he would not allow Holdsworth the pleasure of seeing him bowed. He fixed him with a sightless stare and nodded his assent to hearing the rest.

Clive continued.

The chemistry of relationships had always given him a buzz, especially when he was in control. Like the playground bully sitting astride another's chest, revelling in the fear in his victim's eyes, he administered the *coup de grâce*: that exquisite climax of pain which affirmed his superiority over a meeker mortal. The twist of the nose, the terrifying tug at the ear, the slap or the punch to the cheek or mouth. The blow to the other's dignity that established forever the playground pecking order.

"Teaching and learning," Clive announced. "Any school's core activity. To put it into its statistical context, over forty per cent of lessons were found to be unsatisfactory or to have unsatisfactory characteristics. By any standard, this is a shameful state of affairs. To be blunt a significant number of your staff should never have got beyond initial training. Their subject knowledge is sometimes sketchy. Classroom management and control were often observed to be sadly lacking. In some classrooms the children were dictating the ground rules rather than the teacher. This is not good for the morale of the rest of the staff and should have been tackled by senior management and governors ages ago."

Rogerson nodded without intent. His eyes were stinging with the irritation of salt. He was beginning to feel queasy but he would not let it show. He was determined.

"Achievement. I don't know where to begin. Admittedly, when the youngsters come to you from primary they are already underachieving but, in fact, during their five years with you, most youngsters underachieve dramatically when compared with national, local averages and the averages for similar schools. It would not be an exaggeration to say that the truants, who avoid school for the whole of the last two years of their compulsory education, are no worse placed than the majority of students who *have* attended. In any event, an average attendance of 79% in the upper school is not acceptable. Sad to say, your pastoral staff have made little or no attempt to address the high level of condoned absence among upper school children. The pattern of increasing absenteeism, as the children get older, must be addressed if standards of achievement are to be improved. The school has little or no effective procedures for dealing with truancy."

Rogerson scratched his nose. His eyes twitched a little. He steeled himself against a further onslaught.

"Development planning. Many of your staff thought this was a joke. They had no recollection of being consulted in any planning procedures and no one interviewed could produce any identifiably useful planning documentation. Crisis management appears to be the norm at every level. Most heads of department could not remember the last time they had a formal meeting with a member of the senior management team. My team was not able to trace any planning route through to the governors. One governor questioned said and I quote, 'We leave that sort of thing to the head. After all that's what we pay him for.'"

Rogerson rubbed the corners of his eyes. He stretched the skin of his cheeks with the tips of his fingers until the fingers of both hands met at the point of his chin. His armpits were irritatingly moist. His propensity towards pallor was giving way to an unbecoming ruddiness in the cheek.

"Value for money. The school's budget has been in deficit for three years. It is surprising to me that the local education authority has taken no action to curtail over-spending, which has taken place owing to an absence of careful financial planning. The pre-inspection audit revealed significant levels of poor accounting in addition to some examples of downright misuse of public funds. For example, a few colleagues have claimed inappropriately high levels of expenses and there are no systems in place to identify this kind of malpractice. When taking into consideration levels of funding in relation to national and local averages, the school gives poor value for money. There is an urgent need to reappraise financial systems and to get the budget back on to an even keel."

Rogerson's eyes dropped to the carpet. He could look Holdsworth in the face no more. He placed the palms of his hands flat on his knees and, his breathing noticeably heavier, he contemplated the highly waxed leather of his handmade shoes.

"I know it's painful, Bill, but it has to be said. My written report will, of course, be written in *inspector speak* and will be therefore much more bland than the oral account I have just given you. However, the consequences for you will be the same. I do not see how the LEA or governors will be able to allow you to stay in post. The success of future generations is far more important than the career of any individual. As harsh as it may seem now, you will come to realise this with time. In view of the gravity of the written report I shall be making, it is my duty to inform the director of education of my intentions. I am sure you will hear from her imminently."

With that, Clive Holdsworth snapped shut his folder and acknowledging that Rogerson was beyond solace he restricted himself to a briefly patronising squeeze of his bowed shoulder as he made for the door.

"Goodbye, Bill. I hope things work out for you in the long run," he uttered unconvincingly.

As the door closed, Rogerson slid from his chair and collapsed in a heap on the tasteful rug that Cynthia had bought to smarten up his office.

It was barely an hour since Clive Holdsworth had started his feedback. The bell had signalled the end of another school week. Teachers sprinted for their cars to avoid having their weekend delayed by the mass of heaving youth spewing forth through the rusting gates of academia. The more conscientious colleagues stuffed file paper scripts and dog-eared exercise books into their bags before joining the rush.

For some children getting home was not a happy prospect. Some feared retribution for a recent misdemeanour; a few, the indecent, unaccountable wrath of a drunken parent or the sinister spectre of multifaceted abuse. Others were simply ashamed of what one or other parent might be preparing to do that evening in the name of putting a crust on the table for their family.

These sad children dallied on the corridors finding an excuse to chat with a teacher, picking the flaking paint from the wall, absentmindedly removing the staples from the OfSTED-fresh, only slightly damaged display work and flicking them at anyone who passed by.

Brian Ingleton exhaled a sigh of relief as he saw Clive Holdsworth leave the building and load his multiple plastic boxes of data into the boot of his car. His mind dwelt for a moment on the image of Alison and Clive in deep, hushed conversation in the corridor outside Rogerson's office, before his thoughts turned to Bill Rogerson. Brian was on his last legs but he could not leave for home without enquiring of Bill how the feedback had gone and how he was feeling. It was irrelevant that he knew only too well what the answer to both of those questions would be.

Brian tapped on Rogerson's door. No response. He knocked louder with no greater success and placed his ear closer to the door. He thought he heard a slight wailing, like the cry of a lone seagull hovering offshore. He pushed open the door and hurried inside.

Brian had seen some things in his career but he was not prepared for the pitiful sight that awaited him inside his boss's office. There, curled foetus-like on the rug, which demarcated the conversation space of the room, were the living remains of a broken man. Brian stared and strained to hear the slightest sound. Rogerson's body was rocked intermittently by oppressively silent sobs. He was breathing. Brian stayed there for several minutes, uncertain what to do. Rogerson, facing away from the door made no attempt to communicate.

At last Brian backed away, taking care not to make a sound. His boss deserved at least the dignity of being left alone with his grief.

Brian closed the door soundlessly, wiped his moistened cheeks and nose on the sleeve of his jacket, tapped his jacket pocket to check for his keys and strode towards the three-quarters emptied car park.

25 Wide eyed innocence in the presence of worldly experience

Clive's luck had been in. His longed for opportunity presented itself as he left Rogerson's office, flying high on the adrenaline kick of his post feedback euphoria. His nerve ends were tingling with the power surge that came from seeing another human being so totally in his control, so manifestly at his mercy. Alison was on the corridor, as if by accident, ostensibly going nowhere in particular for any evident purpose. Clive seized the moment.

"Hi, Alison, how goes it?"

"Well?" she demanded.

Clive stared into her eyes just long enough to provoke a mildly embarrassed reaction. His lips up-turning mischievously at the corners, he paraphrased the Oxford dictionary, "Well: shaft sunk into the ground to obtain water, oil or gas."

Alison was not currently disposed to tolerate his puerile sense of humour. "Yes, very funny but you know what I mean. What are you going to do about this mess of a school?"

Clive explored her face for a moment, exploiting every millisecond of suspense to its maximum capacity. Anxiety had accentuated the crease lines radiating from the outside corners of her eyes and beneath her lower lip. This seemed only, in his eyes, to amplify the maturity of her countenance. The years since they had been together had only made her more desirable by endowing upon her face that look which a few women achieve, as they approach middle age, of wide eyed innocence in the presence of worldly experience.

Clive looked away. "It's not good. You knew it was going to be problematic. We have to be grown-up about this Alison. I have my job to do and you have yours."

"Not good? How not good? Are we going into *special measures*? "

"Worse than that."

"I've friends who have been in schools in *special measures*. It's hard to imagine what could be worse, short of a closure, and surely you can't be contemplating that. There isn't another school close enough that is big enough to take all the kids from here."

Clive weighed up his chances. Alison's whole being magnetised him. On the spur of the moment an idea came to him. He pursued it without a thought for the consequences.

"On the contrary, *Andrew Pickersgill* is in line for a major building programme over the next two years. They could set up a few temporary classrooms on that huge expanse of playground that they have to the rear. The LEA would jump at the chance of closing Southdale, even if it meant subsidising buses to run the local kids over to *Pickersgill*."

"You can't be serious." Alison's voice was trembling with emotion. She did not realise until that moment how attached she had become to Southdale's cause in the few short months that she had been there. "You can't do this. Surely you can see what this school would be like," she could not help herself, "… with the right sort of leadership?"

"Hey, hang on a minute. I'm the registered inspector not the chief education officer. I can't make decisions about closures. I can only state the facts, as I see them, about the quality, or should I say lack of quality, of the education that Southdale kids are receiving in comparison with other similar schools."

Clive sensed the time was right to play his trump card. "On the other hand, I *may* be in a position to advise Sarah Koszalinski on what might constitute the *right sort of leadership* to pull Southdale out of the hole that it is in at present."

Alison caught his drift. Myriad emotions besieged her mind within a second. She would never have believed how entangled with Southdale's she had allowed her own future to become. In the face of Rogerson's inadequacy, she had ached to get her hands on the helm, to steer the school out of troubled waters towards a new horizon.

Most of the staff respected her and, after all, what did it matter if they did not? Many of them would have to go, in any case, if the school were to be saved from oblivion. Swingeing changes would have to be made if the inspectors' expectations of progress were to be met. She had never had to sack anyone before but she imagined that you could get accustomed to such things if you really had to. She curtailed her racing imagination and put the onus back on Clive.

"Clive, what on earth are you suggesting?"

"I'm not suggesting anything. I'm just pointing out what would be the likely consequences of my report and wondering if there could be a way forward that would be beneficial to both of us."

Alison's suspicions were aroused. "How could any of this be beneficial to you? You've done your dirty work. It's now up to Koszalinski to come in and wield the axe."

Clive played it cool. "Seeing this school get back on its feet would be reward enough for me, along with the pleasure of seeing you doing the business in the way we all know you can. Listen, it's too public to talk here. Meet me later for dinner and I'll fill you in on the fine detail of the report. That way you'll be well placed to make your move when the question of new leadership comes up."

"So that's what all this is about? Getting me out for dinner? And then what?"

"You misjudge me, Alison. Surely you're not suggesting that I would use my professional position to take advantage of you? It looked to me as if your relationship with *what's-his-name* was built on firmer foundations than you seem to be implying but, of course, if you are up for it, who am I to look a gift-horse in the mouth, so to speak?"

Alison fixed his face with her gaze, trying to penetrate deep into his head, to fathom out his motives.

"What about Dr Rogerson?"

"He's past his sell-by date. The governors will drop him like a hot rock when this lot hits the press. He'll get early retirement with a decent enhancement or a little job in some quiet *niche* in the LEA where he can work out his time without doing too much damage to anyone. That's the civilised way that LEAs work these things out nowadays."

Alison instantly determined not to be drawn into Clive's machinations. Just as quickly she wavered. She thought of Jake. How would she explain going out to meet *someone unspecified* on a Friday night? The idea of telling the truth was a non-starter. Jake was already seething with unspoken jealousy. There was no point in making things worse. But, anyway, why should she worry about Jake? Things had been so strange between them recently. Why shouldn't she go out to celebrate the end of *OfSTED*? Most of the rest of the staff, at any rate those who could still raise the energy and enthusiasm, had arranged to start a pub crawl at the *George*, ending up at Ricky Tomlinson's for a *bring-your-own-takeaway and cheap wine supper*. That was it. She would tell Jake an untruth but the *white lie* would be in Jake's best interests because he had nothing to worry about as far as Clive was concerned, had he?

"OK," she assented.

"OK what?" Clive feigned surprise.

"OK, I'll meet you for dinner to have a professional discussion about the future of this school, provided…"

"Provided what?"

"Provided that talking business is your only agenda," Alison kidded herself.

Jake arrived home half early that night, half intending to have it out with Alison. Talking about his fears would clear the air and begin the process of getting back to normal.

Before he could speak, she was in his face…

"I'm sorry, sweetheart, can you get something to eat on your own tonight? I've promised the staff to join them for their post-OfSTED celebration."

Jake was taken aback. She did not usually join in with staff booze-ups.

"Where are you going?" he hazarded.

"Starting at the *George* and ending up at Ricky's later on. I'll probably be late. Don't wait up!" And she was gone before he could see the guilt shining from her eyes.

Jake stared in astonishment for several seconds at the door as it slammed behind her. He sighed and then went to get something quick out of the freezer.

The coldness between them had been troubling his mind all day. He made a decision. He would meet her at Ricky Tomlinson's. They would walk home together and everything would be all right.

26 The dull ache of suspicion

Those who had gone directly to the *George* from school were already well-oiled and joining Simon Cunliffe in his umpteenth rendition of "There's only one 'f' in OfSTED", when the second wave of Southdale revellers began to arrive. Children had been farmed out to sitters, spouses greeted and fed and the OfSTED survivors were ready to forget their woes and have a really good night.

The few early evening regulars were overwhelmed by the sheer number of weary-looking but exhilarated pedagogues. A leaning tower of fifty-pence pieces festooned the wooden frame of the pool table. Some colleagues sat in twos, threes or fours around the cast iron and wood, heavy-based, pub tables. A few chatted, touching elbows on the bar, best placed but unlikely to order the next round. The smokers' clique sat together, bonded by their constrained staffroom camaraderie. They chain-smoked defiantly, each aspiring to pack the ash trays to overflowing with a score or more of redundant filter tips.

Duncan Lewis and Edith Barker were reviewing their golfing handicaps. It was good to have a topic of conversation other than the inspectors and their antics in or out of the classroom.

Betty Andrews and Henry Appleton formed an unholy alliance at a table for two near the toilets, unconcerned by the constant '*excuse mes*' as the celebrating teachers answered the call of their bulging bladders.

Henry, having a night off from his model making, was holding forth about what it was like in the 'olden days'.

"There wasn't half the violence there is in schools nowadays when we could use the cane. Bring it back, that's what I say. I tell you, Betty, I've seen some of the toughest nuts crack and break into whimpers after three or four strokes on the backside from the *avenger* as I used to call it. It had a wonderful *swish* rating. It was fair musical as it cut the air on the way to its target. I kept it in my prep room for years until Alan Sumner's dad nicked it on his last day at school. Well, at any rate, I always suspected it was him. Dennis, they called him. As hard as nails. Not like that mardy pillock of a son of his. I got it back two days later. Some so-and-so had sawn it into two-inch pieces, put it in a big brown envelope and posted it back to me. Whoever it was they had a bit of aplomb. They put in an anonymous note, cut out from newspapers, you know, like the classic blackmail story. 'Justice is done' was the message or something melodramatic like that. I don't really remember. They had something about them, kids in those days. If you beat them they didn't take it personal. You were just doing your job. They took their punishment like men. If you got caught you accepted it. I clipped some little nerk the other day. I know I shouldn't but old habits die hard when you get to my age. And do you know what? He said he would get his solicitor on to me. *His* solicitor! They're grown up before their time, the kids of today."

Betty nodded and shook and tut-tutted as required and wished she had gone to visit her niece in Pontefract.

In spite of the initial euphoria after the completed inspection, a few colleagues were contemplating its implications. At a table in the bay window, Ricky Tomlinson and Richard Best were in deep conversation.

"I've never felt so much pressure in all my life. Far worse than when I was on teaching practice. At least when I was training you felt as if they were there to help not just to criticise or look for reasons for getting you sacked," moaned Besty.

"I know what you mean," responded Ricky, although he did not know really. Teaching had always come easy to Ricky Tomlinson. He seemed to have that indefinable knack of knowing what interested and motivated young people. Whenever he spoke they listened. Children did their homework for Mr Tomlinson, not because he would put them in detention if they did not, not because he would tell their parents, not even because they might get nearer to passing their exams. No, they worked for Mr Tomlinson because they wanted to. He made lessons interesting. Occasionally even the end of lesson bell was an unwelcome intrusion into their learning experience.

Ricky tried to empathise. "I don't think anyone will be sacking you, Besty. Teachers are in short supply nowadays. Even geographers like you are hard to come by. Brian says that Rogerson receives at least a fax a week from other heads asking if he knows of any teachers who aren't spoken for."

Besty's face was set in a typically perplexed frown. "I don't understand all this recruitment business. One minute they're telling us how rubbish we all are and the next they're mounting multi-million pound advertising campaigns to try to get people to join the profession.

209

Aren't *we* the best advert? If *we* feel valued and reasonably well paid and we have the resources to do the job properly surely we'll be telling everyone that this is the best job in the world. People would be queuing up to join the profession. You'd have to prise out the old timers with a crowbar. Enforce retirement at seventy-five! You don't have to be a genius to work that out."

"How right you are, Besty," agreed Ricky, with a grimace. "Do you fancy another pint? "

Besty resolutely ignored the hint. "What do you think will happen at Southdale, Ricky? Will they close us down, like people have been saying?"

"I don't think for one minute they'll go that far. It's not logical. They couldn't provide enough extra places at *Pickersgill*. In any case, there'd be uproar. The two communities have been at each other's throats since history began. There'd be civil war!"

"But they don't do logical things in education, Ricky. I've heard that Rogerson was cut up pretty badly by the feedback this afternoon. The women in the office said he broke down and wouldn't speak to anyone, not even Brian."

"These things always get exaggerated. All we can do is wait until Monday. Come on, get them in. It's your shout. Look out for low flying moths, everybody! Besty's about to get his wallet out! Mine's a pint of bitter and a bag of cheese and onion crisps. Get your orders in now, folks. We might not see the colour of Besty's money again until after the next inspection. Clear a space at the bar, you lot. He's easily put off. His wallet could be back in his pocket like a ferret down a rabbit hole."

The Southdale crowd abandoned the pub shortly after drinking-up time and caused a brief commotion at the local takeaways before making their collectively boisterous way towards Ricky Tomlinson's tall, narrow terraced house. Any year eleven students who had seen them would have been proud of their teacher role models.

Fortunately, the walls of Ricky's house were thick and his neighbours understanding. Ricky was generally a good neighbour, who did his neighbourly duty by loaning out gardening equipment and taking in parcels, during the school holidays, when everyone else was at work. His immediate neighbours had grown accustomed to Ricky's end of term parties and such like, though they did not feel that they could intrude upon his colleagues' indulgence in spite of his frequent supplications to join in the fun.

Jake heard the thumping of the music from the end of the street. Being Jake, he knocked politely on the door and waited until it was obvious that no one had heard. He pushed the door and met the full force of someone or other's greatest hits of the eighties. Aside from the throbbing beat, it was like stepping into the warm, humid atmosphere of a butterfly house. The reek of re-cycled cigarette smoke assailed his nostrils.

Jake made his way into the kitchen. No sign of Alison. He nodded at faces he vaguely identified. "Anyone seen Ali?" he ventured occasionally, somewhat embarrassed by the puzzled expressions that greeted his every enquiry.

By the time he reached the attic, he had passed through every other room in the house, barring the cellar, and including Ricky's untidy and unoccupied bathroom. Ricky was setting up the *Playstation* in the attic so that some gluttons for punishment could indulge their fantasies in a game of *Who wants to be a millionaire?*

"Hi, you're Ricky aren't you? Remember I bumped into you when I came to pick Alison up after parents' evening a few weeks ago? I can't find her anywhere. You don't know where she is, do you?"

A cloud passed over Ricky's face. "Alison? I haven't seen her. She told us she was too busy to come out this evening. She said she was having a quiet drink at home with you."

Jake turned away without speaking further. She had lied. Why would she lie? His doubts welled up inside him. His head spun. The music and the chatter became oppressive as he fought to control his emotions. She lied. What other possible reason would she have for lying? She must be with *him*.

Jake's ability to think clearly left him more quickly than he left the house. The cool air of the street did nothing to restore his senses. She must be with *him*. Where else would she be? She would not lie for any other reason. What would be the point? There must have been something in it when she came home so late previously. This time he would have the truth. As painful as it would be it would be better than not knowing; better than spending further days and weeks being eaten from the inside by that demon jealousy who had become his persistent inward companion of late.

If she was with Holdsworth where would she go? To a local restaurant? Not likely. If someone who knew Jake saw them together it would be dangerous. Even in the unlikely event of their assignation being innocent, in essence, she would not wish to raise Jake's suspicions again. Things had been too awkward lately.

His room! Of course, his hotel room. Alison mentioned where the inspectors were staying. Where was it? Somewhere cheap and functional, she had said, nothing fancy. The *Travel Lodge* at the roundabout on the ring road. He would find them together and confront them.

The acute agony of knowing for certain would despatch the dull ache of suspicion, once and for all.

27 The increasing intensity of murderous uncertainty

Jake called a cab and directed it towards the *Travel Lodge*. All kinds of emotions were welling up inside him. Anger, loathing, jealousy.... but above all, fear. Fear of losing Alison. Several times during the short drive he suffered a change of heart. Turn the cab around; go back home; stop being stupid. Trust Ali. Or pretend nothing had happened. Even a share of Ali might be better than none of her at all.

Why was nothing in life ever simple? Perhaps it was not just a fling with Holdsworth. Perhaps she might leave Jake.

The fear raged and burst through his fragile composure. His body was shaken by fierce sobs of escaping anguish. The cab driver glanced in his mirror. "You all right, pal? Can I take you to hospital or somewhere?"

"Like I told you, the *Travel Lodge*."

The reddish brick and dark glass fascia of the single storey motel looked sombre in the artificial glow of low profile security lighting. Jake scanned the car park vainly for evidence that Ali might be there. He sensed the obscure contours of a few car-like metal shells. Nothing caught his eye.

Jake forced a note into the cab driver's fist and veered off towards the vacuous glow of *reception*. The double glass doors parted reluctantly to accommodate Jake's determined approach. He stepped into the cold, unfriendly foyer and made directly for the young woman seated alone at the reception desk.

"Holdsworth. Clive Holdsworth," he croaked. "I'm one of his OfSTED colleagues. I have a meeting with him this evening."

The young woman felt a spasm of doubt as she caught the look in Jake's desperate eyes. Having thought twice, she chose the easy way out.

"Room 24. Go back the way you came. Turn right outside the building and it's the last room near to the far end of the car park."

Jake muttered the vaguest of uneasy 'thank yous' and steeled himself for confrontation. Out of the double glass doors, along the edge of the car park as far as he could go.

His thoughts were spiked with an eccentric fusion of horror and elation. His gamble had worked. He had tracked down Holdsworth. He would haul the unsuspecting adulterer from his plasterboard love nest, strike him once on the point of the jaw and, seizing Alison by the arm, drag her dutifully off home, where she would break down, beg his forgiveness and they would begin the process of rebuilding their superficially blemished relationship.

The curtains of number twenty-four released merely an ominous effulgence, disclosing nothing of what was within. Jake succumbed to a voyeuristic urge. He sought vainly to peer through the gaps. He made a superhuman effort to control his heaving breath and placed his ear near the door. He could detect suppressed human sounds within. He strained his senses. Was it conversation he sensed or the abominably matter-of-fact sounds of two humans locked in passion? He could not tell.

All control abandoned him. He rattled the door. He booted it ferociously.

"Open up, you bastard. I know you're in there. Come out and face me like a man." Even in these phantasmagorical circumstances Jake surprised himself by his own descent into comic machismo.

He hammered the door a few more helpless times, then listened. All he registered was a guilty silence.

The sobs seized him again and caused his aching chest to heave with the involuntary effort.

"Ali, come out, please. I love you. I need you. I can't bear to think of you in there with him."

Nothing. Not a sound nor a whimper. No response. No admission. No regrets. Just the increasing intensity of murderous uncertainty. No way forward.

"Ali, I'm begging. Look I'm on my knees. I can't live without you. That's all I know. Come out. Let's talk it through. I won't touch him, I promise. And you know I won't lay a finger on you, don't you?"

Nothing. No response. An empty room where moments earlier human voices had intimated who knows what.

Jake's fear surged upwards from the pit of his stomach, threatening nausea. He retched and coughed and spluttered. He burned with seething frustration. His anger turned to wild-eyed rage.

He flung his shoulder at the door intending to split it asunder. It resisted. Ignoring the intense pain, he repeated the action several times with equal lack of success.

Jake slumped to the ground. He lay there, his crumpled frame shaken by heavy despair. All logic had left him temporarily. Should he lie there all night? They would have to come out sooner or later. But what would be the point of that? He *knew* what he needed to know. His pain had reached its zenith.

Jake was a passionate and caring man. He loved Alison so deeply that it tore at his insides to even imagine existence without her. In spite of his passion, Jake was a man who was capable of exercising control over his emotions. The idea of doing away with himself, melodramatically, on her lover's threshold, only passed fleetingly through his murky consciousness.

Half an hour sobbed by. Slowly Jake's composure began to return. His helplessness metamorphosed into resolve. He dragged himself to his feet and straightened out his crumpled dignity.

He had recovered himself enough to offer a plausible explanation to the occupant of number twenty-three, who, having just parked her car, had wandered over warily and, hesitating at a reasonably safe distance, had enquired about his health. She was unsure whether he was a heart attack victim or just another drunk.

"Fine. I'm fine," Jake offered unconvincingly. "I..er..just lost my footing and hit my head and I must have passed out."

"I'll get a doctor," said the woman, slightly relieved.

"No. No, don't trouble. You see... my wife's a nurse and I only live a stone's throw from here. She'll check me out when I get home. Thank you for your concern. I'll be all right, really."

The woman watched the lugubrious figure dissolve into the gloom, mentally shrugged and went about her business.

It was a long walk home for Jake. He could not face the inane chatter of a cab driver and he did not know the slightest thing about where to catch a bus. Besides he needed time to think.

By the time he set foot on the unwelcoming gravel of their drive, his mind was made up.

Through tear swamped eyes he searched for a few essential commodities and stuffed them into his sports bag. He slammed the front door, without a backwards glance.

As he hurled his paltry baggage into the back seat of his car and hastened away, not even he supposed that he would never set foot again in that place.

28 Chips and scraps for tea

Brian Ingleton was embroiled with a parent. Father and daughter showed clear characteristics of their common stock. He was a little short of medium height, as broad as he was long, with shiny swept back, slightly thinning hair and one of those beards that you would have preferred people not to grow, unless you had seen them without it.

His daughter was obviously his daughter. Tall for a year eight pupil, she echoed both his shape and his demeanour. She wore her hair in an incongruously spiky arrangement, which distracted the observer ever so slightly from the unflattering lines of her oversized clothing.

The Y8 tutor looked on impassively as Brian did his job. He had met with Mr McDonald and Lauren on numerous occasions since she had joined the school some eighteen months earlier. There had been a Mrs McDonald at some time in the past but her whereabouts were currently unknown to the school and her husband was giving no clues. To all intents and purposes Mr McDonald was a single parent doing his best to bring up a damaged and wayward daughter.

Brian Ingleton had always seen his job as doing his best for every child that came Southdale's way. He had his own origins in the region and was still imbued with its culture and moved by its collective sufferings even though his status had been greatly uplifted by the educational opportunities that had been denied many of his classmates at Pitt Street Primary.

The filial bond is self-evident. Mr McDonald loves his daughter with an emotion that transcends and transmogrifies their every day relationship of battles and harsh, hurtful exchanges.

Each time he is called up to school, he vents his frustration on the teachers. It's their fault. Why can't they control his daughter and teach her some discipline? Why is he having to continually come up to school, when they know his health problems? Strain like this could set his heart off and then where would Lauren be?

And then he's convinced by the teacher's argument. Yes, it is Lauren's fault. Why is he blessed with a demon like her? Other fathers have children who are nice and bring credit upon them. Why is she such a disappointment?

Lauren remains impassive. Mr McDonald breaks down in heart-rending sobs and the teacher takes pity.

A new strategy is vainly agreed and Mr McDonald promises that Lauren will be a new person. She will do what the teachers say and will not utter the f-word ever again. In spite of their perilous financial circumstances, she will have her new stereo for the bedroom, if she keeps her promises and, if she doesn't, she'll be grounded and will be banned from using her telly and computer.

"I can't understand why she treats me like this. I've given her everything she wants."

And then he kisses her on her forehead and she, embarrassed by this pitiful man says, without emotion, "I'll see you at home dad. "

The current scene has been played out many times in Lauren's troubled school life. A disastrous breach of discipline occasioned by a child who cannot seem to help herself; followed by recriminations from staff: "There is no way that I'm having that girl in my room again, until she learns how to behave. She's a danger to herself and to others. Why should staff and pupils come to school in fear of what she might do? I'm contacting my union rep."

By Y8, the pattern of meetings with school authority was well established. Brian played out his dual role of disciplinarian and mediator with an ease, born of bitter experience.

Lauren hated herself. She despised her background and could not understand why she did and said the things that got her into trouble.

Too many of her teachers could still remember the days when they could browbeat recalcitrant youngsters into tearful submission. Not so with young people like Lauren, fruit of inadequate parenting, yield of the non-society. Product of that advocate of the cult of the individual, that aggravator of social injustice.

Every confrontation was a platform for Lauren, a stage on which to play out her anger and her frustrations. From an early age at school she had learnt that she was incapable of doing the things that pleased the teachers: passing tests, writing neatly and doing nice drawings, skipping and dancing gracefully, balancing on apparatus without wobbling from side to side, winning the egg and spoon race.

Gradually the rage built up within her until one day, in Y5, she could contain it no more. She burst her banks releasing an inundation of hatred that flooded the room. The teacher looked shocked. Her classmates looked shocked and Lauren was glad. Glad that she had done something, however outrageous, that was bigger and better than any other child, in her class, had ever done.

From that moment on Lauren had been in control. She knew how to get the attention she craved and she exploited her newly discovered talent mercilessly to the extent that her class teacher went down with stress, half way through Y6.

"What are *you* like, Lauren?" asked Brian rhetorically. Lauren remained impassive. "Listen," continued Brian, "if you don't improve your behaviour from this instant I'm going to ask your dad to come into school and sit alongside you every lesson to make sure you are doing what you should."

Lauren remained impassive but Mr McDonald warmed to this theme.

"You know what the trouble is, Mr Ingleton? The trouble is that Lauren's ashamed of me. She's ashamed of her father. And why's that? Well it's simple. She's ashamed of my obesity. That's why she always insists on me dropping her off before we get to school. Well, I'll settle her. I will come into school and I'll sit beside her every day and I'll really embarrass her. I'll lift my shirt up and show my fat belly to everybody. And I'll pull the fluff out of my belly button and flick it at her. And I'll pick my nose and wipe it on the table. And I'll belch and I'll fart and I'll show her up so much that she'll never want me to come into school again."

This was not quite the reaction that Brian had been expecting. He intervened and brought Mr McDonald's outburst to an abrupt end.

"Well, I don't think that will be really necessary, Mr McDonald, and in any case we won't stand much chance of getting Lauren to improve her behaviour if you set the sort of example you've just described."

"I do apologise, Mr Ingleton. I don't know what came over me. I'll leave it in your capable hands as usual."

Brian sighed almost imperceptibly. "Thank you for your confidence, Mr McDonald I'll put Lauren on report. Shall I show you out?"

"No need to bother, Mr Ingleton. I know my way around by now."

Mr McDonald leaned awkwardly over and kissed his daughter on the forehead.

She spoke without the least emotion. "I'll see you later, Dad. I'll bring home some chips and scraps for tea."

29 Grasping the wrong end of the stick

Someone from OfSTED had spoken to Sarah Koszalinski very early about what was likely to be Southdale's fate. The *someone* had mentioned the leadership potential of the deputy head at Southdale. This assertion had been immediately affirmed by *another* someone in Koszalinski's department.

Koszalinski decided on a course of instant action: Rogerson would be relieved of his post, following appropriate consultation with the governors, of course. Additionally Alison Lister would be nominated to take over the running of the school, in the interim, until a *Fresh Start* programme could be worked up and the school closed, then reopened with a new name, a new head and a new future.

Koszalinski need not have worried about Rogerson. He had returned home broken in spirit that fateful Friday afternoon and had made an oath to Cynthia that he would never set foot in the school again. He was true to his word.

In effect, Alison took over the leadership of Southdale in the middle of the week following the inspection. Brian Ingleton was promoted to acting deputy and Ricky Tomlinson took on Brian's job. This, in turn, engendered further 'acting up' roles.

Within a fortnight Clive Holdsworth had made the oral report to a subdued gathering of the governing body. Sarah Koszalinski had made an unprecedented appearance at the meeting to support OfSTED's findings and to express the LEA's determination to see Southdale back on a firm footing. She made it clear that the LEA would be nominating some experienced people to join the governors in the lead up to the *Fresh Start* and exhorted those present to support Alison Lister as she oversaw the drawing up of the immediate action plan. The written report would be released to parents and the press within a matter of weeks so governors should prepare themselves for the inevitable onslaught.

The provisional plan was to advertise for a new head as soon as possible, with a view to closing Southdale at Christmas and reopening, under a new name, in January. All jobs would be re-advertised and existing staff would be free to apply for their own job, or anyone else's for that matter.

Yes, limited funding would be available to provide an essential building programme and to ensure that resources were there to support the transformation. What about Dr Rogerson? Well, the LEA was currently in negotiation with him and his professional association representative with the intention of reaching an agreed settlement.

Gladys Ollerenshaw sat silent and solemn faced throughout Clive's presentation, Koszalinski's exhortations and colleague governors' anxious questions. She cleared her throat dramatically and addressed the assemblage from the chair.

"Colleagues, friends rather, Ms Koszalinski, Mr Holdsworth, please be indulgent of me, I have a few words to say. How ironic it is that financial resources are available now that the school is officially recognised as failing. We've been canvassing for years to get the sort of funding that will enable the staff to give these kids a decent start in life. What a pity that the community has to go through this sort of trauma to get our people their entitlement! Nevertheless, let it not be said that we are quitters. I have first hand experience of Alison Lister's strength and courage and I have every faith that she will begin to put us back on our feet. People around here may be poor and they may not have much time for education, but they are a proud people. I'm only thankful that Ms Koszalinski prefers the option of the *Fresh Start* rather than a definitive closure. I'm not the only one around here who could never stomach our kids being sent to *Pickersgill*. Rivalries are very strong in this neck of the woods and some folk would keep their kids at home rather than send them over there. There may be those of you who are expecting me to follow Bill Rogerson's example and throw in the towel. Well, I'm sorry to disappoint you. I dare say that a 'new' school will need a new governing body and a new chair but until then, unless you have no confidence in me, I am chair of governors at this school and chair of governors I will remain."

Gladys removed her spectacles and dabbed her moistened eyes with the corner of a paper tissue. Her outburst of emotion was met with silent assent and determined nods. This evening was not the time for rapturous applause and further defiance but Gladys Ollerenshaw was the heart and soul of this community and the backbone of this school. She deserved their support in her hour of anguish.

The meeting closed in a state of agonising depression and many of those present left in silence, only to re-group twenty minutes later at the *George* to ease their pain and to revisit more heatedly the words ringing in their ears: *Southdale is a failing school and steps must be taken immediately to get it back on the right track.*

"*Save our school! Save our school!*"

The small but vociferous band of protestors patrolled the pavement in front of County Hall. A single police officer looked on disinterestedly from an acceptable distance.

"*Say NO to closure! Southdale's what we want!*"

The demonstration consisted mainly of mums and toddlers. The occasional dad and school age truant hung warily around the periphery.

"*Hey, Koszalinski, what do you say? How many schools have you closed today?*"

Sarah Koszalinski looked out of her second storey office window on to the pitiful gathering below. She wondered whether County Hall had ever seen another such example of grasping the wrong end of the stick. She concluded that it probably had.

A few bemused visitors to County Hall were challenged as to their credentials and urged to sign a petition in favour of a school they had never heard of. Some, showing mild amusement, signed to avoid a verbal bashing by the angry young mothers. Others just simply brushed past or showed their tight-lipped irritation as they made their way into the entrance hall.

Koszalinski had already been on the telephone to Southdale.

"Mrs Lister, I would really appreciate it if you would call a parents' meeting and scotch this ridiculous rumour once and for all.

Someone connected with the school has obviously leaked confidential information to the *Chronicle* and Sally Mahoney has really made a meal of it."

"Perhaps it was someone in your office, Ms Koszalinski," hazarded Alison.

This had never occurred to Koszalinski and she bristled with self-righteous indignation at the very thought of it. Few people would have been comfortable at the wrong end of one of her rages, when she really let rip.

She withdrew from the conversation with Alison and, aware of the hovering presence of her personal assistant, replaced the handset as firmly as dignity would allow.

The front page of the local newspaper was spread provocatively across her desk.

"EXCLUSIVE: *'Worst school in north of England' to close by Christmas"*.

"Get me a call to the editor of the *Chronicle*. Immediately!"

The plaintive chanting of the protestors could be barely heard, attenuated by the distance, muffled by the double-glazing and disguised by the soft drone of the air conditioning.

"What do we want?"

"Answers!"

"When do we want them?"

"Now!"

Sarah Koszalinski slipped three painkillers into her mouth and washed them down with a plastic beaker full of ice cold water from the dispenser.

30 Don't they teach discipline in schools nowadays?

Bridget and Jeremy Forsyth almost managed to disguise their surprise when Jake turned up, worryingly late and unannounced, at their discreetly elegant detached house in suburban Leeds.

Bridget did not like answering the door late at night, even when Jeremy was around. There were too many reports, locally, of burglaries and street robberies. Bridget felt uncomfortable to the extent that Jeremy had already made secret enquiries regarding a plush, high security residential enclave several miles away. For the moment he would not be discussing the possibilities with Bridget. He liked to have things sorted out before he shared them with his wife.

Only a fortnight earlier he and Bridget had attended a meeting, organised by the Community Forum, at the neighbourhood church hall. About two hundred cynics had turned up and immediately disregarded the rector's intentions. He had intended that the meeting should not dwell on the past but look at positive ways of addressing the gangs of youths that seemed to be aimlessly occupying every street corner.

The gathering was sadly somewhat greater than the Reverend Stubbs' usual audience but he was an accomplished speaker and addressed the meeting with an assurance, born of years of sowing wisdom seeds in the wind.

"Ladies and gentlemen... oh and young people. It's nice to see a smattering of youth among our gathering. I...that is we....the local churches and the community forum working together called this meeting to answer a need...a desperate need. There can't be anyone who is not aware of the problems being caused by a minority of youngsters in our area. We are all familiar with the gangs that hang around on street corners intimidating our old folks by their very presence. We know about the drugs problem. Many of us have witnessed those older youths, not from round here who come in cars and who are constantly surrounded by groups of young people as they deal in goodness knows what. In fact, everyone in the community knows about the problem. What we need to do this evening is to think of some constructive ways forward, not dwell on the past."

"That's all very well, Rector," intoned a pillar of the community, "but we've had enough of these thugs around here. Not all the troublemakers are from outside, you know. That local comp has a lot to answer for. Don't they teach discipline in schools nowadays? I've had eggs thrown at my windows every night for a fortnight now. And it doesn't matter how often I go out and shout at the little bleeders, excuse my French, Rector, or try to cuff them, they still keep coming back and doing it worse."

"Too lenient they are. Too lenient by far," interrupted another voice. It was the genteel tones of Jennifer Maxwell, the manager of the local community centre. "Scum. Low life scum, that's what they are. We should bring back the birch in this country, and national service. Make men out of them. We live in fear of our lives down at the community centre. Do you know, they have tried to set fire to it three times now? And what do the police do? They tell us there is nothing they can do. Insults and threats can't be acted on unless they have been witnessed personally by a police officer. What sort of a justice system is that?"

Jennifer's husband piped up, "We're a marked couple, Jennifer and I. Every time we leave the centre in our car, there's a gang of them waiting for us. Sometimes they just stand in the way and won't let us out of the gate unless we drive straight at them. Other times they hammer on the bonnet or try to open the doors. Jennifer turns up the radio so that we can't hear the foul-mouthed abuse and threats they hurl at us. I'm glad, at least, that the police have had the guts to show up this evening. I've spoken to the community inspector, Fred Johnson, on a number of occasions, and he's a decent chap. All our cars will be safe in the car park this evening, by the way. I noticed as I came in that they have designated a constable to keep an eye on the police car, while the meeting goes on! But let's hear from Inspector Johnson, Rector. It's about time we heard from the police what they are going to do about the situation."

Inspector Fred Johnson was approaching the twilight of his career. A down-to-earth, popular officer, he addressed the audience with a confidence built in a hundred local forum meetings.

"Rector, ladies and gentlemen, I can relate to how you are feeling at present. Remember, we police officers are members of the public, too, when we're not on duty. We live in communities. We pay our taxes. We want the same as you: a pleasant and safe environment in which to live and go about our business without interference from troublemakers. I've been a community policeman for nigh on twenty years now and I've met a lot of young people in that time. Let's not tar them all with the same brush. Most of the youth that you come across are just ordinary decent kids, like kids have always been. It's just that there's nothing for them to do. There's no sports facilities around here, since they closed down the public baths, unless of course you include the private fitness suite up the road there. Minimum subscription, £60 per month. A de-stressing zone for the middle-aged well-off. There was a youth club, of course, until it closed down two years ago because of lack of funding and a shortage of volunteers to help out. Let's try and see it from their point of view. Most of them just want to meet with their friends in an evening. OK, it looks a bit intimidating to older folk when a gang of them block the street corner, bulging out into the road and forcing people to walk around them. They have the right of association in this country. We're reluctant to move them on unless they're doing something wrong. If we do, they just congregate somewhere else. The biggest problem they give us is a lot of litter and a bit of graffiti. Yeah, there are a few villains amongst them, drug pushers and that sort of thing but that's our job to sort them out. We're currently carrying out surveillance on two or three individuals and collecting evidence that will hopefully send them down for a year or two. What we need around here is a few less people moaning about the problem and a few more prepared to stand up and be counted. Those who will face up to their responsibilities as members of the community rather than simply demand their rights. Who is going to raise funds to re-open the youth club? Who is going to chase up potential grants to get a detached youth worker? Who is going to give these kids a chance?"

Apparently no-one.

Fred Johnson returned to his seat, enveloped in embarrassed silence.

Reverend Stubbs resumed his role as chair, "Perhaps a way forward is to set up a steering group, charged with making some recommendations to a reconvened gathering in a month or so's time. Are there any volunteers?"

Miss Hartley, seventy something, raised a hesitant hand. "Reverend Stubbs, I'd just like to ask the headmistress of the school a question about something that's been puzzling me. If these young yobs have got so much time to hang around on the streets, mugging people and taking drugs, shouldn't she be setting them more homework?"

Bridget Forsyth had already retired when Jake arrived. Her husband was idly flicking through the cable channels, when Jake tapped discreetly on the imposing, polished brass doorknocker.

On hearing Jake's voice, Bridget rushed downstairs, fearing something horrendous had happened to her beloved daughter.

Jake reassured her. "It's just that I had to get away. Give me time to think. It's that Clive Holdsworth, remember?"

Bridget remembered only too well.

The fear in Jake's eye was subject only to exhaustion. Bridget knew with the instinct of an adoptive parent that he needed to crash out. The investigation and the recriminations would be better begun in the morning.

31 Deliciously unsaid secrets

Alison cried and cried. She cried so much that she was almost cried out. Jake had left no clues. He had taken his razor and a few things and that was all. She had telephoned his office and they had said he was taking a few days leave to sort something out. A bit irregular, they had thought, but Jake was a conscientious colleague and his boss felt that he should have the space, if he needed it.

She telephoned Jake's ageing and somewhat confused mother, on Tyneside. Jake and his mother had never been close and they only visited when it was absolutely necessary.

The old woman found Alison's enquiry after her health curious to say the least.

"I'm well enough thank you, Alison. And how are your folks?" she asked, fearing news of a bereavement.

"Fine, thanks."

Well, it was not a bereavement, so what did the girl want?

"And how are things at school, Alison? Jake told me that you'd been having a hard time with the inspectors."

Jake told her? Perhaps he's there.

"Oh, it's all over now, bar the shouting that is." How could she probe further without letting on that she did not know where Jake was?

"It's been a while since Jake and I came to visit. When was the last time we were up there? Just before Christmas?"

"Oh, my goodness, no. I haven't seen hide nor hair of either of you since last Spring Bank. How is my lad by the way? I trust you're looking after him in the manner to which he is accustomed?"

"I surely am," Alison lied. Mislaying your husband was, at best, downright careless. Alison was convinced he was not there. His mother sounded too genuinely unprepared for Alison's guarded enquiries.

It was time for Alison to extricate herself from this awkward moment. "Well, it's been nice talking to you. Jake and I are thinking about popping up for a few days next holiday, if that's all right with you? We'll ring again in a couple of weeks' time."

"Of course, it is. My Jake knows he's always welcome here," added Mrs Lister, pointedly. She enacted the niceties and replaced the receiver, even more perplexed than when she had picked it up.

Alison was running out of options. She could think of hardly anyone else to speak to. There was certainly no-one she could confide in. It came home to her how close she and Jake had been, close to the exclusion of other friendships. She was amazed how little she really knew about Jake's past life. Her anxiety not to look back had infected Jake. They had lived only for the present and for their future together.

She had no idea who his school or university friends had been. She had a vague recollection of hazy names scratched on dutiful greetings cards but could not pin them down to a specific connection or location. She recalled the names of a couple of colleagues from work, with whom

Jake had shared an occasional drink. She found their numbers scrawled in the embarrassingly underused household address book. She called them to no avail, now unashamed of admitting she had not the least inkling of Jake's whereabouts.

She called Jake's *mobile* on numerous occasions and left messages when he did not answer. Her unrequited text messages were manifold.

She began to consider contacting the police but dismissed the idea immediately. After all Jake was a grown man. He knew what he was doing. He had not disappeared mysteriously. He had packed his things and moved out of her life for who knows how long

She shivered at the thought that she might not see him ever again. No, she was becoming illogical now. Jake was upset. She really could not understand why but he *was* upset and needed some space. The only thing to do was to give him that space. He would sort it out in his head and come back to her. They would cry, and open their hearts and then they would kiss and make up. Everything would be like it was before.

March came and went. Alison felt the magnolias were in blossom early and noted that, one year hence, she would take the time to enjoy them properly, with Jake, strolling, as they would, in the garden, planning what to dig up and what to plant. A little wall, to break up the monotony of the flower beds. Perhaps a summer house, if we don't get the conservatory? The fence needs repairing down in the bottom corner. Some of the pots appear to have cracked in the frost. We need another ten bags of pea gravel; it's all trodden into the soil. I told you we should put down some of that breathable plastic stuff. That stuff that your Dad used on his, but you never listen. We could do with a little bench over there in the shade. It would be nice for *apéritifs* on a mythically warm summer's evening.

Alison missed Jake more and more. The loss was especially acute on her early spring ventures into the awakening garden. She missed his banter. She missed his smile. She missed his knowing looks, which spoke deliciously unsaid secrets, even in a crowd.

She missed him in the mornings, though she no longer stretched out her hopeful arm to see if he had materialised while she was asleep. She missed him during the day. At first, it was during her rare breaks from activity but as the days drew into weeks, it became a constant, dull ache, which occupied her subconscious, wherever she went and whatever she did. She ached for him into the early hours, until exhaustion robbed her of her consciousness for the shortest of whiles.

Jake had rung her, of course. Even in his anguish, he was too considerate to leave her dangling. He rang from his in-laws'. He explained, distantly, that Bridget and Jeremy had kindly agreed that he could stay until he got his head right. He was travelling to work from Leeds each day and, no, he couldn't envisage at present an opportunity for he and Alison to get together and talk it through. The pain was too severe and showed no signs of abating. No, no, he couldn't stand to talk about what was causing the pain, not even on the telephone.

"But tell me one thing, Alison," he enquired without irony, "are you going to leave me for him?"

"Leave you? Leave you for whom? Oh, my darling, please come home and let's talk. I need to see you face to face. If you won't come here, let's meet somewhere and I can explain what happened."

"So something *did* happen!"

"Well, no, not what you're thinking. It's just that Clive... No, it's too complicated to talk about like this. Please see me."

Jake's sobs continued to reverberate around Alison's head, even though he had long since ended the encounter and rushed off to hide his embarrassment from an overly solicitous mother-in-law.

32 Buzzing again

"Take a letter for me, would you, Rosie?"

Dear Ms Koszalinski,

I should like to invite you and some of your colleagues to come along and have a look at some of the improvements that have been made at Southdale in just a short time since the inspection.

As you are aware, the inspectors made some comments orally, to myself and the governors, and we have decided to act upon them in advance of the written report, so that it can be made clear to everyone that Southdale does have the capacity to improve itself and the potential to raise achievement for all its students. As you can see, we are well on in our thinking and I should be grateful if you would allow the LEA link adviser some time to discuss our formal action plan to address the key issues, once the written report has been published.

The first task for my senior managers and myself was to get the staff back on their feet and convince them that they are the <u>right</u> people for the job. They have been through a lot lately and if you tell even good people often enough that they are rubbish, they begin to believe it! Under <u>Fresh Start</u>, the new headteacher will probably get rid of a significant number of the existing staff, perhaps even myself, but, for the time being, we are the best there is and we intend to show you what we can do.

Brian Ingleton is a good man and he is trusted by the staff. He's a great motivator and he knew just what to do to get the staff 'buzzing' again. He consulted with Staff Committee and they organised a 'get together' at school, one evening. We brought in outside caterers and really let our hair down. I made a short address to the staff to try and raise morale. Brian tells me that I spoke well and that a number of colleagues have expressed their confidence in what we are trying to do.

In the week after the inspection I did assemblies with all the year groups. The youngsters were a bit 'shell-shocked'. A few were very high in the light of the bad publicity we had received and tried it on a bit but the vast majority were very subdued and worried that the school might be closing. They were scared stiff of having to go to another school! Like some wines our kids don't travel very well! Even going to Leeds for the day would be a major event for a few of them. Anyway, I made it clear to all pupils that the school would remain if they rallied round and did their bit. I promised that we would set up a student council to let them air their views and make suggestions for improvement but I made it very clear what was expected of them in terms of discipline and effort.

Of course, it was necessary to back up my fighting-talk with some swift action. The very next day we started the preparation for elections to the student council. To underline how serious we were about improving behaviour, I mobilised all staff. It's amazing how the prospect of losing your job focuses the mind. We were out on the corridors and in the yards. We welcomed the pupils on to the site in the morning and we watched them off the site in the evening.

Brian and I waited at the main entrance each morning for a week and took the names of all youngsters who arrived late. One of the office staff rang home and attempted to enlist the support of the parents in getting their children to school on time. We went through the list of absentees and contacted every parent, even if they were out at work. If any child seriously misbehaved (violence, threats, abuse, bullying) we immediately contacted their parents and asked them to take them off site until they were prepared to give an undertaking to improve.

We are starting to see the benefits of our actions even now. Some parents begin to take their responsibilities more seriously if we pester them enough. We have a calmer, quieter, more business-like school already.

It was obviously important to put parents' minds at rest as well. Following your advice, I called an Extraordinary General Parents' Meeting. Nearly three hundred and fifty turned up! Quite a number when you consider that at our AGM we usually get a maximum of half-a-dozen and most of them have lost their way trying to find the night school pottery class.

They were all very anxious at first and there were a few unpleasant comments made about the staff. Sally O'Mahoney and that scandal sheet that employs her have a lot to answer for, in my opinion. Once I had calmed their fears about the future of the school we were able to have a constructive discussion about the way forward. We are going to set up a PTA. The school hasn't had a PTA since, some years ago, Dr Rogerson instructed the former deputy, Ted Lambert, to spend his time on other things. From now on we will have an open PTA meeting every month. They will elect a committee at the first monthly meeting next week. We are planning to have regular discussions about the life and work of the school as well as organising fund raising events and socials. I am quite excited about the whole thing. There is a small group who would like to see a full school uniform - blazer and tie, the lot - but I think we need to wait for the appointment of the new head before we talk about that.

Given that the school will have a Fresh Start, it was perhaps a little premature of me to talk about the potential for the curriculum. I did it nevertheless, because I can't see the new head not wanting to make things more relevant for our kids. We need some different progression routes for the less academically gifted and we *certainly have plenty of young people who fall into that category. Far too many children are being judged against the wrong criteria and written off rather than encouraged to pursue different ways of achieving the same goals. I have promised some minor adjustments to the curriculum for September and I am sure that they will not interfere with any long-term plans for the school. They will surely move us in the right direction.*

You know I take very seriously the inspectors' views about the quality of teaching and learning. We have some good teachers here but we also have some who have been wearied by all the changes of recent years and feel inadequate in dealing with some of the more challenging situations we face on a daily basis. Most of them are susceptible to being rescued, given a suitable staff development and monitoring programme. However, in the medium term, a minority need to be released, with dignity, to retire or to pursue a career more suited to their gifts. It makes me very angry that the selection system has let them down as well as the countless young people that they have let down through their inability to do the job.

However, this is not for me to worry about at this stage. I am more interested in a very rapid improvement in what we are delivering to the pupils. I have consulted with governors and they are in agreement with my course of action. You will be aware of the good report Ricky Tomlinson got for the standard of his teaching and relationships. He is currently operating as acting deputy. However, I have further plans for him. During the summer term, I want to second him as a staff developer. I want him to research the best practice and I want him to have a free role to work alongside other colleagues and train them on the job.

When teachers have finished their initial training, there is very little on the job training available. They are expected to keep themselves updated on new methods and strategies by going out of school on externally-provided, one-off courses. What a waste of time and effort! After a few days back in the hurly-burly of the chalk face they have forgotten the theory of what they have just learned! I want to change all that. I want teachers being trained in the classroom, on the job, not out in some teachers' centre, divorced from reality.

Just think of how effectively our training money could be spent, used in this way. Think of the saving on staff cover and the increased stability from not having three or four colleagues absent each week on in-service training activities! The mind boggles! Top football clubs don't succeed by simply letting players do their own thing and choose which training sessions they will attend or none at all! They stay at the top level because they put their resources into improving skills on a daily basis. This is the model I want to pursue in any school of which I am head - albeit for a short period of time.

I am afraid I have let myself get carried away with my enthusiasm. I do apologise. I look forward to hearing from you soon.

Yours sincerely

`Alison Lister`

Acting Headteacher

"Mrs Lister, sorry to disturb you but there's a letter from the Director just arrived. You asked me to let you know."

"Oh, thanks, Rosie, bring it in. And will you, please, remember to call me Alison not Mrs Lister."

"I'm sorry, Mrs Li... uh ...Alison. Old habits die hard, you know."

Alison scanned the single sheet of County Hall headed note paper.

Dear Ms Lister

Thank you for your letter. I am pleased to see that you are getting to grips with the job and making a start on much needed improvements. The children of Southdale and their parents deserve far better than they have been getting.

I am sorry but, owing to the pressure of commitments, I will not be able to visit Southdale in the near future. I have asked the link adviser to make time to come over. Please ring his secretary to arrange an appointment.

In your letter, you mention that 'a do' was held for the staff at school. I trust public funds were not involved in providing for this function?

Yours sincerely

Anita Rollinson

ppSarah Koszalinski (Ms), Director of Education

33 Still Alison

"What was that you said, Jenna Bolton?" stormed Verna Richardson. "You just repeat what you said, in front of witnesses!"

"You heard what I said! I don't need to say it again." Jenna spat out the words disdainfully.

"Jenna, just tell me what gives you the right to call me something as detestable as that?"

"Because you are one."

Verna had been teaching for thirty-five years. In her time, few young people had chosen to treat her unkindly. Even fewer would have ever dreamt of speaking to her in the way Jenna Bolton had just done. Verna was a good teacher. All the pupils knew that. She was kind and patient, if a little old-fashioned in her approach. She always insisted on her classes standing to greet her when she entered a room. What is more, they all did it - not out of fear but out of respect.

The youngsters knew she was devoted to them. She came to every out-of-hours event and party that was put on for their benefit. She always helped with refreshments and she was usually to be found helping the caretaker to sweep the floor, long after the pupils had abandoned the building to *have a laugh* on the way home.

If you were struggling with your maths, it did not matter how many times she had to explain it she would not lose her rag with you. If you did your best, she kept a big bag of sweets in the stock cupboard. Everyone knew it was there and that the door was not often locked but only the most reprehensible of characters would have even considered 'nicking' sweets from Miss Richardson's goody bag. That was the level of respect she commanded.

Verna stared long and hard into Jenna's eyes. She could detect not the slightest trace of respect or even pity. Verna, experienced teacher that she was, weighed up the options. Jenna had clearly *lost it*. Obviously, this sort of indiscipline needed to be dealt with but there was nothing to be gained by pouring fuel on to a blazing fire. Verna would calm Jenna down and then discuss it with her somewhere quiet.

"Come on, Jenna, love, you're a bit upset at the moment. Calm down and we'll sort it out later." Verna stretched out a conciliatory hand and made a move to touch Jenna reassuringly on the shoulder. She had not expected the response that she received.

Jenna smacked away the outstretched hand of peace. "Don't you touch me, Richardson, you old cow. Bitch, I'll have my solicitor on you for assault."

The vitriolic outburst in addition to the sharp pain in her hand was too much for even Verna. She snapped.

"You little madam! How dare you treat me in this way? We're going to see Mrs Lister immediately and if she doesn't do something about you I'm out of this place for good. Come here, Jenna!"

"You must be joking. I'm going home. I'm fed up of this school and its crap teachers always picking on me."

"Come back here. I shall be forced to restrain you if you don't."

"I'll knock your head off, if you come near me!"

Verna, reinforced with anger, grabbed Jenna by the forearm and dragged her cursing and screaming down the corridor.

"Child abuse! I'm going to phone *Childline*. Help! Help! Stop her; she's abusing me. Take your hands off me, you filthy cow. You're dead for this, Richardson. My dad'll smash your face in when he hears about this."

Jenna kicked out violently at the classroom doors as she was hauled past them. The few youngsters on the corridor during lesson time stared in amazement at the events taking place before them. Teachers and pupils rushed to classroom doors to see what the fuss was about. Most teachers, though surprised to see Verna in such a rage, concluded that she was in control of the situation and watched from a distance. Not so, Brian. He sprinted to Verna's assistance.

"What's happening, Mrs Richardson? You really should release that child. You could bruise her arm you know."

"I'm not letting go until she agrees to come with me peacefully."

"She's hurting me, Mr Ingleton. Tell her to let go. I'll get her sacked for this."

Helpless to intervene without using physical force on the heaving, sweating duo, Brian settled for *escorting* them to Alison's new office.

Alison was on the telephone as the unlikely trio tumbled in through the door, uninvited. She quickly excused herself and replaced the receiver before the caller had time to hear the profanities issuing from Jenna's mouth.

Verna released her savage grip and the child stood before Alison's desk, dishevelled, trembling and tearful.

"What on earth's going on?" Alison demanded, in the most headteacherly manner she could conjure up at a few seconds notice.

"I want her done for assault," snorted Jenna and she rubbed her eyes, spreading mascara far and wide as she did so.

"And let me tell you, young lady," retorted Verna, "I'm not letting it go. I want my union involved in this. It's about time we teachers made a stand against this sort of abuse and violence."

"Oh, shut up both of you!" Alison had forgotten herself for a few seconds. She quickly recovered her composure. "Let's quieten things down and talk about this sensibly. Jenna, take a tissue from the box on my table, love, and wipe your eyes. You look a frightful sight. I'm going to ask Mrs Richardson to tell me what happened and then, when you've stopped sobbing, you can have your chance to respond. OK?"

Jenna did not reply but the sobs decreased perceptibly in both frequency and intensity.

Alison listened carefully to both sides of the woeful tale, doing her best to be open minded. She had to admit to herself, however, that her knowledge of both parties did dispose her to prejudging the situation before weighing up all the evidence. Jenna did not dispute Mrs

Richardson's version of the events. Alison felt obliged to point out to her that "I'm going to the toilet, you old fart." was not the most appropriate way of responding to Miss Richardson's query as to why she was on the corridor during lesson time.

"But she shouldn't have hit me. Teachers aren't allowed to do that."

"But let's look at this sensibly. You have to be very careful about making accusations, Jenna. Mrs Richardson's version of the story says that you knocked her hand away. That could get serious for you, if you continue to make accusations that can't be proved. I don't really understand why you have reacted in this way. It's completely over the top. Mrs Richardson has every right to question why you are not in class when you should be. I accept what Mrs Richardson has told me and you know what to expect, don't you? As I said in assembly the other day, any student abusing or threatening a member of staff will be taken home immediately and not allowed back into school until their parents have been up to sort it out. Go and wait outside in the foyer. I'll be with you in a few minutes and I'll arrange to take you home."

Jenna's fire had gone out. Head down, hardly smouldering, she withdrew without even the will to slam the office door behind her.

"Thank you, Mrs Lister."

"I'm still Alison."

"Thank you, Alison, but I still fear that the girl is going to get off with it too lightly. If she's prepared to speak to an experienced member of staff in that way what chance do the younger teachers have?"

"I know it hurts, Verna, but we both know Jenna very well. She's loudmouthed and coarse but she has a lot of time for you and this is totally out of character. There must be something more to it. I'll have a chat with her mother and see if something's worrying her."

"Lots of things worry *me*, Alison, but I don't go around using vile language to people."

This was not the time to pursue it with Verna. Alison would get back to her later. For the time being she kept her counsel, smiled supportively at Verna and allowed her to escape to the staffroom to let off steam on anyone who happened to be marking in there.

"Get into the back seat, Jenna. I'll have you home in a few minutes."

Jenna clambered in glumly and sat staring at the back of the seat in front of her. Alison tried to make conversation but with no success. Jenna stared resolutely ahead of her until the car turned into her street. At this point the youngster let out a horrifying shriek and dissolved into a succession of heart-rending sobs.

"Come on, Jenna, love. It's not as bad as all that, surely?"

"I can't go home! I can't."

"What do you mean?"

"I just can't go home. I don't have a home. My mum's chucked me out."

"Chucked you out?"

"Yeah. I was living with my dad until Christmas but I got fed up with him always getting on at me so I went back to my mum's. Well, me and my mum, we love each other but, when we're together, we just don't get on. It's the chemistry, my mum says. We fell out yesterday about me stopping out all night and I ran away. Mum called the police and they found me in town at about four o'clock in the morning. They took me home but mum said I'd burnt my bridges, so they took me to my dad's. He said he had a new family and I didn't fit into his plans so they took me to my auntie's. She's only got one bedroom and three kids so she said I could stop until today but then I'd have to find somewhere else. They're going to put me in a hostel, I expect, and I'm scared because everyone says there'll be drugs and child abuse and all that."

Alison pulled over to the side of the street and switched off the engine.

"Don't take me home, Mrs Lister. It'll all start up again and I've had enough as it is."

"Don't worry, Jenna. We'll sort it." She pondered for several moments and then punched a few figures into her mobile. "Hi, is that Donna? Nice to speak to you as well. I'm afraid I've got a child protection issue. Can I bring a young lady across to see you? We'll be there in twenty minutes."

By the time Alison got back to Southdale, school had long since finished and most people had made their weary way home. Glad the cleaner was busy on Alison's corridor. Glad was cheerful. None of the other cleaners had ever seen Glad as cheerful as she had been for the last couple of weeks. No one had ever seen her elbows move as quickly as they were doing now or the admin. corridor shine quite so brilliantly.

"Hello, Mrs Lister, I thought you were having an early night. I'm so used to seeing you still around when I go off at a quarter past six."

"A chance would be a fine thing, wouldn't it, Glad?"

"I've emptied your bin and I'll be along in a few minutes to dust and hoover for you, if that's all right?"

"Of course, Glad."

As Alison made her heavy-footed way towards her temporarily adopted office she met Emma Inman coming in the opposite direction.

"Hello, Emma. What are you doing here at this time?"

"It's our babby. He were sick on my homework again and my mum tried to wash it in the sink but it got all blotchy and she put it in the bin. She said not to worry because, after all, book-work would be no use to me with what I had to look forward to in life. Anyway, Mrs Brinkhurst said that I shouldn't worry, too, and that she understood but she had to keep me in so that the other kids didn't think I was getting special treatment or summat. So here I am going home at this time."

"Never, mind, sweetheart. Off you go then."

"Bye, Mrs Lister. See you tomorrow. I'm glad we've got you as our new headmaster, Mrs Lister. You're not like a proper one. You listen to us and all and do things for us like that stupid council, or whatever it's called, that you've set up. And we're going to get a drinks machine in the corridor and lockers so that we don't have to carry all that heavy stuff around every day. It's great."

"See you tomorrow, pet."

Alison turned away quickly so that neither Emma nor Glad would see the twin tears track their way down her cheeks to project themselves from her quivering chin and splatter on the glassy surface of the admin. corridor floor.

34 Spring madness

The rowan tree in Alison's garden and her potted, patio rhododendron were in full bloom, though Alison scarcely noticed them. For one thing, life was so hectic and, in a way, so exciting. The school was alive. The staff were beavering and the kids were buzzing. Well, not *all* the kids but not *all* the staff either.

The publication of the OfSTED written report had gone unnoticed in comparison with the furore occasioned by the earlier leak. Sally O'Mahoney had redirected her sights elsewhere. In a way, Alison regretted this but, deep down, she knew that the not inconsiderable tally of positives would have been buried under the more newsworthy, negative conclusions.

Blossom was white and heavy on the hawthorn hedges that decorated Alison's route to school. The swifts had returned and darted busily around at roof height. But how could Alison acknowledge spring when each day without Jake dulled a little more the pleasure of existence?

A creased and greying corner of paper had been pushed under Alison's office door. She unfolded it:

To Mrs Lister

I am happy and smiling again   I will see Mrs Richardson and make things all right with her. I am at my

Nan's. She says I can stay until I am old enough to go on the waiting list for a council flat.

I love you, Mrs Lister.

From Jenna XXX

If Alison had not drained her tear sacks during the night, she would have cried again.

The police had had to be called at lunchtime. Brian had taken the decision. He had received an anonymous telephone message that a number of Southdale students had emerged from the top of the playing field on to the public right of way that separated the school grounds from a non-resident farmer's field. The message had been a bit cryptic but was worrying enough for Brian to grab his mobile, leap into his car and drive round to see what was going off.

The report had been about some of the younger children running around in the farmer's rape field. The caller had spoken of seeing some of them with trousers around their ankles.

When Brian got there he could not believe his eyes. A group of about thirty Y7 children had escaped from the school field, through the permanent hole in the wire netting. Most of them were merely observing as half a dozen boys ran hither and thither amidst the yellow rape in a frenzy of exploded exuberance.

Brian bellowed. Like footballers in a red hot stadium, who, blissfully ignorant of the referee's signal to disengage, push on towards the goal, the children continued their orgy of spring madness.

Brian bellowed again. A bellow that would have made even the most disaffected Y11 student pause to consider the options. No response. Enraged Brian dived into the yellow waves of battered rape.

"Stop this at once! Are you mad? What do you think you're doing?"

It took a few minutes but Brian eventually restored calm and led the erstwhile revellers crestfallen on to the neutral ground of the pathway. He gathered the audience to them and asked the obvious.

"What's going on?"

"It's Daniel Tucker, he started it," called out a helpful Y7 girl.

"Go on, Kimberley, tell me about it!"

"Well, we were just messing around on the field and he says, 'Let's have a laugh. There's no teachers up here.' So we said, 'Yes, let's!' and we followed him through that hole. Then he says, 'You lot are all chicken, watch me!' So we did and he was right rude."

"I think I'm going to regret asking this but, how rude?"

"He says, 'Look I'm going to do a moonie,' and he did. He ran into that yellow stuff, dropped his trousers and showed us his bum. It was right white! Anyway, he says to the rest of us, 'You're all frightened to do it,' and he was right about most of us. After all I don't like going in the showers, even when it's only girls and we have them horrible plastic curtains. But some of the boys weren't so shy and they leapt in there as well and they did moonies. And I'll tell you something else, Greg Bellamy did a front moonie as well as a back one but we couldn't see nothing because he's little and that yellow stuff is quite big."

"Right, that's it. All of you back on the school field at once and try to calm down before afternoon school. You six, get down to my office and wait for me there. I'll be contacting your parents and asking them to take you home. If you want to stay at this school you'd better start thinking of what to say to Mrs Lister and believe me, lads, the only chance you have got is to grovel. Grovel with all your power and strength and then grovel some more."

"It's not fair!" shrilled Daniel Tucker.

Brian was good humoured, "Now, let's get this straight, Daniel. I'm down in school, just about to devour my lovely, squelchy egg and mayonnaise butty when I get a call to come all the way up here to sort out a bunch of lads who are running around semi-clad in the farmer's field and you say 'It's not fair'. Have you tried considering things from my point of view, for once? I don't think it's fair on me, nor on those others who have been subjected to the spectacle of your lily white buttocks, and on a full stomach as well."

"That's not what I mean, sir. If we're going to get done that man should get even more done for what he did."

A dark cloud passed over Brian's mind. He became serious.

"Which man? What did he do?"

"He was hiding over there in the bushes. He pointed a gun at us and it went off and we thought we were dead but some like, little bits hit us and it hurt."

"I think you have been fantasising, Daniel."

"No I haven't, Mr Ingleton. I've got some marks I'll show you."

Daniel revealed his limbs and his back but, having regained his modesty, did not offer to show Brian the stinging weal on his left buttock.

The other boys rolled up sleeves and trouser legs and lifted shirts to reveal a similar pattern of red marks, some still indented and some slightly swollen.

"This is serious, boys, and will have to be treated very seriously."

Brian went for his mobile phone and activated the school number. "Hello, Rosie, it's Brian here. No, I can't deal with an incident in the dining room at the moment. I'm at the top of the school field on that public footpath. Yes, that's the one. No I'm not having a walk. Actually there's been quite a serious incident. Would you ring the police, please? Yes, of course I'm serious. Well, yes I know Mrs Lister has a code and when she says to you 'Ring the police' she really means 'Hang on for a few minutes to see if it passes' and when she says 'Ring 999' she means 'Get the police at once because someone's got me by the throat!' OK, ring 999! Can I make it any plainer than that?"

The police came and looked around the area but could find no trace of a man or a gun, though they admitted that the wounds did look reminiscent of cases of shot gun wounding that they had dealt with in the past. Unless there were any leads there was nothing they could do except report the incident and ask other officers to keep their eyes open for similar happenings.

The boys' parents were called and predictably some believed that the school, and Brian in particular, should never have let it happen. And as for the police, they were useless as well. Weren't they going to arrest someone?

Brian's protestations, on behalf of school and police force, fell on deaf ears and the parents departed in high dudgeon with more than a hint that solicitors would be appointed with great alacrity and that the school and the police would be sued for every penny they had.

"They've not got much to come, then," thought Brian. "And, oh, by the way thanks for rounding up our little dears when they decided to leave the site without permission and reveal their bums to all and sundry."

When Alison heard about the lunch time goings on she was not able to share in Brian's chuckles. She said to him, "For goodness sake, tell the kids they mustn't say anything to the press. On second thoughts, don't. If we tell them not to do something one of them is sure to do it. Or their parents may feel that they can get something out of the paper for tipping them off."

35 Bye-bye, Pepsi

The *Fresh Start* sped ahead apace. The LEA consulted with the governors on the appointment process. "It's like asking a condemned man what he wants for breakfast!" joked Gladys Ollerenshaw darkly.

The advertisement for a creative, tough, resilient, ambitious, determined super hero, with excellent communication skills, willing to work excessive hours, eating every other mealtime, was placed in the *Times Ed*. The half page panel, featuring an 'attractive remuneration package' conjured up five applicants through its national exposure. Four of them, including Alison, were felt to be interviewable. The fifth applicant was rejected, after a short debate instigated by Sarah Koszalinski's representative from the LEA, on the grounds that his previous experience as a chartered surveyor and chair of governors of a primary school, did not fulfil the criterion of an experienced professional, in quite the way that had been intended, when the advertisement had been placed.

The interviews were scheduled over three days for just before half-term so that the successful candidate could be free to open the 'new' school the following January. Alison, not expecting to be that person, was quite relaxed about the whole business, a factor which probably contributed greatly to the eventual outcome. In the meantime she had other more mundane but nonetheless necessary tasks to fulfil.

She had made it her business to observe each teacher personally so that, at the very least, she could compare her opinion with that of OfSTED and be in a position to advise the new head about which staff should be kept at all costs.

Though she found him a bit on the adolescent side, she liked Simon Cunliffe and appreciated the way he got the best out of some of the less motivated students in his PE lessons. Alison had arranged to watch him teach a Y7 class in the gym.

Alison had made up her mind that she would take nothing with her into lessons when she was observing. Teacher colleagues had had enough, for the time being, of serious-faced individuals, carrying clipboards and writing copiously and mysteriously throughout the allotted time. She had determined to look for the successes and not the failures and to give the most positive and encouraging feedback to both teacher and class. She had asked herself the simple question, "Do I get more incentive to improve from being told I am useless at something or from being told that I am being successful at some things and should now use that as a basis for improvement on others?" Undoubtedly the latter was more motivational to her and she could not, for the life of her, imagine why OfSTED and its masters should think otherwise.

Simon was on good form and the diminutive Y7s were loving his keen exhortations to warm up, bend and stretch, run, jump and climb their way to a more healthy lifestyle.

Alison had had some thoughts about how health affected education as well as life in general. The pale demeanour, slight build and lack of energy of the pupils at Southdale, were thrown into acute relief when they played sporting fixtures against the rosy, rounded individuals from the more leafy quarters of the borough. Southdale's defeats were often more attributable to difference in physique rather than differential levels of commitment and effort.

Alison had read fervently a series of articles by healthy lifestyle enthusiasts in her favourite education journal. She was easily convinced by their assertions that too many E-numbers in fizzy drinks and chips-with-gravy every lunchtime were serious factors in poor behaviour, concentration and achievement. She blamed the fast food revolution for the deterioration in the pupils' table manners. She was saddened to see this reflected in the eating habits of some of the staff. It was now common place for people to use their chips as dippers and their gravy as dips. Alison, however, had drawn the line when she observed a Y9 pupil chasing her baked beans around the plate with an overdone, largish, flat chip serving as an improvised scoop.

Alison was convinced of the deleterious effect of fizzy drinks on concentration, behaviour and consequently on young people's learning. As soon as she took over the temporary headship she was resolved to do something about it.

"It really is contradictory," she informed Jake, in one of the many imagined conversations she had with him, "that we try to teach the kids about healthy eating habits and then the school meals people fill them full of gunge every lunchtime."

"You're quite right, Al," he imaginarily replied.

They say that fortune favours the bold. Coincidentally and quite fortunately as it turned out, some of the Y9s and Y10s, in their quest to find ever more devious ways of causing lunchtime mayhem for the supervisors, had taken to smuggling the little plastic bottles of fizzy pop from the dining room. Subsequently, they would loosen the cap slightly and launch the bottle as high as they could into the atmosphere. The theory was that the bottle would land on the tarmac of the yard with a stomach-churning thud and dispense the agitated liquid over an extensive arc of lunchtime loungers. The theory was fine and the practice caused much amusement to the bystanders until they, in their turn, became the bespattered. As with most prototypes, however, there were considerable teething problems. Ever more frequently people's persons got in between the bottle and the tarmac. When a Y7 girl was knocked nearly senseless by a downwardly mobile carbonated missile, Alison imposed a ban.

What an opportunity to impose a healthier regime on her young charges! She stormed to the kitchen and boomed that bottles, cans and other such containers would be banned from sale until further notice. She convened a *Student Council* and went into powwow with them.

The councillors understood Alison's dilemma but they also had a duty to uphold students' rights.

"Surely, Mrs Lister, you are not going to punish all of us for the misdemeanours of a few?" asserted a serious- looking Y10.

"You have a point, Curtis, but I have a responsibility to ensure that no one is injured. I think that student councillors should go back to their year groups and attempt to get other students on board. We cannot allow someone to be seriously hurt. "

"I agree. We'll do what we can," responded Curtis ponderously.

"But hang on a minute," intervened Becky, an equally serious Y10 rep, "I should like to question why we are selling such rubbish in the first place. I read in my Dad's *Mail* the other day that all those additives are making us barmy and affecting our learning."

"Yes! Yes!" thought Alison and she seized the opportunity. "Since that is the feeling of Student Council, I will set up a meeting with the school meals people and we will see what alternatives can be made available. Thank you. You may return to your lessons."

The Councillors traipsed from the room, not quite sure if they had won a resounding victory. Curtis turned to Becky. "Thanks a lot, Becky. I suppose I can wave bye-bye to my dinnertime *Pepsi* because of you!"

Alison had no difficulty in convincing Brian of the validity of her argument though the longer term fear of losing his chips and gravy did rest a little heavily on his mind for a while. They consulted with pupils, parents, the LEA and the school meals people. Fresh fruit juice would be served and cooled milk with the possibility of milk shakes, depending on what was in the flavourings. A state-of-the-art water cooler would be ordered and, in the meantime, little plastic bottles of still mineral water would be served, with the tops removed to discourage abuse.

The idea seemed to work well. After a bit of initial moaning, most students started to try out the milk and the fruit juice and more and more began to discover that cool, filtered water was more thirst-quenching than sugary, fizzy pop.

One lunchtime, Alison was approached on the corridor by an obvious deputation of determined Y9 girls. At their head was Katy Howson, a student not known for her sense of responsibility towards others.

"Hey, Miss," she began, "I want a word."

Alison bit her lip. "Yes, Katy, what can I do for you?"

"Well, Miss, I've just bought this bottle and they taken the top. It's my top, I've paid for it and I want it. If I don't get it I'm going to complain to Councillor Todwick, who lives on our street. He told my Dad that, if anyone messes us around at school, we should be round and see him like a shot."

Alison resisted the intense temptation to say, "Go away and don't be so stupid!" Instead she set about trying to explain to Katy why she had taken the action. When it became obvious from the obtuse expression on Katy's face that she was getting nowhere, she simply stated, "I suggest you take it up with your Student Council rep." She walked swiftly away hoping that her annoyance had not been as evident as she would have liked it to be.

Alison was roused from her reverie by the sound of Simon Cunliffe's voice.

"Come on you lot, get into twos! Hey, Lester Bennett, are you daft or what, I said get into twos."

"I am in twos, sir," said Lester defiantly, standing resolutely alone.

"Don't be so…"

"Um! Um!" coughed Alison.

The penny dropped. Simon readjusted. "Get into twos all of you except Lester. Lester, you get into threes."

"Right, sir," said Lester and danced off happily to find a partner.

Simon sidled over to Alison. "Sorry, Alison, I nearly forgot about Lester's imaginary friend!"

36 Twenty per cent less fat

"**A**rsehole!"

Brian did worry from time to time that his hearing was beginning to fail but it had not failed enough to prevent him discerning hissed insults – especially when they were delivered almost directly into his auditory canals by a student passing closely behind him.

He had just departed hurriedly from the dining-room in pursuit of a Y11 girl. Brian had been observing her antics at table as he lazily wiped the vestiges of congealed gravy from his plate with an endangered fry. She had, somewhat warily, ordered one of *Mrs Lister's* new, twenty-per-cent-less-fat, healthy-eating yet still of indeterminate origin, burgers. Having extended her purchase with an uncapped bottle of water, a miniature *Tetra Brik* of fresh apple juice and a revealingly flat sachet of ketchup, she found a seat next to a friend and stared at the burger. Brian chuckled inwardly as the bizarre concept of *an uncapped bottle* tickled his imagination. "Perhaps with a few more years' experience and a lucky break it will play for England one day," he snorted, almost choking on his soggy chip. The girl lifted the burger's dry bread lid. She stared at it some more and Brian thought she was about to lick it. Instead, table manners won the day and she merely inhaled any potential aromas with the enormously capacious sniff of a wine connoisseur. She tore the sauce sachet with her teeth and squeezed out a blob of bright red gunk. She then used the redundant sachet to smear the ketchup, thinly, of necessity, over the whole surface of the burger. She shook the sticky sachet from her fingers on to the floor beneath the table.

Still unsure, she let the lid flop back into place and raised the whole to her tentative lips. She nibbled the bread cake and wrinkled her nose. As if unaware of Brian's fascinated gaze, she spat the barely masticated bread bits on to the table, peeled the bread cake from its burger and deposited it on the floor, under the table. She picked up the burger and bit hesitatingly into its circumference. Her face became a picture of unconcealed disgust. She coughed the morsel of almost untouched burger on to the table and flicked it to the floor with her thumbnail. She perused the remainder of the unappealing disk for a few, long moments and then slid that too between her knees to the floor. She wiped her greasy ketchup-stained fingers on the sleeve of the hapless Y7 seated to her left, stuffed the *Tetra Brik* into the pocket of her jeans, pushed over the capless bottle of water and headed for the exit.

Brian snapped out of his trance. "Young lady, "he called "come back here at once!" The *young lady* was in selective hearing mode. She passed through the door and went up a gear as she entered the corridor to the yard. Brian caught her up at the half-way point. "Young lady!" No response. Brian gently placed his hand on the girl's shoulder and halted her progress before firmly encouraging her to turn towards him and engage with his words of wisdom. The girl briefly entertained the *how dare you lay a hand on me, you'll hear from my solicitor in the morning approach*. However, spotting that her *assailant* was Brian and not one of the

269

younger, easier to wind-up sorts, she half turned towards him, curled her thin lip, inclined her head to one side and squinted up at him with undisguised disdain.

"Just remind me of your name, young lady."

"Stacey."

"Stacey what?"

"Stacey, sir."

"I'm glad you've remembered your politeness belatedly but I meant your second name. "

"Louise."

"No, your family name."

"Lacey, sir. Stacey Louise Lacey. "

"Stacey Lacey?"

"Correct."

"Thank you. Well, Stacey Lacey, you must be new to the school otherwise you would have known that we always display our best manners when in the dining-room."

"I don't know what you mean."

"I mean that it is very bad manners to put your food on the floor and walk away."

"It wasn't me. I put mine in the bin."

"I've just seen you do it with my own eyes."

"Not me."

"Are you calling me a liar?"

"You must be lying because I didn't do it. I had curry and rice and scraped my plate into the bin like it says on the notice near the door."

"Arsehole!"

Brian spun round to see two Y11 boys shuffling along the corridor. "Who said that?"

"Who said what?"

"Arsehole."

"Aw, sir swore," said a stunned Y8 passing by. "I'm going to tell me mum."

"I never said nothing," complained one of the Y11 boys.

"If it wasn't you, it was him."

"Oh, there you go picking on me again. Whenever, anything goes wrong, it's always me."

"I want to know who said 'arsehole'.

"Well, it wasn't us so can we go to our mates, all right?"

"No. Down to my office now. I'll be there in a couple of minutes. Stacey Lacey, you wait here and don't you dare move."

"But I need a wee. I'm desperate and if I wet myself my mum'll have you in court."

"Give it a rest, Stacey. Just be there when I get back, all right? Hey, you two, I said *my office*. OK?"

"Right, now which one of you called me an arsehole. "

"Not me."

"Not me."

"All right, you can stay here until one of you tells me the truth."

"Aw, that's not fair. We want to see our mates. This is our lunchtime. We have a right to... "

"And *I* have a right not to have students call me an arsehole. And, anyway, by keeping you here I'm helping you to address your nicotine addiction. You've got fifteen seconds to tell me the full truth or I'll take you to Mrs Lister."

"Wow, we're really scared."

"15, and that will mean contacting you families, 10 and an exclusion 5, and an appearance before the governors, 4 and if you've already had a written warning..."

"OK. OK, I'll come clean with you, sir. It was him."

"You what?"

"Straight up, it was him but he didn't say *arsehole* because that would be disrespectful, wouldn't it, sir? He actually said *rarsol*."

"Rarsol! Rarsol? What's rarsol?"

"It's like a slang word, sir, that we use in our community."

"And what does it mean?"

"Well, it means tramp."

"And why on earth would your friend call me a tramp?"

"That's just it, sir, he was talking to Stacey Lacey, weren't you? She's a real *rarsol*."

"I still think I heard the word *arsehole*."

"Me and my mate would like to, sort of, apologise. Say we're sorry, like, for us, well him, making you think that we were talking about you, when we were talking about that *rarsol* Stacey Lacey."

"I can't believe what I'm hearing. I am one hundred per cent sure that I heard the word *arsehole*. Come with me. We'll ask Stacey what she heard."

"Stacey…"

"Sir, sir, I'll wet myself. Can I go to the toilet, *please*?"

"Yes… just as soon as you tell me what you heard one of these boys say when they walked past me earlier."

"I heard it very clearly, sir, he said *dick head*."

Stacey rushed off to relieve her bladder.

"My office at the end of the day." And Brian strode off with as much dignity as he could muster.

"Do you know, Wes, if I said *arsehole* as many times as Mr Ingleton, I'd get excluded."

37 ILY

The silky, pinkish petals of the wild roses, that briefly embellished the extremities of the school field in late spring, were still precariously clinging to the briars when Alison made use of a walk in the noonday sunshine to calm her nerves for the big interview.

She had got through two and a half days of presentations, in-tray exercises and psychometric tests and, genuinely to her surprise, had made it to the formal interviews on the last day. One of the four candidates had been rejected on the second day, on the grounds that he would have driven everyone crazy with his endlessly regurgitated data and his file full of tick boxes.

Alison convinced herself that she had got through, with a woman from Leicester and a man from Manchester, as a backstop and to recognise the efforts she had made to drag Southdale from the depths in the last couple of months. "It will be good experience for eventual headship interviews," she had told herself. She had found the whole process quite draining but was astonished how much she had enjoyed some parts of it. Once she had got over the butterflies and the worries that the video projector would do strange things to her, she wowed the panel with the simple common sense of her presentation on how to hoist Southdale to safety in the league tables. Alison was a born teacher and she had revelled in the interchange with the student panel. It appeared that the Southdale students were rooting for her on the grounds that the other candidates looked and sounded a mite intimidating.

Another of the activities in the interview process was a spontaneous debate. The four candidates had been seated around a table while observers observed them from the corners of the room. They were each given a piece of paper, face down, bearing the subject to be debated. Alison turned over the paper, scanned the only sentence on it: *Special Needs students should not be made to learn a foreign language* and returned the face of the paper to the dimly elegant surface of the careers library reading table. All traces of graffiti and chewing gum had been banished for the occasion and the table was resplendent with the nearest it could accomplish to a decent shine.

Alison calmly folded her arms and waited. Soon to be rejected *data man*, determined to be the first to speak, cleared his throat nervously and jumped in. "Well, of course, I agree entirely. Statistics show that very few young people with special educational needs, who attempt a GCSE in a language, get a G grade or above. It is a waste of their effort and the teachers' time. They'd be better off doing more maths and English. That would improve their chances of employability, which according to the Chief Inspector's latest report is the greatest need for youngsters of that sort."

"Oh, come now," interrupted Leicester woman, "you can't be serious! Which century are you living in: this one or the one before last? It's quite clear to me that learning a modern foreign language can improve any young person's confidence in using their own language. That is provided that the quality of the teaching and the teachers' empathy with the students are what they should be I..."

"I agree entirely," interpolated Manchester man determined not to be left behind in the scramble to impress. *"In fact, I agree with both of you, in a sense. You're both right and yet you've both got it wrong."

And so the debate continued for five minutes or more, three of the candidates arguing with gusto and Alison just waiting.

Manchester man noticed that Alison was not participating. Anxious to display his inclusive credentials, he turned to Alison solicitously, "Alison, I apologise, we've not given you the chance to join in. What have you got to say on the subject?"

Alison seized her chance.

"This is getting us nowhere. It's no way to run a debate with everyone chipping in when they feel like it. We need to do things properly. I'll chair," and looking in the direction of Leicester woman, "Right, you were just talking about the huge potential that the human brain has for absorbing language. Would you like to come to your point quickly and I'll bring in the others to challenge or support your standpoint as they see fit?"

In one of the corners of the room Gladys Ollerenshaw nodded contentedly.

That was yesterday. The waiting seemed interminable. Alison went to Brian's office. She could not face going to the staffroom to socialise with whichever of the two others was not being interviewed at the time. Brian was teaching, so she could slouch in his sumptuously sagging old swivel chair without fear of human contact. She felt that if anyone spoke to her a thread would snap and everything would unravel leaving her limp and resourceless for the approaching ordeal.

Manchester man went in first and came out very quiet and reflective. Noting this boosted Leicester woman's confidence and she went in knowing that Alison was the only other contender and that it would be no contest; a successful headship of a failing school behind her and membership of one of the Secretary of State's consultative committees. She came out buoyant and glowing with the sure expectation of success.

Alison went in last. Some said that it was an advantage. Others said that the long wait could make you stale. Alison could not care either way. She thought she would vomit. She just wanted to get it over with.

She entered and hovered near the high back chair, the obvious focal point for the panel seated behind a table at a slightly intimidating distance from the candidate's position.

"Welcome. Do sit down, Mrs List... Alison," smiled Gladys Ollerenshaw in an attempt to repair Alison's frayed nerve endings.

Alison scanned the beaming panel, beaming that is except for Sarah Koszalinski. Alison wondered if Ms Koszalinski ever smiled. She could recall the odd smirk or sneer at a meeting but a genuine, warm, welcoming smile seemed to be alien to Koszalinski's nature.

"Anyway, I mustn't be fazed by the ice queen," thought Alison, a trace of amusement flitting mischievously across her lips. Five panel members. Five lots of questions to be had. Forty-five painful minutes at least. She acknowledged two governors: a parent and that LEA nominated governor who hardly ever came to meetings but had a lot of influence when he did. Gladys sat in the middle of the five. To her left was Sarah Koszalinki and at Koszalinksi's side a faithful lapdog, that senior adviser, what's-his-name, the one that is always going on about league tables and value added and coasting schools and underachieving schools. Used to be on secondment to the DfES. "What on earth is his name? I do hope I don't have to address him by name."

"I'll not bother with the introductions, Alison. You know everybody here don't you?" began Gladys unhelpfully.

"Yes, yes...of course. Good afternoon, everyone."

Gladys hurled the first question at Alison. Alison connected with it, like a rounders player striking the ball just right. She was off and running, first base, second base, third base and home. "Fling whatever you like at me I can handle it!"

It was nearly five-thirty. Manchester man was pacing up and down the staffroom carpet. "No danger of him wearing it out," thought Alison and her mischievous smile returned briefly. Leicester woman was whispering loudly, as people do, into her miniature mobile. Her conversation was of no interest to Alison but it sounded sort of business-like; perhaps talking to her secretary, making plans for the morning.

Five-thirty came and went. Manchester man seemed unaware of his audible sighs.

At five forty-two, the staffroom door opened, straining against its spring loaded mechanism and the entire panel walked in, looking drained and worn.

"I'm sorry to keep you waiting. I know what a long three days you have had but it has been a very difficult decision. You are three very strong candidates."

Manchester man swallowed dryly, appreciating Gladys's diplomacy and her concern for his damaged feelings.

"Anyway, you're all very tired and you don't want to listen to me prattling on. And by the way Ms Koszalinski and Mr Johnson are prepared to offer all candidates a professional de-briefing either now or at another convenient time."

"Johnson! Johnson! That's his name, Tom Johnson. How could I forget that?"

"After a long, long discussion, we have decided to offer the post to..."

All eyes turned towards Leicester woman.

"Alison Lister," declared Gladys with a smile of immense satisfaction.

Alison telephoned her parents with the news. They were ecstatic. She hoped that Jake would be there, having a meal with them, perhaps, but they were not giving any clues and she was too afraid to ask directly.

She tried to call Jake on his mobile. She let it ring and ring until a cold, digital voice informed her that the recipient was not available and advised that she should try again later.

Alison pressed exit and hurriedly fingered a text message: "Got the headship. Love, Ali."

She went to the kitchen and poured herself an overdue dose of alcohol.

Her heart leapt into her throat as her mobile beeped in the dining-room. She snatched it up and fumbled the keys.

"Well done. ILY."

38 Whistling like Ashley Hardman

Clive Holdsworth came around that evening.

"I told you that you'd get the job, didn't I?" He thrust a bottle of cheapish champagne into her startled hand. "It must have been the word I put in for you with that cow Koszalinski."

"You'd better come in," Alison suggested, against her better judgement.

Clive did not need asking twice. He strode into the living-room and instantly made himself at home.

"Come on, Ali, get that bubbly opened."

Alison took the less than chilled bottle into the kitchen and grabbed two flutes from the cabinet.

The telephone rang. Before she could shout to him, Clive picked up the receiver, "Hello?" and replaced it after a few silent seconds.

"Who was that?" Alison called out.

"Must have been a wrong number. Nobody there."

It was eleven-thirty when Clive left her in peace. She closed the door and rushed to the telephone to punch in 1471.

"You received a call at eight thirty-one today," droned the electronic voice. "The caller withheld the number."

Alison dragged herself upstairs and robotically straightened the wrinkled sheets. She flopped down on the bed and unable to distinguish between the heights of joy and the depths of sorrow cried herself to an eventual, shallow sleep.

Ashley Hardman whistled while he worked. Staff and students looked at him in amazement and some said, "Why on earth are you so cheerful, Ashley?", though everyone knew really. Ricky Tomlinson, in his acting-up capacity, was getting things organised to the extent that Brian had put in several good words with Alison in the light of job adverts looming for everyone's posts.

Ricky had begun to line manage Ashley Hardman and his team, by default. He had had several meetings with them, light refreshments provided, of course, and had complimented their commitment to the school and the effort they put into their job. He had asked the simple question, "How can we get even better?" He had been inundated with suggestions.

"We work our socks off trying to keep the toilets clean," asserted someone. He did not actually say *socks* but Ricky let discretion get the better of him as he reported back to the newly elevated Alison. "Yet, those kids trash them every day. They're always complaining about no toilet paper but if we put it in they use it for streamers. They stuff all sorts down the toilet pans including food and some of the girls do unmentionable things with female hygiene products. We're sick and tired of cleaning off foul graffiti. There have been three wash basins smashed in the last month or so. Just coming into work depresses me. I'm thinking of jacking it in and getting a job cleaning in a hospital."

"I'd be very sorry to see you go, any of you," interjected Ricky. "Let's see if we can come up with a system that will improve things." And he did. Toilet passes were provided for all teachers and any student *really* needing to go to the toilet had to take the pass to reception, sign in the record book and bring the key back. At break and lunchtimes, staff were exhorted to pay regular, unexpected visits to the students' toilets to keep an eye on things, as it were, and some of the less easily intimidated of Alison's newly instituted band of prefects were allocated, 'bog duty', as they called it.

All this was so successful in returning and maintaining the basic standards to the sanitary installations, that even the hard set group of youngsters who had never relieved themselves at school, on account of the poor state of the facilities or the nightmare of having to partially divest in a lockless cubicle, actually asked for the pass and went to the toilet. Several letters of appreciation from equally relieved parents were well received. They could relax from now on, knowing that their offspring would not be 'holding on to it all day', as they had been doing prior to Ricky's incursion into this former staff no-go area.

Ricky also organised *clean-up kits* for the departments: plastic bags and litter pickers, graffiti spray, cloths and scouring pads and protective wear, including masks and goggles. Ricky met with the caretaking team, periodically, and concluded that they had begun to enjoy their job more.

More whistles and hummed tunes and even the odd cheerful, "Hello, Mr Tomlinson. Lovely day, isn't it?"

Now that the behaviour of the young people had begun to improve, staff expectations were higher and they were no longer prepared to tolerate disobedience from any quarter. They became frustrated and a few became very angry with the minority of refusers.

"Take your coat off in the classroom, please."

"I'm not. Why should I? You can't make me!"

"Oh, yes I can."

"You want to bet?"

"Leave my room at once."

"No. Don't you dare come near me. I'll have a lawyer on you."

This type of interchange was being witnessed increasingly frequently, with a small group of very challenging students who had so little going for them, in life that they did not care in the least about any consequences that the teacher could possibly dream up. "Lines, detention? You must be joking!" Incidents of the like sometimes resulted in foul and abusive language from one party and occasionally both. From time to time minor physical contact was greeted with horror as a teacher tried to shepherd a student from the class and the student, mule like, resisted the impulse to go in the required direction.

Brian was delegated by the staff to nag Alison into taking action.

"Hi, Alison, have you got a few minutes?" Alison recognised that tone. Brian was very good at getting his way, when he had something in mind, and they both knew it.

"Come in, Brian. Ten minutes and then I must get on with these unanswered letters. Some go back to Dr Bill's time, things have been so hectic."

"I'll not keep you long. Provided you agree to my plan," Brian thought to himself.

Two hours and five minutes later Brian emerged from Alison's office, a hint of satisfaction on his lips, but eager to find out if Ricky Tomlinson had taken steps to replace him on lunch duty. He need not have worried about it.

Alison, thoughtful, gently squeezing the tip of her nose with her thumb and forefinger, remained at her desk for several minutes longer. She hoped she was doing the right thing in letting Brian have his head. Some of what he was proposing seemed to clash with her personal philosophy on dealing with difficult young people but, if she really did believe in the principle of shared leadership, she had to gently ease her hold on the reins.

Brian cancelled departmental meetings and got all the staff together in the staffroom. He announced his scheme for dealing with disobedience and backchat. His audience, at first sceptical, warmed to Brian's theme as he extolled the successes that similar actions had achieved in the school where his cousin taught. Staff went home that night visibly heartened.

The next day assemblies were held for each year group. These were led by Brian and Alison with Ricky Tomlinson in the wings making helpful suggestions and ensuring that the students arrived, waited, listened and departed with the maximum of decorum.

Letters were delivered home and it was made clear that the new scheme would start the next day. Alison, who always liked to *sleep* on an idea and consult everyone before implementing it, was a little wary of what Brian was undertaking but she bit her lip and let him get on.

The next morning, since Y11 had finished their examinations, the hall was able to be set out with empty examination desks. At registration the students were reminded of the content of the assembly and the letter they had take home. Anyone who had not brought back the reply slip had better bring it in by tomorrow.

Laura Dunne was in Verna Richardson's Y10 maths class, period one. She drifted in late with the challenging smirk on her face that all staff knew only too well. Her face was probably a pretty one, but so smeared in make-up that it was difficult to be sure. Her fingers and neck were overburdened with outrageously obvious jewellery. She understood the game but had no intention of playing by the rules.

"Good morning, Laura, nice of you to join us."

Laura scowled. She found a place the furthest possible from the teacher's location and tossed a rolled up exercise book on to the table before scraping a chair back and forth on the wooden floorboards and throwing herself down on it for maximum effect.

Verna remembered Alison's advice that teachers should *model* the sort of behaviour they were expecting from the students. She found it hard but she kept her cool. "Did you have a late night, dear?" she enquired. Laura's scowl became a sneer.

"Well, OK then. I see you have your exercise book. Get your pen, pencil and ruler out, turn to page 43 and let's get on. And oh, by the way, Laura, take your coat off, there's a love."

Verna moved to the board and was poised to continue. "Laura, love, I don't think you heard me. I asked you to take your coat off and get on with your work. Keeping your coat on and putting your feet on the table doesn't seem to me to be very co-operative."

Laura's sneer turned to a snarl and the feet remained on the table. Aggressively folded arms showed that she had not the least intention of removing the coat, the badge of her defiance.

"Laura, you are being told, remove your coat now! You have five seconds." Verna began to count down dramatically.

Laura's arms and legs twitched involuntarily as if something deep down inside was impelling her to comply but years of custom and practice held the sway and she symbolically tightened the grip of her already tightly folded arms.

Verna took a laminated pink card from her drawer. "Take this card to Mr Ingleton in the main hall." Verna wondered if she would move but she did. Reluctantly, belligerently, kicking things out of her way but she went. She slammed out of the door and along the corridor to the main hall where Brian greeted her with a sinisterly cheerful, "Hello."

"Candidate number five for the sin bin, hey? Go and sit at desk number 12, no, not there next to him, three rows away. You must sit there in silence. I will find some work for you to do when you have had a chance to think through what you have done. You were warned yesterday: any disobedience will be treated most seriously indeed. You will continue to work in the hall and spend your breaks and lunchtimes here until your parents have been in and we have drawn up a contract together about your future behaviour."

On the first day of Brian's scheme, there were around two hundred students in the hall at one time or another. Colleagues rallied round and the telephone lines were hot with staff trying to establish parental contact so that an apposite discussion could take place. The second day saw a hundred and fifty there and by the third the total had dropped to sixty.

As Kevin Breeze went home that Friday evening, he called out, "All power to your elbow, Brian, I think I could even start to enjoy teaching again."

Brian smiled the smile of the deeply self-satisfied and answered his telephone.

"Hello, Mr Robinson, thanks for phoning back. I"ve been trying to get hold of you all afternoon. You see your Danny is one of the last ten detained in our hall because of his disobedience to staff. I wonder if you could get over here straight away and we can get him sorted in time for Monday. Thanks very much for your co-operation. Sorry we had to ring you so often at work. Was that your boss we spoke to? She sounded a nice woman, if a little irritated by our repeated calls. See you in twenty minutes, Mr Robinson. Tea or coffee? OK, thanks. Goodbye."

Brian could not resist a mischievous chuckle as he replaced the receiver and returned to the hall, *whistling like Ashley Hardman,* as the staff had begun to describe that tunelessly cheerful shrill.

39 Mingled tears

Out of the blue Jake telephoned. Her heart was thumping. She could not get her breath. She thought her chest would explode.

"Hi, Ali. I thought I'd ring to see how you're getting on with the new job. Just because we're not together any more, it doesn't mean I shouldn't take an interest in how things are going."

Not together any more. It sounded so, sort of, decided, as if their futures had already embarked on a journey of irrevocably divergent pathways.

Alison bumbled a bit about school and Brian and Ricky and how good she felt about working with the pair of them. And somehow, in her confusion, she blurted out those fateful words that live with her still to this day. "And Clive's been very helpful. I probably wouldn't have got this job without his advice. He pops in from time to time to see how things are."

Why did she say it? So many times she had rehearsed the scene where Jake rang. Never in a single *take* had she even considered letting Clive's name slip between her lips.

There was an aching silence on the line. "Jake, are you still there?" He sighed. "Oh, thank goodness I thought we had been cut off."

"Ali, I can't go on like this. You know what I'm like, I can't deal with uncertainty. I need to be clear about us so that I can start to live my life again."

Perhaps there was a glint of hope in what he was saying? She seized the initiative. "Let's meet somewhere, on neutral territory, so that we can tell each other why we are hurting. Maybe we can find a way out of this mess?"

His heavy-hearted sobs were audible. "Only if... only if...there's a chance..."

He had set her off. Her emotion escaped in wave after wave of anguished hiccups. "Oh, my darling, after all we've shared together, there has to be a chance. Let's talk."

They arranged to meet in a pub that they never frequented. Jake had found it in the yellow pages. It was near enough to be convenient but far enough away not to be visited by people they knew. It felt like an assignation.

When Alison arrived she discovered Jake sitting at a small round table for two in a quiet corner of a dimly lit lounge. It was early in the week so the whole pub was pretty deserted.

She had forgotten how adorable she found the look of him but she sensed that he was not as immaculately shaven as would have normally been the case. He was in his work suit, a little crumpled but fairly business like. He had removed his tie and his pure white shirt yawned between the collar and the second button down. It was the same Jake that she had once fallen for. His slightly casual elegance had been his major charm but now his eyes were reddened and heavy and betrayed weeks of anguished struggle against bitter heartache.

On the small table in front of him were two froth stained pint pots and a third, part full, that he dangled between the thumb and forefinger of his left hand.

"Can I get you a drink?" he asked shakily.

"Just an orange and soda."

"Off the alcohol?"

"I'm just not in the mood."

Jake returned two minutes later carrying Alison's soft drink and another pint glass with a thick frothy head. Alison looked disapprovingly at the fourth pint but bit her lip. Now was not the time. Jake drank off the remainder of his third pint and having gulped down a deep draft of the fourth, wiped the foam from his lips inelegantly with the back of his hand.

Neither was in the frame of mind for small talk but did not dare broach the subject that was eating both of them from the inside.

As she asked the question Alison realised how bizarre it sounded, "How are my Mum and Dad?" She felt guilty that she had not visited them for ages. Jake clearly had. "They're OK. I was there for a meal the other day. They send their love."

Alison's throat was dry and anxious. She salved it with a mouthful of orange and soda and then tentatively, "How are you feeling?"

"Pretty crap."

"That's not surprising really...you...we've been through a lot recently... "

"Yes, all that business at school must have been pretty taxing... "

"That's not what I meant..."

"Let's not argue, Ali. I'm on a knife edge."

Alison took a deep breath, "Do you want to give it another go?"

There was a silence long enough to tear at Alison's insides. "I simply don't know, Alison," he used her full name, "I need to know what has happened between you and Clive – get it out in the open – then I can decide if..."

"Don't you love me any more?"

"It's not a question of love." Alison's face twisted slightly in frustration. "I've loved you since the moment I saw you. I love you now and I probably always will. It's just that I can't bear to think of you with someone else. It's more a matter of trust really."

Anger flashed within her but she resisted the temptation to let him see or to stand up and walk out.

"If it's a question of trust are you saying that you don't trust me now? Because, if that is the case, what can there possibly be between us any longer? If every time I leave the house, you think that I'm going off to meet someone else or, if I'm back late, you are burning with suspicion, how can that be a return to what we had. It was... it is something special, Jake."

"I need your word that you'll never..."

"My *word*? Don't you remember our marriage service? We exchanged *words* then. As far as I'm concerned the promises we made then still stand."

"But have *you* honoured them?"

"Have *you*?"

"I don't know how you can ask me that question, Ali."

"Well, if you won't answer it than neither will I!"

"Is that because you've got something to hide?"

"It's because I'm making the same point as you did: marriage has to be based on trust. If there is no trust then there is no point in trying again."

"I'd like to trust you but I need to know, sort of clear the air, have a fresh start."

They both felt awkward and this led to an uncomfortable silence. Jake nearly finished his fourth pint and Alison pretended to sip at her orange and soda. They both looked as if they were going to start up again but then Jake quaffed his beer and seeing that Alison's glass was barely touched made a half-hearted gesture of offering another drink. She shook her head nervously. Jake went to the bar returning with what looked like a double whiskey.

She could not hold back this time, "Jake, you're worrying me. You never used to drink like that. You can't possibly drive."

"That's my business."

"It's mine as well. I care about you and I don't want to see you hurting yourself or anyone else for that matter."

Jake looked her straight in the eyes. "*Hurt*, that's what all this is about, Ali. You've hurt me and I need you to help me lose that hurt."

"How?"

"By telling me what went on between you and Clive."

"We're back to trust again. There's nothing of any substance between Clive and me. We go back a long way but that's all there is to it. End of story."

Jake suddenly found the courage to blurt out the question that was haunting him, "Were you with him when I came to the motel that night? No matter how bad the answer I need to know it, Ali, for my peace of mind."

"I've said what I've said, Jake. There is no longer anything between Clive and me."

"But that could mean anything."

"It means what it means, my darling." She could no longer hold back the flood. "I love you. I need you. I want you to come back to me. There will never be anyone else for me like you."

They grasped each other's shoulders across the small round table. Their cheeks touched, moistened by mingled tears.

Had the landlord come through to collect the mounting glasses he would have wondered at their bizarrely held pose. Had they suffered a mutual bereavement? Were they coming to the conclusion of an illicit affair? Perhaps one of them had decided not to abandon a long-standing partner and had called the whole thing off. He would have asked himself if their embrace had an air of the inevitable about it. But the landlord stayed resolutely behind his bar in the distant well-lit part of the pub, looking everywhere except in the direction of the sad couple locked in anguish in the gloom. There were some places that you just did not go.

"Jake, come back to me."

"I need to think. Love you."

40 No room a refuge

Jake swallowed the residue of his umpteenth *Jameson's*, tossing his head as it scorched the back of his throat. He made up his mind. He hauled himself to his feet and snatched up his crumpled jacket from the back of the armchair, where he had abandoned it earlier, squeezing the pockets to locate his car keys. Several blades of serrated metal validated his supposition. The effects of the alcohol caused him to reel perceptibly as his face hit the cooler air of the darkening evening. After several clumsy attempts he tottered into the driver's seat and fumbled for the ignition. The car lurched forward into the spreading darkness. He *must* see Alison.

Traffic was light. Jake soon left behind the pale amber topped lamp posts and sped on into the gloom. The occasional oncoming vehicle seared his optic nerve with the ghostly glare of its tear-smeared headlamps. The intermittent white road lines, camouflage grey, strayed about before his eyes. His tyres squealed at every curve and bend, such is the de-skilling effect of excessive whiskey on the brain.

She could not settle. Alison's head was brimful to exploding. She had not been able to stomach the notion of food. No seat was consoling; no room a refuge. She picked up the newspaper and laid it down as quickly. Her quivering hands poured a leftover glass of warmish *chardonnay*. She moistened her salted, splitting lips, then abandoned it on top of the television.

Rousing her from her supplications, slivering shafts of light splintered on the feebly lit walls of the living room. A vehicle's headlights fleetingly illuminated Alison's sorrowful surroundings. Heavy-laden footsteps scrunched the gravel of the drive like boot-clad feet on frost hardened virgin snow.

Alison hurried into the hall.

Please let it be Jake.

Post scriptum

The rowan tree in Alison's garden hung blood-red in its heaviness. As she turned her face from the window, a single tear found its way to the point of her chin and exploded on the scribbled draft of her start of the year exhortations to Southdale's staff.